# THE LAW OF ATTRACTION

BRITS IN MANHATTAN BOOK ONE

LAURA CARTER

Boldwood

First published in 2017. This paperback edition published in 2024.

I

Copyright © Laura Carter, 2017

Cover Design by Rachel Lawston

A CIP catalogue record for this book is available from the British Library.

Paperback ISBN 978-1-83533-956-5

Large Print ISBN 978-1-78513-527-9

Hardback ISBN 978-1-78513-526-2

Ebook ISBN 978-1-78513-524-8

Kindle ISBN 978-1-78513-525-5

Audio CD ISBN 978-1-78513-532-3

MP3 CD ISBN 978-1-78513-529-3

Digital audio download ISBN 978-1-78513-523-1

Boldwood Books Ltd
23 Bowerdean Street

London SW6 3TN
www.boldwoodbooks.com

*For everyone who believes in second chances.*

# 1

## DREW

I slip out of the bed, naked, and head into my en suite. While the shower heats the wet room, I look out over Manhattan. From this angle, I see the spring sun rising through the multitude of the city's skyscrapers. On the other side of my apartment, the view of Central Park is lush green.

When I step into the shower, I'm blasted from all angles by the spray. Closing my eyes, I lean my head back and let the jets clean away the mild fog I feel from last night's scotch. I didn't have much, just enough to take the edge off the stress of today's hearing.

It's time to bring my game face. In a few hours, I'll be in court, defending another millionaire accused of white-collar crime. Today, I'll be convincing Judge McAvoy that my client isn't guilty of insider trading, despite the fact he placed trades that made him more money than even the Einstein of Wall Street could have managed.

Hey, he pays me a hell of a lot of money to keep him out of pretty-boy prison, and let's be real here, it's not like he killed anyone.

Knocking off the shower, I shake out my dark-blond hair, flick water from my ears, and tie a towel around my waist. After wiping down the steamed mirror, I brush shaving cream on my face and get on with making myself appear court presentable. By court presentable, I mean a cut above the average man's best day. I'm a big hitter on the circuit and I have to look like one. It's all part of the show.

When I'm finished, I slip out of the bathroom and pad quietly through the bedroom to my walk-in – not intentionally quiet because I don't want to wake the sleeping brunette in my bed but because my feet are bare on the thick rug.

The hanging racks are full of suits and shirts but there's only one suit for court. The don of all suits. The pinstripe.

I dress in my shirt and pants, wiggling the knot of my tie until it sits just so. My vest is next; judges like a three-piece. I leave my jacket until last, carrying it with me to the kitchen as I go in search of my best friend. I hear her percolating and smell her rich aroma before I see her.

Meet my coffee maker. The most reliable and dependable thing in my life. Black coffee in hand, I head back to my bedroom to wake last night's conquest. She's wrapped loosely in only my white, cotton sheet, her slim, tanned body displayed in all but the most important places. Her hair and makeup aren't as pristine as they had been when I'd picked her up in the bar, but I can still see why I brought her to bed.

'Janey,' I say, standing on the threshold of the room, sipping my Italian coffee. 'Janey, wake up. I've got to go.'

She moans and rolls over in a way I imagine she thinks is erotic. Last night, I probably would have thought so. Now, I have shit to do, places to be. It's not like I'm being disrespectful. We both knew what this was. I'm just the first of the two of us to call the bluff.

'Mm, coffee,' she whispers, bringing herself up on her elbows. 'Maybe you'd like some breakfast with that?' She rolls her finger across her lip and bites down on the end. Enticing but, again, not right now. The fun's over.

'This is my breakfast. And you have five minutes to pull on that little black dress and be at my front door ready to leave. Otherwise, you'll have to find your own way home.'

She sits up. That pretty face twists into a frown. 'You're an asshole.'

I take another gulp of coffee as I leave the room. Walking away, I call back, 'I told you I was an asshole last night, Janey.'

'Janette, dickhead. I'm fucking Janette!'

I hear something crash against my bedroom wall and hope it's a pillow. Ten minutes later, I'm shutting the door of the Mercedes that belongs to my regular driver. Outside on the sidewalk, Janette flips me the bird through the window. My driver meets my eye through the rearview mirror. He chuckles and maneuvers out into the building city traffic.

We pull up outside a high-rise in the middle of bustling Midtown Manhattan. The modern glass building is home to Statham Turner, one of the top three law firms in New York and one of the best law firms in the world. That isn't just because I happen to be a partner at the firm; that is coincidence, mostly.

I tug the cuffs of my suit jacket to straighten the arms as I step onto the sidewalk. Once I've closed the door, I pat the roof of the car twice. Dipping my head in acknowledgment to a familiar suited colleague, who definitely works at the firm but whose name I can't remember, I stride past the revolving door of Lexington Tower.

At the end of the block, I find my destination. Fabio's bagel truck. There's only one thing for it, pre-court. Jarlsberg. A bagel crammed full of copious amounts of melted Jarlsberg.

Fabio leans out of the truck to hand a customer a foil-wrapped bagel. He clocks me when he lifts his head and flashes me a toothy welcome. 'Drew. My main man.' His Italian accent always makes that sound peculiar to me.

I'm just yards from my breakfast. I open my mouth to say, 'Hey,' but some blonde woman moves into my path and steals Fabio's attention.

I'm going to line up for a bagel? Seriously?

Fabio shrugs when I shake my head but serves Blondie. I check her out from behind, and I check out her *behind*.

If she's going to make me wait, it's not like I have anything better to do. It's either ogling or foot tapping, and I don't feel like tapping my foot today.

She's petite. Slim shoulders and waist. My guess is she's about five four, maybe five five in her flat shoes. Small though she is, that ass could wreak havoc on a man. Perfectly sculpted in tight jeans. Her T-shirt sits just below the waistline of her pants and lets me see those two cup-able globes. 'Erm, what do you have?' she asks Fabio. Her accent is British. Like the kind of British in movies. The kind of British my wealthy clients from that side of the pond speak.

'Bagels, lady. I got bagels.'

'Erm, right. I guess I'll take cheese?'

I can't help but roll my eyes, already knowing what Fabio's next words will be.

'What kind of cheese, lady?'

'I'm not sure. What kind do you have?'

I hang my head back and look to the clouds for the strength I need to get me through this painful experience. This is why only New Yorkers should eat from New York food trucks. The growl of frustration inside my mind must actually come out loud because Blondie turns her head across her shoulder to look at me. There's no mistaking her expression for anything other than a wicked scowl. She tuts and turns back to Fabio. Annoying as she is, she's hot. Fully hot.

As I'm having that thought, she throws me a second glance. It's fleeting but long enough for me to see her big, beautiful, alluring, blue eyes. The blue is dark, like the deep sea, but they seem to sparkle like diamonds catching the morning sunlight.

As pretty as she is, this is not a bar at midnight, and I have places to be. I raise my arm, unsubtly, and stare at the minute hand of my Omega. I receive another tut in response. Maybe I do want to tap my foot after all.

'Whatever cheese you have that melts. And tomatoes, please.'

Fabio sets about making her food, and I give myself another moment to indulge in that fine body.

'You want coffee?' Fabio asks.

Christ, don't ask her another question.

My thoughts must have left my mouth because Blondie says, 'Yes, please,' to the coffee, then 'Are you always such a dick, arse-hole?' to me.

I'm not sure if it's the level of feistiness coming from such a small thing, the hands on her hips, or the insult itself, that makes me smirk. 'Which is it, dick or asshole?'

She huffs her next breath as Fabio tells her she owes him four bucks. She takes the small satchel she's carrying from her shoulder and starts rummaging around.

And she rummages. And rummages.

For the love of God.

I take a ten-dollar bill from my wallet and hand it to Fabio. 'Here, it's on me.' I step around her and tell Fabio, 'I'll take my usual for court day.'

'Sure thing, Drew.'

He's already made my bagel, knowing from yesterday that I'm in court today, and knowing how I like my Jarlsberg on court days. He pours me a black coffee and tells me the ten will cover both Blondie's breakfast and mine.

I strip back the foil wrapper around my bagel. I'm taking my first, sensational bite as I turn from the cart, only to find my path blocked by Blondie.

'I didn't ask you to do that.'

'I know,' I manage through my full mouth as I walk past her.

'You're so bloody rude, do you know that? People in this city, damn it.'

Riled, I turn back to face her. She hasn't moved. Her lips are pressed tightly together. 'People in this city know how to get shit done. You tourists shouldn't come out to play during work hours. I have to be in court in an hour.'

That scowl is back. Her brows are furrowed. And damn, the woman looks fine when she pouts. Especially with that chest puffed out, drawing me in.

'For your information, I'm not a tourist. This is actually my lunch break. While you New Yorkers are sleeping, I'm killing myself in a patisserie kitchen from 4 a.m. So, shove that in your bagel and eat it.'

I never laugh on the morning of a trial. In fact, I don't laugh all that often. But a laugh comes from so low in my gut, it rocks my body. 'Shove that in my bagel and eat it?'

Her frown is broken by a smile that I can tell she's trying to fight. Dimples form at the sides of her pink lips. Sweet, charming dimples. She forces them away. 'Whatever. Thanks for breakfast.'

She turns on her heel, and I could let her go. Instead, I call out, 'I thought you said it was lunch.'

'Whatever, smart arse. I thought you said you had to be in court, like, yesterday.' She shouts her words down the sidewalk as she comes to a stop by a crossing.

'I do have to be in court. I guess you have to go back to making cupcakes, Blondie.'

She shouts something that's lost in the sound of cab horns and the subway running beneath my feet. I'm pretty sure she used at least one expletive, and I'm almost certain she doesn't make cupcakes for a living. There's a good chance she also likes birds.

I head to my office but not without casting one last glance at the curvy, stubborn woman with the sweetest damn smile I've ever seen. She has crossed the road but turns to look right back at me. I raise my coffee and shake my head.

Crazy, indecisive Brit. Manhattan is going to eat her alive.

\* \* \*

'Holy crap, you're smiling. Is the world about to end? Give it to me straight.'

Meet Sarah, my overpaid legal secretary whom I couldn't live without. She falls into step beside me as we head from the elevators to my office: the corner office, on the fifth of five floors the firm owns in the building. Incidentally, the top floor of Lexington Tower, also known as 'where the gods sit.'

I straighten my lips. 'Are my briefs ready?'

'They're already at court with your associate.'

'Good. I need you to file the Donatella application for me by eleven, latest, so that I can—'

'Already done.'

We step through the glass door into my office. 'Good. Is my tie crooked?'

Sarah stands in front of me and tugs on my tie, wiggles the knot, then sets it right. 'Better,' she says, patting my chest.

'Do I look like I'm going to kick ass?'

She winks. 'Damn straight.' With the dramatic flair only she possesses, she turns on her stiletto heel and struts out of my office, flicking her long, brunette waves across her shoulder as she goes.

Thirty-five minutes later, I'm pulling up outside the courthouse.

I fasten one button of my suit jacket as I step onto the sidewalk, almost in sync with Charles Wickman. He's the lead attorney for the US Securities and Exchange Commission, more commonly known as a spineless jackass. Oh, and the guy I'll be facing in court today as he tries, and inevitably will fail, to put my client behind bars.

Wickman finishes the bite of breakfast roll he's chewing. 'Ah, if it isn't the infamous Drew Harrington.'

The guy has one of those faces. You know, the type you want to smack and watch rebound into your fist over and over again like a speed bag. We studied at Columbia Law School together. He was a nerd back then. Realistically, he still is. But four years ago, he made his name taking out a big city gun in front of a grand jury. Since then, he's been slicking his greasy hair to the side and strutting around Manhattan like he runs the place.

'Wickman, I see they let you out of your pen.'

'Make all the jokes you want, Harrington. Let's see who's laughing when your guy is sitting behind bars.' He finishes his sentence with a sniff, flicking a knuckle under his nostrils. He could be wiping away a crumb. More likely, he's just being a pretentious dick.

'The only joke is that you think my guy will end up behind bars.' I take a step toward him, close enough that I can smell egg on his breath. 'I don't lose, Wickman. I'm the best goddamn defense money can buy.'

'There's a first time for everything.'

I lean closer so that passersby won't hear when I tell him, 'There is. And by the way, after the trial, if you still have a problem, we can always step outside to discuss it.'

For some insane reason, I want to finish that statement with, *Shove that in your bagel and eat it.*

# 2

## DREW

'A toast. To the most ruthless son of a bitch in the state.'

I raise my glass of scotch level with Marty's. That's Marty Statham, by the way. Of Statham Turner. The named partner who will end up backing me to get my name on the door one day. And one of my closest friends.

We met when I was new to the firm and he was a jumped-up associate who thought he could order me around. It was the definition of a love-hate relationship. We both hated each other and... Nope, it was just a hate relationship and we eventually came to respect each other. The thing is, if you spend enough hours locked in a glass tower together, respect and a good working relationship eventually blur the line between business and friendship. A mutual love of sports and good liquor got us a long way.

'Ah, Jesus, Drew, Wickman didn't know what hit him. You came at him so hard and fast, he didn't even see your turbo ass blazing right by him to the finish line.'

'You say that like I was ever behind him in the race.' I sip my fine single malt on the rocks.

'Our man was as guilty as sin, and Wickman had one hell of a witness. He definitely started in poll position.'

I can't help feeling smug. 'Too bad he got caught out doing shady shit to get his witness.' I won the case on a technicality that meant Wickman's key witness testimony was inadmissible. That's the only part about the win that sucks. I would have liked to kick his ass in a real dogfight.

As if his thoughts mirror my own, Marty tells me, 'A win on technicality is still a win, buddy. What are you eating?'

There's no need for me to open the black, leather-bound menu on the table in front of me. We've been celebrating big wins at this same place for years. It's the city's finest French restaurant and there's only one thing for a win like today's... *steak au poivre*.

Despite being a big, modern space, the restaurant is packed, and the atmosphere is buzzing. The only nights this place isn't teeming with people are Sundays and Mondays, and that's because it's closed. But the crowds never affect the quality of the food. Edmond Devereux is a five-star head chef, and I know personally that he is all about his standards. He employs only the best.

It's a good thing really, since his poker skills are awful, at best, and he does like a poker night with the boys.

Our order is taken by a waitress. I watch through the window to the open kitchen as she hands the ticket to Edmond. When he reads it, he seeks out Marty and me and holds up a hand in greeting.

'I don't need to tell you, Drew, this case won't hurt your chances of taking a named spot next to me.' Marty leans in and lowers his voice. 'I didn't tell you, obviously, but Turner is on his way out. He's talking about giving notice of his retirement soon. Very soon.'

Outwardly, I remain cool as I sip from my crystal glass. Inside, I'm buzzing. I was the youngest junior partner ever at Statham Turner. I busted a gut to make it to senior partner two years ago, when I was only thirty-two. If I made named partner by thirty-five... Shit.

I'm about to respond to Marty when a loud clatter pulls my attention to the service counter in the kitchen. Three staff bend to the ground to pick up whatever just spilled. One head pops up before the others. Blondie. She's apologizing profusely to Edmond who, oddly for him, seems to be taking it well.

'New girl,' Marty says. I imagine he's rolling his eyes and shaking his head, but my focus is on the petite blonde. She glances around the restaurant, her eyes full of apology. The fire I saw this morning is lost behind something... embarrassment, maybe. Her hair is tied back from her face, and her cheeks flush pink. Even that's a good look on her.

'You know her?' Marty asks.

I tear my gaze from Blondie, confused. I thought she made cupcakes. Well, okay I thought she made some kind of cakes. What is she doing in Edmond's restaurant?

'Not exactly. I bought her breakfast this morning.'

'She's the one you picked up last night?'

I can't resist another glance, but when I look at the station, the mess has been cleared and Blondie is nowhere to be seen.

'Ah, no. She was at Fabio's truck this morning. Long story. I ended up paying for her breakfast, that's all.'

He whistles through his teeth and leans back, jiggling his tie for effect. 'Didn't hook up with her and you still got stung for breakfast. Some might say you're losing your touch, Drew.'

It irks me that he's talking about the woman as a lay, and I have no idea why. Brushing off that alien feeling, I tell him, 'No chance, Marty. You're way off base. I'll keep smooth talking my way to the best picks, and you can take what's left in the draft.'

We eat steak and drink wine, moving from talking NFL references to talking about the Yankees' upcoming game against the Red

Sox. More than once, my attention drifts as I search the visible kitchen area for Blondie.

Our plates are cleared, and I'm looking for her again. 'Drew, what's up with you tonight?'

I finish the wine in my glass – specially paired to the steak – and play ignorant. 'What do you mean?'

'You've had half an ear at this table all night.'

'Sorry, man. I guess it's been a long day.'

Marty sits back in his chair and accepts a dessert menu handed to him by a waiter in a vest. 'Nothing to do with the fact you've been looking around the place like a hungry tiger?'

A tiger. That's right. That's who I am. Aggressive. Always on the prowl. King of the circuit. Not a guy who wants to know more about the petite, yet perfectly curved, indecisive Brit with the most incredible smile I've ever seen.

Clearing my throat, I drag my head back in the game. 'You haven't moaned like a fly hitting a windshield over the Giants' draft this week. You finally made peace with the selections?'

'Fuck no.' And we're back. Marty spends the next ten minutes crying like a little girl with pigtails and a pretty pink dress over the shit storm he predicts in the next NFL season.

I'm leaning back, laughing at Marty, because he's now so worked up, he's pulling his hair out. I'm not even speaking figuratively. His knuckles are white as he tugs on his roots.

'You need to calm down, Marty. I think I see you thinning on top.'

'Fuck off.'

'Yep, there it is. Just around the crown there.'

I spring forward, and my laughter dies instantly when Blondie's striking blue eyes are looking right at me. 'Erm, hi again.'

There's a moment of silence between us. I must have lost my mind somewhere between scotch and wine because I can't think of a damn thing to say. I'm just staring. Possibly memorizing every contour of her face. Frozen.

For the record, this never happens.

I feel Marty's focus flick between Blondie and me, and I come back to life.

'I didn't realize you were a waitress. I thought you made cupcakes.'

'Ah, I'm not.' She gestures to her white coat and the apron that's tied tightly around her slim waist. 'And like I told you this morning, I don't make cupcakes. But I do prefer being hidden behind those walls to being out here.'

Hidden? She should be on display. The comment seems entirely at odds with the confident, back-chatting woman I met this morning.

'Anyway, I, erm, wanted to give you this.' She places ten dollars on the table in front of me. 'Turns out I left my purse here this morning. Thank you for your help.'

I slide the bill back toward her. 'Don't worry about it. I don't need reimbursing.'

Her features visibly stiffen, and I start to see the feisty woman from the bagel truck. 'I'm sure you don't. But I don't want to owe you anything.'

'I wasn't holding a debt against you. Call it part of your tip.'

Her eyes widen, and I realize how shitty that remark must have sounded. 'Wow, you really are arrogant.'

Marty leans back in his seat. He looks primed to retort. I won't let him have a go at her. But I will take it on myself.

'I'm not sure you're supposed to insult paying customers. Is that a British thing?'

She opens her mouth as if she'd like to counter. From what I've seen of her so far, I'd expect nothing less. But she must check herself at the last minute because she closes her mouth and twists her lips into a fake smile, as if she's a wind-up toy. She leaves the bill on the table between us, Alexander Hamilton staring up at me, and asks, 'Can I get you any dessert?'

I almost scoff at how clearly annoyed she is.

'I'll take the cheesecake,' Marty tells her. She nods, and her tightly held jaw seems to relax momentarily before she looks back to me and raises her eyebrows.

'I'm not a sweet kind of guy,' I tell her.

'Funnily enough, I didn't have you pegged as a sweet guy, but I would like to know if you want pudding.'

Now I can't help the pfft of humor that escapes me. 'All right, I'm not a dessert man.'

Her scowl seems to disappear and she bites her lip. I think she's fighting a smile.

'That's because you haven't had my desserts,' she tells me.

'That's right, your cupcakes.'

She all but growls through her teeth. 'I don't make cupcakes. You're impossible. Has anyone ever told you that?'

'Lots of people, actually. I'm still not a cupcake fan though, thanks anyway.'

Shaking her head, she walks away from the table.

'What in the hell was that about?'

I take another second to watch that ass walk away, then give Marty my attention. 'Since when do you order dessert?'

'Since the pastry chef looks like her.'

I hold up a hand to the barman at the far side of the room. He knows my usual.

As I'm enjoying my cognac, Blondie returns with four plates, two on each arm. She grips a plate of cheesecake in her right hand, with another plate stacked behind it, balanced on her forearm. She holds out her arm in front of Marty. 'I'm so sorry, I'm a chef, not a waitress. I've worked out how to carry this many plates but not how to put them down. Would you mind?' Marty's eyes run all over her as he takes the plate with cheesecake. His interest makes me want to tear his eyes from their sockets.

Blondie doesn't seem to notice it. She turns to me and inclines her head to the plates she's holding. 'Your turn.' The remaining three plates contain exquisite-looking desserts. Not cupcakes at all but fine cakes, decorated in what can only be described as art. Intricate sugar and chocolate art.

'Opera with a Twist. Violet Passion. Red Silk. That's my take on red velvet cake.'

I stare at the plates, honestly, a little wowed.

'Well, help me out here.'

I feel my brows furrow as I take the Opera cake from her right arm. Gold dust decorates the plate and what looks like gold leaf has been crumbled into flakes and scattered around the top, making the thing look like a million dollars. Blondie puts the other two plates down on the table in front of me, shuffling my cognac aside to make room.

Nope, these are definitely not Granny's homemade cupcakes.

'They're on the house. You can thank me by enjoying them. Enjoy the rest of your evening, gents.' I notice now that her white uniform has been replaced by jeans and a blouse.

'Where are you going?' I ask, without knowing why.

'To bed.' The thought of Blondie in bed has me swallowing so hard, my Adam's apple is practically grating my neck. 'It's been a long day, and yours is the last table for desserts, so I'm off duty. Plus, I have to be up at 4 a.m.'

I watch her leave. I'm still looking as the door to the restaurant closes behind her. And I'm still looking when she walks by the window and glances back at me.

# 3

## DREW

Towel drying my hair, I move around my apartment, blissfully naked. Dropping the towel around my neck, I pour myself a black coffee and look at the three takeout boxes lined along the granite top of my kitchen counter. The woman made me take a doggy bag, for Christ's sake. The thought makes me snicker. Drew Harrington took a doggy bag from a restaurant and actually headed home, alone, after dinner. It's not like the coming-home-alone thing never happens. But it never happens the night after a big win in court.

Ignoring the white cartons, I take my caffeine hit to the wall of windows and watch the rising sun. But they're leering at me. I can feel the calories goading me from the counter. The sugar and fat staring at the muscles of my back that I work damn hard to keep in good shape. I had tried the Opera cake in the restaurant. I'd eaten a quarter, and though I didn't think I reacted to the most delectable thing I have ever tasted, something made Marty lean over the table and cut off a forkful. The remaining half of the Opera cake, along with the Violet Passion and Red Silk, were placed into cartons and bagged up for me to take away.

It left me no choice but to come home alone. It's not like I could have taken my doggy bag to another bar.

I turn my back to the window and stare at the three boxes. I can almost taste the sweetness of Opera with a Twist. The bitter aftertaste of something, dark chocolate, perhaps, left in my mouth. My tongue slips along my lip as I remember the way the ganache dissolved: light, slick, delicious.

Screw it.

I grab a fork, pull up a stool at my breakfast bar, and open the lid of each carton. I start with Opera with a Twist. I need just one more mouthful. And whoa, Opera plus coffee. Now there's a match made in obesity heaven.

I take every last piece from my fork, licking the sides; then I open my eyes to Red Silk.

White chocolate flakes – not flakes, something fancier than flakes – decorate the top of red waves of smooth, glossy icing. It really does look like silk. Suddenly, my mind is no longer on cake but the thought of Blondie in a red, silk lingerie set. Maybe something trimmed in black lace.

Jesus, Drew. It's only a cake.

Cracking my neck and clearing my throat in an extremely masculine way, I slide my fork through the lingerie topping and into layers of red velvet cake and cream. The cream oozes as the steel cuts through the dessert. I'm fighting to keep my filthy mind on cake as I bring the fork to my mouth.

Damn. I was wrong. This isn't just cream. It's... more. White chocolate. Vanilla. I have no idea beyond how good it tastes on my tongue.

I wonder how Blondie would taste on my tongue? I wash away the thought immediately and turn my attention to the third and final cake. Violet Passion. But just whispering the name to myself has my member stirring. This. This is exactly why I need to get laid after a big win. Now I have excess testosterone that I'm going to have to take care of before I go to the office.

Violet Passion is cylindrical. A purple, shiny finish, as shiny as Red Silk, covers the entire cake. A simple yellow and purple flower sits in the middle. I hope that's edible.

My fork glides through the cake like a hot knife through butter. As the round bursts, syrup spills through the layers of purple and yellow, the exotic scent of passion fruit striking my nose. Taking a piece of everything and pushing syrup onto my fork with my finger, I taste Violet Passion.

Sweetness. A sour kick. If a cake can be quirky, this is quirky. This is... this is Blondie. Those sweet dimples. That perfect smile. Her Britishisms.

Holy crap, I have a thing for the indecisive, kind of obnoxious patisserie chef.

'That's ridiculous,' I say for the benefit of no one other than my sanity. I like brunettes, for a start. Tall, leggy brunettes. I like women who are less interested in bickering with me and more interested in getting laid.

I close the lids on passion and silk and head back to the shower. This testosterone has got to go. Now.

\* \* \*

As I stand on the sidewalk outside Lexington Tower, I'm feeling better. A heap more rational now that my right hand has straightened me out.

I consider avoiding Fabio's altogether. I definitely don't need anymore to eat for breakfast after those cakes. But I do want a coffee.

Marty opens a car door and steps onto the sidewalk in front of me. I break my pace to allow us to walk in sync. 'Fabio's?' he asks.

I nod. 'You look rough.'

'I call this look Veronica.'

'Veronica for the third time in two weeks. Are you sure she's still just a lay?'

'Are you keeping tabs on my sex life now, Harrington?'

'No. But I am keeping tabs on your impending matrimony.'

He chortles. 'No chance. I'm like the Dean Martin of the circuit.'

I scoff. 'The hell you are.'

'Actually, let's go with Sinatra. Still a notorious ladies' man but more classy about it than Dean Martin. That's me. Classy bachelor.'

This time, my scoff turns to a laugh. Fabio waves a hand at us from his truck. 'The usual?' he shouts.

I tell him just coffee for me. Marty gets his standard turkey bacon bagel and a coffee.

As I take my first mouthful of caffeine, Fabio leans on his forearms and asks, 'What happened yesterday, my man?'

'Fabio, you need to ask? I won the case,' I tell him.

'I know you win your cases. I meant with the girl. I could feel that chemistry from my truck. Could have fried bacon on that heat.'

Marty's eyebrows are raised as he wipes crumbs from his mouth.

'I bought the woman breakfast. You two need to calm the hell down.'

Fabio holds up his hands. 'Whatever you say, my man. Whatever you say.' As I'm shaking my head, I take a look over my shoulder. Am I making sure she isn't here or wishing she was?

Dismissing the two assholes trying to get a rise out of me, and my own wayward thoughts, I change the subject. 'Did you get that mess straightened out with your street license, Fabio?'

'Yeah, thanks, Drew. Got the new one here.' He holds up his mobile food vendor license with pride. 'You fixed me right up. Are you sure I can't pay you?'

'Forget it. Just keep making the best coffee in the city; that suits me.'

'I appreciate it, Drew. Really.'

I nod, not wanting to give Fabio a chance to get all sentimental on me, and make my way to the office.

* * *

I'm standing behind my desk, waiting for my laptop to boot, when Sarah steps inside.

'Smiling again. Who was last night's celebratory lay?'

'Sometimes you cross the line, Sarah, you know that?'

'Please. I'm Sarah. I define the line.'

I look down to hide my smirk. She's clearly been binge-watching *Suits* again. 'How many times have we had the discussion about you blurring the line between boss and friend?'

She starts counting on her fingers. When she's used them all up, she shrugs. 'Nope, sorry, too many to count.'

The woman drives me mad, but she's the feistiest woman I know, and I like that. I like that she challenges me. It's part of the reason we're such good friends. I just don't need to tell her that.

'I've dealt with your post-court filings. You've got a ten-thirty with Carlton Best. And Preston Hamilton asked if you can move your three o'clock to four.'

'Can I?'

She tsks. 'Already done. Remember, I have a half day today with full pay.'

I lift my head sharply from where I'm typing my password. 'Did I authorize that?'

She smiles and turns on her heel to leave my office, purposely swaying her hips as she moves. 'You sure did. You said I should consider it part of my birthday gift.'

I stand up straight. 'Is that right? What else did I get you?'

She reaches her desk and holds up a scarlet leather handbag. 'This limited-edition Dior.'

'I'm a hell of a boss.'

She sits and spins in her chair to face her computer screen. 'The best.'

I should sit. I should start trawling through my inbox. But I don't. With one hand on the waistband of my gray, tailored pants, I rub my other hand over my day-old stubble – yep, it's definitely a non-court day. Then my fingers find my lips. The lingering taste of coffee reminds me just how good that cake was with my morning blend. And I get the most ridiculous, impulsive idea I've had in a while.

I pull a piece of paper from the top drawer of my desk and grin to myself as I write.

*Blondie,*

*Thanks for the desserts and the hours I will now need to put in at the gym. For your information, I'm STILL not a dessert man. As they were on the house (kind of), I think you deserve some constructive feedback, so here goes:*

*In third place, with a score of 5/10, we have Opera with a Twist. In second place, scoring 5.75/10, Red Silk.*

*The winner of mediocre desserts (read: glorified cupcakes), is:*

*Violet Passion. 6/10.*

*See you around, Cupcake. Drew x*

'Sarah, I'm going out. I'll be back before my ten-thirty.'

\* \* \*

I walk through the glass door of Edmond's restaurant. Part of me was hoping it wouldn't be open because on the short walk here, I started to wonder what on earth I am doing. Why I'm sending notes like a kid. And doing it in person. Impulsive is not who I am. Instinctive, yes. Impulsive, no way.

Edmond is sitting at a table with Beatrice, the restaurant manager, documents and coffee laid out in front of them. He looks up first. 'Drew, how are you?' His French accent has softened over the years.

'Edmond. Beatrice. I'm good, I'm good. I, ah...' Suddenly feel like a total idiot. 'You have a new girl working for you.' And I don't even know her name. 'Patisserie.'

They exchange looks, then Beatrice responds. 'Do you mean Becky?'

'Is she blonde with...' – a body I want to roll around the sheets with? – 'ah, blue eyes?' Quick thinking, Drew. Nice.

Amusement is splayed all over Beatrice's face as she tucks her auburn hair behind her ear and stands to walk over to me. 'That sounds like Becky. She's been here nine months.'

'Nine months? I've never seen her before.' God knows I'd remember.

'Mm-hm, nine months. She's always tucked away in the kitchen, I guess. Do you want me to grab her for you?'

'She's here?' My words come out too high-pitched, as if someone just grabbed my balls and squeezed. My heart starts thumping in my chest. I think I might be having some kind of medical condition here. I press the side of my fist to my chest. What the actual...?

Edmond moves over from the table. 'She's not here. She finished her morning shift early, and I sent her home. She'll be back in for tonight's service.'

My breathing calms. 'Right. Would you just give her this note for me? She, ah, asked for my feedback on one of...' I give up because the look on both Beatrice and Edmond's faces tells me they see right through my façade. 'Could you just give this to her? She'll know who it's from.'

Beatrice grins. 'Sure will.'

I make some kind of frustrated grumbling noise and rub my fingers along my jaw. 'Thanks. Edmond, we still on for poker Saturday, my place?'

'I'll be there as soon as service is finished.'

I bolt from the place faster than lightning: idiotic, caught in the act, not fooling anyone. I head to the sanctity of the Drew I was before tasting those damn cakes. The Drew who kicks ass. The Drew who keeps women around long enough in the morning for seconds of the meal he had the night before, and no more. I head back to the office to prepare for my ten-thirty.

# 4

---

## DREW

I'm sitting at the head of the oval board table, just off center. Marty and Richard Turner are in the chief seats. Opposite me is Patrick James: the joker who thinks he'll be my competition for named partner. No chance. I mean the guy has two first names. Come on.

The other Statham Turner partners fill the sixteen seats at the table. Other attorneys stand or perch on the window ledges. Some are dialed in and viewing the monthly partners' meeting via videocon. We've covered most items on the agenda, but we're running over.

A tentative knock on the door tells us breakfast has arrived. Marty flicks a finger, beckoning the kitchen staff to come in.

'Put it in the middle,' he tells the woman whose name I do not know, despite her working here for years. 'All right, everyone, let's grab a bite and we'll finish up,' he tells the rest of us. He glances at his watch. 'I appreciate some of you have places to be. For those of you who don't, you ought to.'

Like me, Marty can be a class A jerk to work with. We know it but that's part of what makes us good lawyers. But it wasn't his arrogance that helped get him named partner at thirty-six. What did help was that his father was the Statham predecessor. I don't mean Marty didn't deserve it on merit, but on personality alone, he might not have won the vote of all the partners.

The server leans between Marty and me, putting down two plates. She's a middle-aged woman. Kind of plump with a bad perm. She mustn't have got the memo that the eighties are over.

One of the plates is stacked with turkey bacon bagels; I can take a good guess at who ordered those. The other hosts a selection of French pastries. As I consider the French pastries, I suddenly feel like the arrogant ass I am.

This woman has served me for the better part of a decade, as a junior and a partner, and I've never given her the courtesy of asking her name. In fact, I've possibly never even thanked her for her service. She comes and goes largely under the radar. She probably gets a train from some working-class suburb and puts up with the commute and minimum wage to feed and clothe a family.

I look at her, then the plates, and this time I don't just see food; I see bread that someone has baked this morning because Statham Turner considers itself too highbrow to order in. Maybe this lady even baked as well as serving. I reach out for a bagel and find my lips curling. *Shove that in your bagel and eat it.* I can't stop the pfft of amusement that breaks my lips.

I rub my mouth quickly and clear my throat, disguising the humor and regaining my composure.

'A plate, Mr Harrington?' The server holds out a side plate. I take it and, for the first time ever, I say, 'Thank you, ah...?'

The fact that she looks startled makes me feel like an even bigger ass. Then, as if one 'thank you' can make up for the countless times I haven't thanked her, she beams. 'Tricia.'

I nod. 'Thank you, Tricia.'

'You're welcome, Mr Harrington.'

'Drew.'

She presses her lips together with two quick nods, but her eyes continue to smile. And I feel... good?

I take a bite, then set down the bagel in front of me. My mind goes right back to the bagel truck and, I've now decided, the most stunning woman I've ever seen. I've seen hot women. I've had hot women. But Blondie... she's hot in a different way. Like the kind of beautiful you want to keep in your bed not just all night but all the next day too, even when the makeup has come off and the mini-dress and heels are on the floor. She's natural, fresh. The kind of mesmerizing you don't just see in a club but the kind you want to take to the Hamptons and roll around in the sand with for an entire weekend.

What the heck am I thinking?

'Drew. Drew?'

I jerk back to reality, where all eyes around the table are on me. In the process, I knock my coffee cup on its saucer, spilling coffee. 'Shit.' I look up to see Marty's scrunched brows. They're somewhere between questioning and pissed. Tricia is still in the room and comes to my rescue with a towel to mop up the coffee. 'Sorry, I was thinking about the strategy for the Harbandon case. Something just came to me.'

Marty is still looking at me the same way but he says for everyone else's benefit, 'Always got your mind on the game, Drew. Take note, folks, this is what a top dog looks like.' I breathe subtly and straighten my shoulders. 'Looked like you were going to make love to your bagel to me,' Patrick mutters.

I lean across the table and whisper. 'I don't need to put my dick in bagel holes, Pat. That's for people like you. You know, the kind of people who don't have women falling at their feet.'

Marty sniggers. 'As I was saying, Drew aced it. It was a big win for the firm, and the coverage of the case won't harm our profile either.'

'All in a day's work,' I say, back to slick, confident, best goddamn lawyer at the table.

Blondie needs to get the hell out of my head. This firm is my focus. This is what I do. This is what I've been working twenty-eight hours a day, eight days a week to achieve.

'To our final matter then. Richard, I'll let you do the honors.'

Marty glances at me and this time there's a subtle curl of his lips at one side. It's my turn to frown questioningly.

'Thank you, Marty.' Richard rises from his leather chair and fastens one button of his suit jacket. 'As many of you know, I have been considering retirement for some time. I was here at the very beginning. I helped build this firm from nothing. And I'm incredibly proud of what we've achieved in the last thirty years.' He runs a hand through his thin, gray hair. 'The time has come for me to hand over the reins. I wanted you all to know together. Today, I will formally serve my notice to retire. I'll be here to oversee a vote on my replacement as named partner and to assist in the handover process. However, from today, I won't be taking new cases.'

I don't hear the rest of his speech. I'm too busy throwing my bring-it glare across the table at Patrick. Statham Harrington. That's what this firm will become, whether Patrick wants to cry about it or not.

When the meeting is wrapped up, I head with Marty in the direction of my office. 'Why didn't you tell me? You knew when we had dinner the other night. You had to have known. It was two days ago, for Christ's sake.' I'm annoyed, but my voice is at a level below conversational as we walk the corridors, keeping beneath the earshot of the secretaries in the open-plan pool.

'He wanted to announce it, Drew. I owe the man that. He's a big reason this firm is Statham Turner and not Wilson Turner.' He's referring to Richard having his back when he was running for named partner. 'It makes no difference. You know you're front runner. Everyone in that room knows you're front runner.'

I scoff. 'Patrick?'

'Well, no, he doesn't seem to have caught the ball.' He stops in front of his office door. 'I've got to tell you though, Drew. While Patrick doesn't have your balls, or your financials, the other partners like him. You might want to think about that in the run up to a vote. God knows I had to think about that once too.'

'Are you telling me to stop being an asshole like you, Marty?'

He shakes his head with a smirk. 'Something like that. Just don't give them a reason not to vote for you. Maybe let them see that as well as being a shark, you're a human too.'

'That's not my style, Marty. You know it. They know it. They'll vote me in because I'm a shit hot attorney, not because I bake cupcakes with my granny.'

His face distorts. 'Cupcakes with your granny? What the hell kind of reference is that?'

He turns his back to me, and I continue toward my office. What the hell kind of reference *was* that?

I need to brush off that girl. I need to stop thinking about stupid cakes. I need to be Drew. King of the courtroom. Not the goof ball who spills his coffee and starts thinking about a woman instead of becoming named partner. Jesus, I must have looked like a dumbass in that meeting.

My anger thickens when I reach Sarah's desk outside my office and she isn't there. Where the hell is she?

I stop dead in my tracks on the threshold of my office. Through the glass walls, I see the last woman I want to see right now.

Opposite Sarah, who is sitting with one leg crossed over the other on the arm of my leather sofa, her head thrown back as if she's laughing at something, is Blondie. Yes, Blondie. She's sitting on the sofa with... what the hell... chocolates set out on the coffee table.

I clear my throat, unmoving. God, she gets more attractive every time I see her. She's the Devil. The actual, distraction-that-I-don't-need, godforsaken Devil.

She stands, adjusting her striped shirt and tucking it into her skinny jeans. Her blue irises are bright, like she's smiling in her eyes. And they're staring right at me.

'So, my desserts are mediocre?' Her hands come to her hips, and she pouts playfully. The attitude that seems to have stuck in my head for the last two days is back. Proof of the interruption she's causing to what my mind should really be focused on.

'What are you doing here?' My words are more curt than I intend, but I am pissed. More at myself than her, for sure, but pissed nonetheless. She can't just come in here, all gorgeous as hell and... I turn my attention to Sarah. 'Why did you let her into my office?'

Sarah stands and holds up two hands. 'Whoa, calm, Drew. Becky was—'

'Becky? That's right; that's your name.' I remember from Beatrice at the restaurant yesterday. I'm still being abrupt and, frankly, shitty, but she needs to leave. This force field she seems to have around her is pulling me in and threatening to tilt my axis in the entirely wrong direction. She needs to get out of my space.

She looks at me, then places a hand gently on Sarah's arm. 'It's okay, Sarah. I'm sorry. I misunderstood. I don't know many people in the city, and I thought your note... I guess I thought it was an invitation to be friendly. I got it wrong. I'm sorry. Really sorry.'

She starts packing the chocolates on the table in front of her into a plastic tub. As she does, Sarah's eyes shoot daggers at me. They're no more painful than the daggers I feel in my gut when I notice Becky's shoulders sag.

Sarah strides past me and out of the office, glaring at me as she goes. Becky picks up her bags and moves toward me, her head down, her eyes on the ground. That fiery temper I seem to be crazily addicted to is gone. I hate that I'm the reason for its disappearance. When she's in front of me, I reach out to her shoulder. 'I'm sorry, I didn't mean to upset you. I just have a lot going on. This is my workplace.'

The smile she gives me is obviously forced. It doesn't reach her eyes. Those eyes, wide and truly entrancing. 'You didn't. This was my mistake. It won't happen again.'

She heads quickly toward the elevators, and I look after her. That was the right thing to do. I can't deal with her. A woman. I mean, I can deal with a woman, women. Just not her. Not now.

'If that was the best way to handle that situation, why do you feel so shitty about it?' Sarah is leaning back in her chair, judging me. Nailing my thoughts better than I can understand them myself.

Damn it.

I jog down the corridor and toward the elevators. As if Drew Harrington runs after women. Christ. When the car opens, Becky steps inside. I get there just in time to jam my hands between the doors and push them open. 'Becky.'

As the doors move farther apart, I see two suited men in the elevator with her. One is an associate at the firm, whose face I recognize. The other is a junior partner in the Insolvency team. There's no way I'm looking like a pussy in front of these men. I should have thought this through. I should have planned what to say. I should have expected other attorneys to be in the elevator.

Becky looks from the floor to me. I try to apologize silently because I can't say the words. Not here. Not now. I step back from the doors, wishing they would just close. Close on this pathetic version of me.

The doors start to move. She looks so hurt. I can't give her nothing. 'You were right about the letter,' I tell her.

Then she's gone, and I'm staring at closed elevator doors, looking and feeling like a dick.

When I get back to my office, Sarah is standing by my desk, arms folded.

'It's for the best,' I tell her.

'Whether it is or it isn't, you just had a real bad attitude with the sweetest girl I've met in a hell of a long time. What gives?'

I move behind my desk and fire up my laptop, still standing because I'm too worked up to sit. 'Nothing gives.'

'She told me about the note you left, Drew. She's wrong. It wasn't just friendly. It was flirting. You went out of your way to get her attention, then she shows up here to reciprocate, and you basically punch her in the gut.' I wince at her words, and in my mind, I see Becky standing in the elevator, her gaze on the ground. I did upset her.

I sit in my chair and type my password. 'I've got work to do,' I growl.

'She made chocolates for you. Handmade. And instead of going home to bed after her early morning shift, she chose the chocolates she thought suited your personality and brought them to your office.'

She did?

'Yeah, well, I told her I'm not a dessert person. I don't even know the woman. I didn't even know her name until yesterday.' Sarah starts to speak but I hold up a hand, cutting her off. 'Nor do I want or need to know anything about her.'

She storms toward the office door. 'Sometimes, Drew Harrington, you're an insensitive piece of work. The girl is asking for a friend in this big old city.'

'If you want her to have a friend, why don't you befriend her?'

'For your information, we're going to brunch on Saturday.' She tugs the door closed behind her.

I stare at my inbox, trying to focus. But I can't. Sarah's right. Marty's right. I don't show I have a human side. Based on this morning, I'm not even sure I do have a human side.

* * *

I have spent the rest of the morning trying to convince the CEO of one of my biggest clients not to sell out his business to an investment firm. Two reasons. Now is not the right time for a shake-up at the client who earns me my biggest income at Statham Turner. But it's also sound advice. That investment company would swoop in and have him out of his throne in a matter of months. It would take away everything he has built from scratch. Everything he has worked so hard for would be thrown away with one quick signature. I don't want to see that happen.

Yeah, I know, I sound like I give it shit. Truth is, I do. I've worked for the guy for years. I've had dinner with his wife and kids. I couldn't let him make such a mistake without at least trying to get him to see sense. By the time I finally hang up after the call, I think I have convinced him.

I swivel my chair from my window view to my desk. There's a white paper bag next to my laptop. Reaching inside, I find a pulled pork baguette. Not just any pulled pork baguette: a Hog Heaven pulled pork baguette. The best pig in the city.

I hold up the sandwich and wink at Sarah. She rolls her eyes and wafts a hand flippantly. I guess we're back on good terms.

I take the food to my window and look toward Staten Island as I eat. I was brought up on Staten Island. My folks still live there. I haven't since I went to Columbia, and I definitely don't go back as often as I should, but it will always be home. It will always be a place to get away from the hustle and bustle of the city. I haven't needed that for a while but sometimes, the city, the law, the constant dogfights, they can grind a man down.

As I'm staring out to the distance, I think about Becky. She just wants a friendly face in the city. I scoff through a bite of my sandwich. She chose the wrong man for that. Yet I still feel bad about the way I dismissed her.

I ball the empty paper bag in my hand and take aim at my waste basket, nailing the shot, as I always do. Then I put my hands in my pockets and, with a sigh, I resolve to at least apologize to her, the prettiest, most annoying damn Brit in New York.

I pass by Sarah's desk as she's taking off her headphones to end a call. 'You win. I'm going to apologize.'

'While I fully endorse that decision, you might want to hold off.'

'Why?'

'That was Archer Williamson's secretary on the phone. Archer is on his way down here. He wants to explain in person, but the gist is unsavory photographs in the hands of the media. Again.'

Archer Williamson. One of the slimiest, fakest sons of bitches walking the earth. The man's had more affairs than I've had cheeseburgers. And I like cheeseburgers. The greatest irony is that his logistics company is all about 'going green' and supporting women's and kids' charities. The guy has one of the cleanest public reputations in the world, and he's a total scumbag. Now he'll want me to work all night to get him another injunction to stop the press from going public with whatever his latest seedy shit is.

'That son of a—'

'Bitch.' Sarah finishes my sentence.

# 5

## DREW

'I brought you another coffee,' Sarah says, setting a mug on my desk. 'Can I get you anything else? A bite to eat? I can order in for you.'

I glance at the clock on my laptop and drag my hands over my face. 'No, I'm good. It's after one in the morning; you should go. You've been great tonight, thanks.'

'Any time, boss man. How's it going?'

'I think we're set. I just got off the phone with the judge. The injunction should be granted. That dirty, lying cheat will be off the hook, again.'

Don't get me wrong. I've been with a lot of women. But I would never cheat. I have more respect for myself than that, and I'm certain, if I ever found the right woman, I would have too much respect for her.

This isn't even my line of work – injunctions against the media – but Archer Williamson is a big client. Morals and the law are an interesting thing. They're both meant to keep us all on the straight and narrow. The problem is, when one fails, the other tends to follow suit. Still, if Archer's family is going to be hurt by his actions, he should be the one to break it to them. Airing his filth in public is not what his family needs. That's the only thing that stops me hating myself for protecting his ass.

'You did your job, Drew.' Sarah places a hand on my shoulder, and I cover it with my own. She's my accomplice in all of this, and I know she's just as uncomfortable about defending Archer as I am. To the other partners, I might seem impenetrable on all fronts, but Sarah knows some things get to me. Screwing over family and friends is high on that list.

'You too,' I tell her. 'Make sure you get my driver to take you home, all right?'

She nods. 'You know, I was thinking. If you're going to be here any longer, you won't have much time to wait before Becky starts her morning shift. Maybe you could still squeeze in that apology.'

I want to tell her she's crazy. Becky doesn't start for hours, and I'm wrecked and ready for sleep. Yet I don't say that because, more than once tonight, between calls to the judge and waiting for associates to draft court papers, my mind has wandered to Becky. Each time I think about how I treated her, I feel worse about how I handled the situation. I encouraged her to come here, and I charged through her like Babe Ruth would go through a bush league pitcher. She didn't deserve my anger. I was frustrated with myself and how I behaved in the partners' meeting, not at her, not really.

'Sleep tight, Sarah.'

''Night, Drew.'

When I finish my coffee, I head down to the kitchen and make myself another.

\* \* \*

I'm standing on the corner of the block with my hands tucked into the pockets of my overcoat. It's spring, but it's still cold at this ungodly hour of the morning. I watch Becky climb out of her Uber. She looks up at the restaurant and smiles. It's a serene smile that makes her button nose crinkle. She's happy here. She might still be finding her feet in the city, but she looks like she's sticking around. I don't even know her and that thought warms my chilled body.

She doesn't notice me as she walks to the glass door of the restaurant and fumbles with the lock, then the alarm inside. When she's in and the lights are on, she holds up a hand to the driver and he pulls away.

I move to the door but don't knock, not yet. I just watch her take off her coat and hang it up. She drags her fingers through her smooth hair and pulls it into a knot on top of her head. I flex my fingers in my pocket, desperate to know exactly how silky those blonde locks feel.

Friends. That's it. There are bigger things at stake right now. Becoming named partner has been my goal for a long time. My sole goal. And it needs to remain my one and only focus. I've worked too hard to mess with my life plan now.

Eventually, I knock gently on the door. At least I thought it was gentle. The way Becky screams and practically jumps out of her own skin makes me realize otherwise.

She stares at me, her eyes locking on mine, which probably look wild from caffeine.

'Are you going to let me in?'

She approaches the door cautiously. 'This is a bit creepy, Drew. You're not going to make me use my pepper spray, are you?'

I chuckle. 'That's not my intention, no.'

She unlocks the door and opens it but doesn't step aside to let me in. That happiness I saw just moments ago has turned to a frown that honestly looks adorable on her. 'I guess it's my turn to ask what you're doing here at my office?'

'I guess I deserve that.'

She drops one hand to her hip, the other still holding the door and blocking my entry. 'You sure do.'

Hmm, this isn't quite what I had planned. Not that I had had a plan beyond my impulse to see her.

'Right. Look, I came to apologize. I was a jerk with you, and I'm sorry. If you're looking for a friendly face in the city, I can be a friendly face.'

Her brows furrow. 'What makes you think I would want a friend like you?'

Ouch. I take a breath that leaves me on a tired exhale. The effects of my coffee might be starting to wane. 'You've got me. I don't even want to be your friend, but it's after four in the morning, I've been working all night, and I would really like those chocolates now.'

I count the seconds I wait for her response. One. Two. Slowly, subtly, that glower dissipates and her dimples start to appear on one side of her inviting pink lips. 'I thought you said my desserts were mediocre?'

I step forward and take hold of her hand, peeling it from the door. That small touch, my big hand folded around her small, delicate fingers, is like a blanket wrapping around my body. I find myself wondering how nice it would be to lie with her now, and sleep, actually sleep, in her arms.

She swallows deeply, as if she might have had the same brain fart I just had. I drop her hand and scratch the back of my neck for something to do with my fingers. She moves to close the door behind us, and I follow her to the kitchen. All the while, trying to shake the feeling that I'm the one who can't handle being a friendly face and only a friendly face.

The palpable awkwardness in the air begins to fall away as she sets about turning on ovens and taking bowls from stainless steel racks and cupboards. When she disappears into the refrigerated room, I try to calm my unusual nerves. I take off my coat and rest it on the bench, then I grab a stool from the bar and bring it into the kitchen.

I take a seat at the worktop, opposite where Becky is spreading out ingredients – flour, eggs, sugar – and quite obviously avoiding my eye.

'Are you going to look at me, British Becky the Cupcake Baker?'

She lifts her head sharply and, waving a wooden spoon at me, she says exactly what I expect her to say. 'I don't make cupcakes.'

She disappears to another part of the kitchen, which is larger than I had realized from the restaurant view. She returns with a box I recognize from my office yesterday. She takes off the lid and places a tray of chocolates in front of me.

'If I did make cupcakes, they would be like this.' She takes one more thing from the box, and it is very definitely a cupcake. I tell her so. 'Just wait.'

She slides it toward me and hands me a fork. 'Go ahead.'

I peel the paper from the sides of the cake and slide a fork through the creamy looking icing that's piled high like a whippy ice cream cone. I cut straight through the middle of the confection, and the yellow cake bursts with some kind of soft center. I look up to find Becky grinning.

I take icing, cake and the gooey center and put the hefty forkful into my mouth. My eyes close when I wrap my lips around the little bite of heaven. Mango. Cinnamon. Vanilla.

When I reluctantly peel open my eyelids, she's cocking one eyebrow at me, looking defiant and supercilious in equal measure.

'I want to lie so bad right now but this... this is no ordinary cupcake.'

She nods. 'I know. But I still don't make cupcakes.'

I laugh, hard. I have no idea whether I'm high on coffee, delirious from the combination of flavors in my mouth, or whether being around this woman somehow just makes me happy. 'You're modest, British Becky.'

'That makes two of us, Yankee Drew.'

As I begin working down the line of chocolates in front of me, Becky cracks eggs into bowls, sifts flour, and starts to hand whisk things, because she says that's how you get the best feel for the mixture.

'How come you're in New York?' I ask her.

She dips her little finger in the mixture and sucks. The things that action does to me have nothing to do with friendship. I force myself to look away. When she starts whisking again, she replies, and I finally brave facing her.

'I worked for Edmond in his London restaurant.' She shrugs and stares into the bowl. 'A job came up here and... I mean, Edmond works here in New York, mostly. What an opportunity, right?'

I nod, wondering why her expression tells me there's more to this story. I say nothing.

'So.' She plants the bowl on the counter, and her contemplative look switches to a smile. 'I thought, why not?'

'That's it?'

There's a slight pause that doesn't escape my attention before she says, 'That's it. Here I am.'

'Do you like it?'

'The kitchen?'

'The kitchen. New York.'

'I love working for Edmond. The pastries I get to make are amazing. But one day, I'd like to have my own place. A patisserie, not a restaurant. Something quaint. A place where I have regulars and I know their names and which cakes their kids and wives and husbands would like for their birthdays.'

'You're a family person?'

She shrugs and casts her attention back to her bowl. 'I guess. There's something about the idea of a family looking out for each other. It's... special.'

'And New York?'

She scoffs, and her momentary melancholy lifts. 'Well, so far I've met a lot of arrogant people. You know, specifically at bagel carts. It seems arrogant men in suits hang out there, and they just latch on.'

I'm laughing again as I suck chocolate from my fingers. 'Latch on?'

'Yeah, kind of like ticks. They get under your skin, uncomfortably so, and they won't let go.' Her smirk breaks into a giggle, but all I heard was that I'm under her skin. Yeah, well, that makes two of us.

'Hey, why am I doing all the work here? Get over here and help.'

Now it's my turn to raise a brow. 'You want me to make cakes with you?'

'Oh, come on, it's half past five in the morning and there's no one here to see you.'

As tired as I am, I slip off my suit jacket and roll my shirt sleeves up my forearms. After being told to wash my hands like a boy who's been playing in dirt before dinner, I'm on the other side of the counter beating cake mix in a bowl.

'Which chocolate is your favorite so far?' she asks.

'I think the one with the purple stuff inside.'

She's beating her own mix beside me and rocks into my side. 'That *stuff* is blackberry. And I don't think that one will be your favorite. Look out.' She puts a hand on the small of my back to nudge me out of the way and leans across the counter to pick up a chocolate. Her hand is warm through my shirt. As I'm thinking that, she leans further, and her ass moves dangerously close to my crotch. I'm staring, unashamedly so, and I'm pretty damn sure she catches me when she turns around. She's now facing me, close enough I can smell the sweet scent of shampoo or soap on her hair and skin. Vanilla. Coconuts. I fight the urge to press my lips to her skin and taste her.

Too much coffee and sugar, that's all it is. Coffee and sugar.

I set the mixing bowl on the bench and in doing so, I bring us closer together. My lungs force my breaths to come quicker and shallower. Jesus, I'm fifteen again.

'Try this one. This will be your favorite,' she says. There's a huskiness to her words I haven't noticed before. She lifts the chocolate, and my lips part as I get lost in her. In her beauty, her scent, the pheromones that ooze from her and infiltrate my mind.

Then I remember where the hell I am and jolt back from her. She drops her hand in response. 'Sorry, I, ah, here.' She takes my hand and puts the chocolate into my palm, then slips away from me.

My breath seems to remember its natural rhythm. I put the chocolate in my mouth. As soon as I crack the bitter dark chocolate shell, there's a rich, sweet burst of flavor. Not too sweet. Just sweet enough for me.

'Well?'

I cross my arms and lean back on the bench. 'You might be the one to make a sweet man out of me yet.'

She bites her bottom lip, and I realize she's probably uncomfortable under my ogling.

I have to do something to take the heat out of the air between us before I forget why I'm here. To be polite. Friendly. Human.

'So, besides ticks, what have you seen of New York?'

She exhales, probably as happy to escape the intensity that was just between us as I am. 'Between my shifts here and sleeping, not much.' She moves around the kitchen, taking cakes from the ovens and lining the various shapes, colors and sizes along the work benches. 'I'm actually on vacation next week, so I'm going to make a start. I have a list of things I want to do. I'm going to go up the Empire State Building. Take the subway to see Yankee Stadium, maybe do a tour or something because I don't actually know the rules of baseball. Mm, ride the ferry to Staten Island and take pictures of Manhattan and the Statue of Liberty as I pass by. Walk South Shore Boardwalk.'

She continues to talk and, sensing I've been relieved of cake-baking duties, I continue to listen to her from my stool. I could listen to her all night. That accent is actually kind of sweet, not at all irritating. Her voice is soft and gentle, but animated. Not for the first time this morning, I'm feeling like someone just wrapped me up in a thick blanket.

Suddenly, my lack of sleep is taking its toll. I rest an elbow on the worktop and lean my chin against my hand. Those dimples are back, and she's waving her wooden spoon in the air as she talks about a cute Italian restaurant she's heard of by Central Park. Apparently, it does the best pizzas in the city. When my eyes close, I still see her, like bright light that still shines through your eyelids when they're shut. As I drift into a calmness I haven't felt since... I don't remember... I take her with me. The sound of her voice. The curve of her lips. Her button nose. That sweet giggle.

\* \* \*

'Drew.' Her whisper floats into my ears like a song. I feel her fingertips against my temple. Then I smell cake. Moaning, I reach out my arm to wrap it around her. Instead of a beautiful woman and a soft mattress, my hand finds a stainless-steel work surface.

My eyes dart open, and I sit up quickly, glancing around Edmond's kitchen. 'Shit.'

Becky is no longer in her white chef uniform; she's in jeans and a T-shirt and she's biting her lip to stop herself from laughing.

'You fell asleep, Mr Big Shot.'

I scowl, despite being more embarrassed than angry, and stand. As I do, I find we're no longer alone in the kitchen. Ah, Jesus.

'Good morning, sunshine,' Edmond shouts across the space. I'll never hear the end of this with the guys.

Four other chefs are doing some kind of prep and clearly all fighting to hide their own amusement.

Well, there's nothing else for it. I stand and take a bow. 'Thanks for the service, guys.'

I pick up my suit jacket and coat, putting them on as I leave the kitchen. Becky follows me through the restaurant and pats my back, 100 per cent patronizingly. 'Come on, tough guy, I'll treat you to a breakfast bagel.'

I turn to face her and raise a finger in front of her nose. 'You.'

'Me what?' she says through a giggle.

I lose all my conviction and end up shaking my head, my smirk betraying my attempt to be angry. 'You shouldn't have let me sleep. And you shouldn't have put me in a sugar coma.'

'Oh, come on, even the best lawyer on the circuit needs a nap.'

I find myself wrapping an arm around her shoulders and pulling her to my side without conscious thought. 'You can buy me a bagel for that.'

\* \* \*

Once we're served, we stand to the side of Fabio's truck, eating our bagels and sipping coffee. 'Were you born here?' she asks.

I nod as I chew. 'Staten Island.'

'Do you have family?'

'My parents are around. They still live on the island. I have a much younger brother, and a sister who's a couple years younger than me. She can pretty much get anything she wants out of me.'

'That's what big brothers are supposed to be for, right?'

There's something almost wistful about the way she says it that has me wondering whether she has a brother she misses.

'Do you have a brother?'

'Yep. Older. I have two, actually. Two half brothers and two step-sisters. I'm the youngest. Three dads between us.'

'Do you miss them?'

She raises one shoulder and picks at the edge of her bagel. 'We're not really a close family. I needed and wanted a change.' She pauses, then, as if a wave of something comes over her, she lifts her head and smiles. 'Hey, if I ever want to see them it's only a flight away, right?'

I wait a beat, expecting her to say more. Nothing comes, and I get the feeling she might never want to see her family again.

I can't remember the last time any woman, other than Sarah, made me curious to know more. Like why did she need a change? I decide now is not the time to ask. In any event, why would she want to share her life story with me?

'Well, British Becky, thanks for the stainless-steel bed. I need to work now.'

'You're crazy. You need to go home and go to bed. Real bed. Or at least shower and change.'

'I can do that in the office.'

We both trash our wrappers, and we're left standing facing each other, an awkward silence descending. How on earth is this supposed to end? How would it end with Sarah? We're friends; it's just the same thing, right?

She gets there first. 'Okay, well, I guess I'll go decorate those cakes.'

'Right. Sure. And I'll go get my injunction.'

'Yep. Okay then.'

She turns to walk away, and I'm about to breathe a sigh of relief when she spins back around. 'It was nice to get to know you. Someone. In the city. Thanks, Drew.'

I nod because I'm not sure what else to say to her. Then I start to walk away. God, she's so great and so grateful that someone in this city spent time with her. She shouldn't be grateful. She's so... she's...

'Becky!'

She turns in the street and I'm shouting across the suits walking between us. 'You can't go to Yankee Stadium without actually watching a game. There's like a law against it. And I would know.' I feel passersby looking at me like I'm some kind of weirdo. I couldn't give a... 'Let me take you.'

'Okay!'

'Okay?'

'Okay!'

'I'll send a ticket to the restaurant.'

'Okay.' She's laughing as she walks backward away from me, not considering how many people will knock into her. Christ, she really is a tourist.

\* \* \*

'You're looking especially happy, considering you were here until the small hours.' Sarah carries her daily bowl of porridge as we walk the corridor. It's some quinoa thing that sounds healthy until you see that it's drowning under Manuka honey: Sarah's latest fad.

I try to rein in the grin I hadn't realized was on my face. Before I manage to do that, Sarah halts on the spot and sucks in a breath, making me stop alongside her. 'Are those yesterday's clothes?'

Ah, crap. I resume the walk to my office and she totters in her heels to catch up to me. 'They are, aren't they? No wonder you're smiling. I just told you to apologize to the woman. Although, wait, in Drew language that probably did mean sleep with her.'

'You've got the completely wrong idea. And don't you have work to do?'

'My job is to see and hear everything that goes on in this place and report back to you. What I'm seeing and hearing is that you slept with Becky.'

When we reach her desk, I press a hand to her shoulder and encourage her to sit. 'No, I didn't. If you must know, I fell asleep in these clothes. Now, I'm going to grab a spare suit from my office, shower and change. Then I'm going to do my job. Like you should be doing yours.'

She raises a hand and leans back in her desk chair. 'Hold up. You went to her apartment?'

I growl and screw my knuckles into my suddenly tired eyes. 'No, I fell asleep in the kitchen at the restaurant.'

She presses a hand to her mouth, but her bellowing laugh still finds a way out. 'You're such a loser.'

'I'm not a loser, I'm your boss.' I make a move toward my office and call back to her. 'Can you get me two tickets to the Yankees and Royals on Tuesday? Pull some strings and make them good ones.'

'We're going to the game?' comes another voice.

Stepping into my office, I find the source of that voice. Marty is sitting on my sofa drinking a coffee that looks like it came from Fabio. His legs are spread in his black suit pants. His free arm is draped lazily along the top of the cushions.

'No, we're not. I'm taking a friend.'

'I'm your friend.'

I move to the standing wardrobe in the corner of my office and pull out a dark-gray suit, white shirt and blue silk tie.

'A different friend.'

'Which one?'

'Christ, what is it with the Spanish inquisition from you and Sarah this morning? What's up, anyway?'

He stands, drains the last of his coffee and fires the empty cup at my waste basket. Miss.

'You've moved the basket,' he says. 'I came to tell you I've been putting out feelers among the other partners, trying to get a sense of whether they'll vote for you or Patrick when it comes to naming Richard's replacement.'

I scoff. 'Please, if they know what's good for their earnings, no partner in their right mind is going to vote for Patrick over me.'

'Right there, Drew.' He points at me with one hand and presses the other into his pants pocket. 'That attitude is losing you votes. I've got to tell you, buddy, the guys on the forty-sixth floor are all for Pat.'

I lay my suit on the desk and prop my ass onto the edge of it. 'Who gives a shit about the guys on forty-six? They're real estate attorneys, for Christ's sake. They hardly even qualify to be taken seriously.'

'Yeah, well, they'll be taken seriously when it comes to a vote. Right now, I'd say you're looking at evens. You need to do something to tip the scales in your favor. Our favor.'

'Like what?'

He holds out his hands. 'I don't know, Drew. Take them for steak. Buy them Yankees tickets. Whatever you have to do. I'll be damned if my name is sitting alongside fucking Patrick's.'

'I'm not bribing a bunch of real estate jokers with good meat. That's not my style, Marty, and you know it.'

'It's up to you, Drew. But it's on your stubborn head if this vote doesn't go the way we want it.'

With that, he leaves. At the door, he twists back to me, his hand braced on the handle. 'Is that the suit you were wearing yesterday?'

Goddamn it. 'No.'

# 6

## BECKY

*Twenty years ago*

Mummy stops the car outside Nanna's house. I'm already excited. I love Nanna's house. It's nicer than ours. Not bigger. It's quite small. It's a white house in a row of other white houses. But Nanna's house feels nicer. I like how it smells of her, and I like that she lets me watch cartoons. And we always have fun, Nanna and me. I like that too; it is always just Nanna and me, no one else. She listens to me and sings to me. She's the best nanna in the whole wide world.

I unfasten my seatbelt and slip from my booster seat onto the path next to Nanna's front garden. Her roses are big and pink. She loves her roses. She spends a long, long time pulling yellow leaves off them and pouring special grow juice on them.

Mummy stays in the car and winds down the window. 'I'll be back later. Tell Meg to give you lunch and dinner.'

I pull on my backpack and wave, but Mummy is already driving down the road. It makes me sad that she never says goodbye. Nanna says maybe it's because she is sad to be leaving me.

I shrug and head to the house. Nanna is already coming down the drive to see me. Her arms are stretched out wide.

I run to her, and she scoops me up. I wrap my arms around her jiggly belly and she squeezes me tighter, kissing me on the head. She smells like the talcum powder she puts on me after a bath. 'Oh, hello, my baby. I've missed you.'

She tickles under my arms. It always makes me giggle. 'I've missed you too, Nanna. Mummy said she was too busy to bring me last weekend. And the weekend before, Stella from next door looked after me and my brothers and sisters.'

Nanna pushes her head against mine in the way she normally does. Her curly, gray hair is fluffy like a teddy and tickly on my skin. 'Well, you're here now, sweet pea. Guess what?'

She starts walking us into the house, still carrying me. There are so many things, I can't think of what to guess.

'What am I wearing?' she continues.

I open my mouth wide. 'A pinnie! Are we making cakes?'

'We sure are. What's in this bag of yours today?'

I wriggle out of the pink backpack that Nanna bought me and unzip it when she sets me down on a wooden chair at the kitchen table.

I take out my school workbook. 'I bought this to show you.'

Nanna leans her head to one side, and I know what I did wrong. 'You bought it, or you *brought* it?'

'Oops.'

'Remember, Rebecca, *brought* is when you have brought something along with you. *Bought* is when you've bought something from a shop.' She's told me this before, but I always forget. Some words I'm good at but bought just sometimes slips out. I do it at my house, and Mummy never says anything, but Nanna *allllways* catches me.

'Now, let me see.' She takes the orange book from me and opens it to the last page. She draws in a big breath and smiles. 'You got ten out of ten? This is the spelling test we worked on last time, isn't it?'

I nod, and my smile hurts my lips because it is so wide.

'Well, it's a good thing I bought you an extra special treat for baking today, isn't it?

I feel my eyes open wide. Nanna takes a paper bag from the kitchen bench and hands it to me. I look inside and slide out pictures of all the princesses I love. Cinderella – she's my favorite – and Belle, and Princess Jasmine.

'They are to go on top of the cakes we make.'

'Really?' I stand up on my chair and wrap my arms around her neck. 'Thank you, Nanna.'

'You're very welcome, sweet pea. Now, let's get this jacket off and start baking, shall we?'

She takes off my pink coat, leaving me in my dungarees and flowery T-shirt – an outfit my Nanna bought me. She combs my hair, hurting me when she tugs on the tangles, but she puts it into a plait and I like it when she does that. It feels nice to have someone play with my hair. When she's done, she makes me stand on a stool and wash my hands in the sink.

When I'm clean, she holds a big bowl and tells me to put in flour and eggs and sugar. She beats them all together until all the lumpy bits are gone; then she lets me have a go. It aches my arm, but I keep going because it's so much fun making cakes with Nanna.

'What do you say to doing some vanilla cakes and some choco-late cakes?' She takes a bar of chocolate from the fridge and wiggles it in front of my face.

'I think you know the answer to that, Nanna.'

She laughs. Her laugh is pretty.

When our mix is done, we pour it into colored papers inside a tin. I have to stand on my stool and watch Nanna put the cakes in the oven because she says it's burny.

'Right you are then, why don't you spell the word' – she looks in my orange workbook – 'pottery for me, and if you spell it correctly, I'll let you lick the chocolate bowl?'

I clap my hands and try to think. I remember how the word looks from my school class. 'P O T E… no, P O T T E R Y. Pot-tery.'

She tucks a paper towel into my T-shirt at the neck, then we sit at the kitchen table, and I lick the chocolate bowl and the wooden spoon. Nanna tries not to, I can tell, but she ends up putting her fingers in the vanilla bowl and licking them more than one time.

When our cakes are done, Nanna says they have to cool before we can do the best part and put icing on them, but we get to make the icing with butter and a different, fluffy kind of sugar. After, we put it in the fridge and eat ham sandwiches at the table. I only ever sit at the table to eat at Nanna's house.

Finally, Nanna feels the cakes and says it is time to put the icing on. I climb back up to my stool beside her, and we use a spoon to ice the cakes. She gives me some shiny silver balls and some sparkly glitter and the princess stickers.

I start with my favorite. I poke Cinderella's face until she sticks to the icing. 'When I grow up, I'm going to be like Cinderella. Except I'm going to have wings too, so I can fly anywhere I want.'

'And where would you like to fly to, sweet pea?'

'Mm, where does Prince Charming live?'

'Well, I suppose he lives in Disneyland, which is in America.'

I lick icing from my finger. It's yummy. My finger makes a popping noise when I pull it from my mouth, which makes me giggle. 'Then I'll fly to America and I'll find Prince Charming, and he'll kiss me and I'll wear pretty dresses.'

'Now, now, you don't need to be thinking about kissing boys just yet.' She lifts me to the ground. 'We'll let these set and have one later with a nice cup of tea.'

I scrunch my nose. 'I don't like tea.'

'You can have orange juice.'

We go to the lounge and put on *The Little Mermaid*. I sit next to Nanna and she puts her arm around my shoulder. 'I don't like Ariel's daddy; he's mean to her,' I say. 'I wonder if my daddy would have been like him or if he would have been nice.'

'Your daddy was a lovely, lovely man, Rebecca.'

'Mummy said that he left us and didn't want to see me.'

Nanna pulls me tighter into her side. 'Maybe when you're bigger, I'll tell you the truth about why your daddy left, but you should know that he loved you very, very much.'

'Do you think I'll ever see him one day?'

Nanna's eyes go wet. 'Well, you'll see him in heaven, with the angels, but hopefully not for a long time yet.'

'Mummy said Daddy isn't in heaven.'

Nanna seems to get very cross. 'He most certainly is there, sweet pea, and he's watching over you all the time. Even when you are sad at home with your brothers and sisters, your daddy is looking out for you. Okay?'

I nod and tuck myself to her side. 'If he is watching me, maybe he can make them all just disappear.'

* * *

Nanna packs me a box with seven cakes inside: one for me, two for my half brothers, two for my stepsisters, one for Mummy, and one for Mummy's new friend, Dave.

'Can't I just have them, Nanna? I don't want the others to have our cakes.'

She bends in front of me by the front door and kisses me on the head. 'Maybe they'll like your cakes so much, they'll be nicer to you.' She pulls me into a tight hug.

It is dark outside – and cold. Mummy must think so too because she stays in the car and shouts for me to hurry up. Maybe it's because it's so cold that I start to cry. 'Nanna, let me stay with you. Please. I'll be good. I'll stay here and we can make cakes.'

Nanna's eyes are wet again. She tugs the sides of my coat closed. 'I wish you could stay here, sweet pea. I wish for that more than anything.'

'Rebecca, come on! I don't have all night.'

Nanna rubs her thumbs under my eyes and tells me, 'Stop crying, darling. Don't let them see you cry. And like I've told you before, you have my telephone number, and if anyone ever hurts you, you call me.'

I nod.

They don't hurt me: Mummy, Dave and my brothers and sisters. They just aren't nice to me either.

'I love you, princess.'

I sniff. 'Love you too, Nanna.'

She stands on the doorstep and watches me get into the car. Mummy pulls away before I have my seatbelt on or a chance to wave at Nanna. I reach in my bag and hold out the box of cakes between the front seats. 'I made everyone cakes today.'

Mummy glances at the plastic box. 'Rebecca, I'm driving.'

I keep holding out the box. 'Will you give them to the others, though? I don't want to.'

'Rebecca, you need to learn to be nice to your brothers and sisters.' She tuts. 'For God's sake, here.' She snatches the box from my hand and throws it onto the front seat.

I hope the stickers didn't come off the top, or she'll have ruined them.

# 7

## DREW

The intercom buzzes. I walk through my apartment in my jeans, towel drying my hair, which is still wet from my post-workout shower. When I pick up the intercom, the building concierge tells me Marty, Brooks and Kit are downstairs. I tell him to send them up and go to pull on a T-shirt. By the time I get back to my apartment door, my buddies are knocking.

Brooks and I finished sparring at his gym less than an hour ago. I set the poker table and showered when I got home but Brooks has still made good time. Especially since the stacked, six-four, inked giant is holding four boxes of takeout pizza.

'I bought it, you can serve it, man,' he says, dumping the pizza boxes into my arms.

All three men head down the corridor to the open-plan kitchen-living space, all three carrying boxes of beers. I kick the door shut with my heel and follow.

'Man, I forget how sweet this pad is,' Brooks says, walking to the floor-to-ceiling windows and looking out at the lights of the city against the black sky. I watch his reflection as he folds his arms across his chest. It's subtle, but his shoulders sag.

Marty and Kit are in conversation as they make their own way around my kitchen, finding large plates for the pizzas. I take the caps off of two bottles of Bud and walk over to Brooks.

'Everything okay?' I ask, handing him a cold beer.

He reaches for the bottle without looking at me, and I watch his reflection as he takes a swig. 'Yeah, man. I'm good.'

Brooks was one of the smartest kids I knew growing up. He wasn't interested in studying, but he knew shit without having to study. Not academic stuff, but he could read people. Even when we were teenagers and everyone else just wanted to get laid – and that was an emotion to most of us – Brooks was tuned in to the things people couldn't see. He guessed Tom Harrison was getting a hard time from his old man while the rest of us believed the kid was just clumsy. He realized his parents were getting a divorce six months before they told him. For a man who looks like he should be hanging on a wall in the Louvre with all the art covering his body, Brooks is deep.

'How's work?' I ask, taking a shot at what he's feeling and thinking.

'Yeah, busy.' His city gym is thriving, but Brooks isn't the type to brag. We swig our beers in unison.

'Have you looked into franchising the gym anymore?'

One side of his mouth curls into a smile that doesn't reach his cheeks. 'Someday, Drew. Someday.'

He pats my shoulder to tell me we're done talking, and I take the cue, heading into the kitchen where the pizzas are now on plates.

Kit is leaning his head back, holding a slice of Meat Supreme in two hands, dropping the nose of the triangle into his mouth.

'Christ, he's like a five-year-old,' Marty says.

I pat Kit's increasingly chubby stomach and lean back against the kitchen island. He's about forty pounds heavier than he ever was when we shared a house at Columbia. After majoring in mathematics, he got a desk job, and I can't remember the last time the man did physical exercise beyond walking the pathetic excuse for a dog he and Madge have.

'How are Madge and the kids?' I ask.

He doesn't bother to swallow before he speaks. 'Jesus, Drew, I just got here. Give me a break. This is the one night a month I'm allowed Kit Time. I swear my kids are possessed, and for some reason, when I say that to Madge, she thinks I'm saying she's a bad mother so she should get a job. She thinks I'm criticizing her for being a stay-at-home mother. I'm telling you, and I tell her, I would take a job as a janitor over looking after those spawn of Satan every day.'

Marty chortles. 'I can't imagine why Madge is pissed.'

Kit looks at him, deadpan, and says, 'Exactly.'

Now I'm sharing in Marty's amusement. 'You should cherish it,' I tell him. 'Time flies, buddy.'

He rubs the back of his hand across his pizza-stained lips. 'Right, like you'd give up the high life. Drew Clooney-Harrington, right there.'

'Hey, I'm a godfather, aren't I?'

'Drew, you know I only chose you because you're loaded.' With that, he picks up a beer and moves into the living room toward the round poker table.

'He's right though,' Marty says, clinking the head of his bottle against mine. 'We wouldn't give up our lives for a nagging wife and kids.'

'Marty, I can fucking hear you. I can say what I like about my wife, but you can keep your thoughts to yourself.'

Marty raises his arms from his sides in surrender. 'I overstepped. Sorry, buddy.' He speaks quietly this time when he says, 'Doesn't make it untrue though.'

We stand around the kitchen, eating pizza and drinking beers, waiting for Edmond to finish for the night at the restaurant. He usually takes off when all main courses are served and gets to us around ten thirty.

By the time I tell the concierge to send him up, the rest of us have worked our way through a box of beers and two pizzas. We're limbered up and ready to play some cards.

Brooks answers the door while I'm taking a leak. When I come back into the room, Edmond is in the kitchen, flipping the top off a bottle of beer, talking to the others who are sitting around the poker table.

'Drew, my friend,' he says, his French lilt coming through his American-accented English, showing his years spent between his signature restaurants in London, Paris and New York. Since his family moved to New York, he's spent more and more time here. 'This is for you.'

I pick up a bottle and knock it against his in greeting. Then I contemplate the white cardboard box he slides along the counter toward me. 'What is it? Aw, have you brought me food, Ed? You know how I love when you treat me.'

'Not me. Open it.'

I do as he says and see what I know is Violet Passion. There's a handwritten note.

*I had a spare mediocre dessert.*

  *BB x*

BB. British Becky. I realize I'm grinning down at the box, and something flips in my stomach. Like when you drive too fast over a speed bump: an exhilarating kind of sickness.

'What did you bring us, Ed?' Kit asks, pulling me from the

image in my mind of Becky and me, by a fire, feeding each other desserts and drinking wine. We'd be naked. The heat of the fire keeping us warm. And we'd touch, kiss, have our limbs wrapped around each other, just because we could.

Because we couldn't get enough of each other. I would listen to her talk all night. That insanely gorgeous voice.

Holy hell!

I hold my fist to my mouth as I do something between coughing and choking. I take a step back from the box, as if it has a contagious disease.

'Help yourselves,' I manage through my dry throat. I drag a hand through my hair and nail half my bottle of beer in the next gulp. All the while, Edmond's eyes are fixed on me.

Kit bounces like Tigger from Winnie the Pooh. He locates forks and takes the box to the poker table.

'She's a good person, Drew, and an even better patisserie chef.' Edmond speaks for my ears only. 'She's been squeaky clean since she came to the city. By all means, if you like her... But please don't make me lose my best chef.'

I don't know what to say.

*Don't worry, I don't do relationships*, I want to say. *You've got nothing to stress about, Edmond. I haven't even thought about Becky like that.*

*I haven't thought about lying her back on your kitchen worktops as she whispers everything she wants me to do to her in that damn sexy British accent.*

'I hear you, Ed,' I say instead. 'She just wanted a friend in the city. That's all I am.'

'You're being a friend?' Marty asks across my shoulder as he comes for another beer. 'Is this that chick you met at the bagel truck?'

I just look from him to Edmond because I'm still trying to make sense of my spinning head and erratically beating heart.

'Hold up! Is she the reason you didn't change your clothes the other night?'

'That wasn't what you think.'

'You did. You fucked her.'

'Christ, Marty, are you twelve?' Who am I kidding, lays are quite often a topic of conversation between us. But Becky... I don't want to talk about her like that. 'I didn't sleep with her. I went... There was something I had to take care of, and I fell asleep.'

'I can vouch for that,' Edmond says. 'I've never opened my kitchen to find a grown man drooling on my benches.'

Marty starts laughing. 'You went to see her and fell asleep? Jesus, I've heard it all now, Drew. First you buy breakfast without getting the night-before screw. Then you fall asleep on her. You like this woman.'

Growling, I tip my head back and drain what's left of my beer. 'I've got a lot bigger things to deal with than relationships, Marty. Like getting my name on the door of our firm.'

'Damn right you do.'

'Joking aside,' Edmond says, sober and straight-faced, 'Do not mess around with this girl. I know what you're like and I don't want her running back to Britain with a broken heart. She's been through enough.'

I nod. That's the end of the conversation, but my problems aren't over because now I'm also wondering what Becky has been through.

The top and bottom of it is, I have to get British Becky out of my head. For my sake. I have to focus on my career. For hers, because Edmond is right, I could hurt her if she falls for me. If nothing else, to make sure I don't piss off the best steak chef in the State.

I hang back in the kitchen and open a new bottle of beer while the others sit around the poker table. I lean forward on the breakfast bar, my back to the others, my hands gripping the edge of the work surface. I contemplate canceling on her, maybe telling her I couldn't get Yankees tickets after all. But I can't do that to her. She has a list of things she wants to see in New York. And she wants some company in this city, that's all.

No. I'll go. I'll go and I'll make it clear that there can't be anything between us. I'm not that kind of guy anyway, and I have a lot more important stuff to work on. I don't have time for her... for anyone. Not nagging wives or the Devil's kids. I'll let her cross the Yankees off her list, then I'll step out. Maybe leave friendship to Sarah and Becky. I'll just be the guy she bumps into sometimes at the bagel truck.

Why in God's name does that thought bring a dull ache to my gut?

I join the guys, and we finally play some poker. We talk, we laugh, we take the piss out of each other, we drink far too much beer.

Four hours later, four grown men are making their way unsteadily out of my apartment.

Brooks is last to leave. The booze is affecting him less than the others, but the hand he lays on my shoulder is still heavier than it needs to be. 'I gotta tell you, man. I haven't seen you smile like you smiled when you opened that box of cake since... Man, I don't ever remember seeing you grin that big.'

'Cake will do that to a man. Catch you later, Brooks.'

He nods, then thumps the side of his fist into my chest. 'You don't even like desserts, man.'

I never used to.

When I'm left alone, I grab a final beer and drop back onto my sofa. I didn't realize I was drunk until my mind wanders to British Becky. Her soft skin. Her silky blonde locks. That body.

I've had too much beer to fight it. I'll find willpower tomorrow. Tonight... I'll let my mind indulge in the only dessert I've craved for days.

* * *

I wake with a dry mouth and a heavy head. There's only one thing to get rid of it, and that's to sweat the beast. I pull on my workout clothes and head for a run.

An hour and a half later, I'm showered, I have a full pot of coffee to go at, and I'm sitting on a stool in my kitchen making notes on a new case. The dial tone of Skype sings through my laptop speakers when I'm mid-sentence. Grumbling, I pull a hand back through my damp hair. Then I see it is my sister calling.

The case can wait.

I hit 'Connect', and Millie's face shows on the screen. She's sitting in the kitchen of Mom and Dad's house. She lives in Jersey now with her husband and two kids, so she often stays over when she visits our parents. Free sitters and a better alternative than making her way home after a glass of wine or two.

'Hey, handsome,' she says. Her smile is a mirror of my own. She's four years younger than me, but you could be forgiven for thinking we're twins. We have the same dark-blond hair, although she has highlights. The same straight nose. Even the same blue eyes.

'Hey, yourself.'

Before we can get into conversation, the screen shakes, and the image of Millie blurs. I'm staring at the kitchen floor in Mom and Dad's house, then the ceiling. I hear my niece and nephew arguing, then my sister grabs hold of the laptop, and she's back on the screen.

'Stamping down your authority there, Mill,' I tease.

Ignoring me, she brings the kids into view, both propped on stools and looking as mischievous as ever in matching jeans. Poor kids.

'Now, one at a time, say hello to Uncle Drew.'

Annalise goes first, wiping her wispy, white-blonde hair from her baby blue eyes as she does. Cute as heck. 'Hi, Uncle Drew-bew.'

'Hi, Uncle Drew-willy.' That's Timmy. Two years older than Annalise, he's six going on thirteen with that attitude. But I'm telling you, one flash of his big childish grin, and I'm putty.

'You know that doesn't rhyme, kiddo, right? Drew-bew rhymes. Drew-willy is just silly.' I force my eyes to turn in to look at the tip of my nose and rotate a finger around my temple to tell him he's crazy. He laughs. He has this huge laugh for a kid, like it comes from his toes. It's infectious.

I talk half-sense to the kids for a few minutes, then they're bored of me and running off to terrorize someone else. Maybe their grandad. The thought makes my lips curve up. Watching my dad play with the kids, watching them penetrate the grumpy façade he tries his best to maintain, is a secret indulgence of mine.

I've just opened my mouth to pick up conversation with Millie when Skype tells us someone is joining the call. And then Jake, our younger brother, appears on screen, taking up half the shot, with Millie still on the other side. Looking at him next to Millie, I'm reminded how little he looks like us. He's younger, twenty-five. But his hair is dark brown, almost black, and his eyes are deep brown with gold flecks. He looks more like Dad.

'Hey, dickhead,' he says. I know that's to me, not Mill.

'Hey, accident,' I say back.

'Fuck off.' Almost immediately after the words leave his mouth, a dish towel moves into view and slaps the side of the screen. 'You will not curse in my house, young man.' Mom leans into the camera and points. 'And you stop calling him an accident.'

In unison, my brother and I apologize.

This is my family. Nuts. All nuts. God love them.

'Listen, I can't stay,' my brother says. 'It's like four in the afternoon over here in London, and I didn't get much sleep last night. I might still be drunk. I just wanted to say hi.'

After a brief lecture from Mom on the topic of alcohol poisoning and liver damage – she ignores the reason he probably didn't get much sleep – Jake leaves us to it.

'Are you coming for lunch today?' I'm back to just Millie.

'Sorry, Mill, I'm working.' Guilt churns in my stomach. I haven't been to Mom and Dad's for Sunday lunch since... I can't even remember. The fact that my dad is the only one who didn't crop up on the laptop screen has something to do with that, I'm sure.

'You're always working, Drew. You look tired. You need to take a break.'

'Did you get the flowers I sent this week?'

'Yes. And they were beautiful. But I'd rather you brought them in person every week.'

I hear my dad in the background. 'Now, Millie, leave your brother alone. He has more important things in his life than family.' His lack of interest only confirms my suspicions.

I chomp down on my gums. Thing is, I'm angry at myself because he's right. I should make more of an effort. It's just work can't wait. When shit hits the fan, I'm the person who's supposed to fix it. That's why I'm going to make named partner. It's how I'm going to repay my parents for everything they ever did for me growing up. My old man will see that soon enough. I hope.

Millie rolls her eyes and leans in to the screen to whisper, 'I know you don't think that.' She leans back and talks at normal volume. 'You'll be here next weekend though, won't you? It's Aunt Nellie's sixtieth, and Mom is making Key lime pie on Friday night.'

Mom does make an awesome Key lime pie. In fact, it's the only dessert I really eat. Or it was before this week.

'I'll see what I can do.'

Disappointment drops her shoulders an inch, and I feel like the worst brother in the world.

I am.

# 8

## DREW

Scrutinizing my reflection in the mirror that's usually hidden on the inside of my office wardrobe door, I pull my jacket over my white T-shirt. I drag a hand back through my hair and shake my head at the nervous loser in front of me. When I've studied him enough, I bend to adjust my jeans over my boots.

'What's this? Has a client requested dress down?'

I stand to face Chewie. Variably known as Chewbacca – owing to the hairs that poke out his shirt collars – wanker from the forty-sixth floor, the partner heading up real estate. Malcolm Eddy. I want to throw out a snide remark. Hell, more than anything in the world right now, I want to throw out a snide remark. But Marty's words are still rolling around in my head. *The vote. Be human.*

'What can I do for you, Malcolm?'

He looks visibly taken aback. His second chin wobbles as he draws his head into his neck like a cock... erel. Cockerel. *Be nice.*

'I just wondered if you've got two minutes to talk over something. It's more your bag than mine.'

I check my watch. I really don't. Trying not to roll my jaw, I tell him, 'Sure, take a seat.' I move to sit on the window ledge behind my desk and give him his two minutes.

See, this is the thing with real estate lawyers, they know jack about anything other than buying properties. By the time Malcolm leaves my office, two minutes have turned into ten.

I need to get him on my side, then the rest of the forty-sixth floor might follow suit. There's still work to be done, but I've made baby steps.

Now rushing, which is not like me at all, I grab the suit I changed out of and hand it to Sarah as I head out of the office. 'Could you get this dry-cleaned?'

'No problem. How are you feeling?'

Sick. Nervous like a kid with zits asking a girl to prom. But I'm not going on a date. I'm being sociable, kind even, and taking a woman who is relatively new to the city to a Yankees game. 'Fine. Why wouldn't I be?'

One side of her lips curl and she waves a hand in a way that tells me she can see right through me.

'What's this?' Marty's voice comes across my shoulder.

I roll my eyes before turning to him. There really is no hiding from these two. 'I'm taking the afternoon.'

'What do you mean, you're taking the afternoon? You never take the afternoon. You're Drew. Workaholic.'

He sounds like my sister. 'Yeah, well, you told me to start behaving like a human. Reap what you sow, Marty.'

* * *

By the time I reach the subway station, I'm hot in the day's humid air. Great. Not only am I being forced to take the subway, but I'm hot as hell. I hate the subway, for the record. I haven't ridden the subway since I was old enough to afford not to take the subway. But

British Becky wants to ride the subway, so it looks like I'm taking the sweat oven right up to the Bronx.

'Hey!' I swivel to face the person whose hand is on my shoulder. Her hair is loose around her shoulders. Her lips are kissed with gloss. Her cheeks are pink, and her eyes... Those eyes are going to be the death of my self-restraint.

Put the brakes on, Drew. There are bigger things going on in your life. I'm about to do just that but I open my mouth and no words come out. Air passes my lips, but my synapses refuse to send a message to my voice box. I can't speak as I drink her in. Who knew a baseball jersey and little denim shorts could be so damn sexy?

'Are you okay?'

The hell I am. I need to get a serious hold of myself.

'Yeah, just wondering whether you bought that jersey especially for this game.'

Her eyes narrow. 'Well, duh. You can't go to your first Yankees game without a Yankees jersey.'

'Christ, I feel like a tour guide. Come on.'

I lead us down the steps and to the station's metro card booth. But when I go to take my wallet my from pocket, I find two Yankees tickets, a cell phone, and nothing else.

I try my other pockets. I didn't do this. Come on.

'Everything okay?' Becky asks.

'I forgot my wallet.' When do I ever forget my wallet? Jesus. Where is my head? 'Give me two minutes. I'll run back to the office.'

Becky nudges past me and hands a twenty-dollar bill to the man selling metro cards. 'Forget it. Let's just go. I can pick this up. We can get your wallet on the way back.'

'I can't let you pay.'

'Drew, you're doing me a favor. It's not like this is a first date or something. You can pay next time.'

She's right. This isn't a date. We're friends. I'm being a buddy. I'm being human. A human who wants to tear those tight little shorts off with my teeth. 'You're right. I'll pay you back later. I'll need a hot dog too. You can't do Yankees without a dog and fries.'

She hands me my card. 'Deal.'

As I watch her push through the turnstile, it dawns on me that I didn't refute the fact there'd be a next time.

'That was worse than a slow and painful death. Just so you know.' I breathe the infinitely less stuffy air as we follow the crowd up the steps to exit the subway.

Becky nudges her shoulder into my arm. 'Oh, come on. It wasn't so bad.'

'You're right. I especially enjoyed the five-hundred-pound sloth who put his sweaty paws all over me for the last five stops.'

She laughs, and I think I might write a list of things I could say that would let me hear that sound. 'Right, tour guide, where do we find these infamous hot dogs?'

'This way.' My hand is wrapped around hers and I'm moving us through the crowd before I comprehend what I've done. Thing is... it feels... nice. Her petite fingers. Her gentle grip.

I don't move my hand from hers until we're through the crowd and at the back of the line for the hot dog stand. When I finally let go, she looks from my hand to hers, then lifts her gaze to mine. Something so intense, charged even, passes between us that I have to drag air into my lungs, desperate to feed my mind.

'Listen, Becky, I need to be straight with you.' I look away and into the crowd, buzzing happily with either pre-game excitement, or because they have the afternoon off work. It helps calm the rate of my blood pulsing through my veins enough that I can look back at her. 'This... us... it's not going to become a thing. I have too much going on. And, honestly, I'm just not the kind of guy who does relationships.'

Her eye visibly open wider and she pulls her head back. 'Relationships?' Her face contorts, and I instantly panic. She's going to cry. Shit. Then she bends from her waist and laughs. 'Crikey, Drew, did you think I was going to jump your bones for bringing me to a baseball game? I didn't move to New York searching for love. Quite the opposite, believe me.'

Whether it's the fact that I deservedly feel like an idiot or that she sounds like the Queen of England when she says, 'Quite the opposite,' I find my lips curling up.

She places her hand on my shoulder. 'Plus, you're kind of an arrogant arse. That's not exactly my type.'

Now my smile is gone as I stare at her back. I fold my arms, annoyed and, yes, offended. But then, I am 'an arrogant arse', as she politely puts it. So why am I so irritated? And what did she mean by 'quite the opposite'? What are you running from, British Becky?

When we reach the front of the line, I order two hot dogs.

'Anything else?' the guy asks.

'Chips, please,' Becky says.

The server asks her what flavor chips she would like. Becky's look in response is completely perplexed.

'She means fries,' I tell him.

'Gotcha.'

'Darn, I forget that every time,' Becky tells me.

I take hold of our food as Becky pays. I still can't believe I forgot my wallet. We eat and walk, which is Becky's idea, but clearly she hasn't thought this through. Eating a hot dog and walking is not an easy feat.

But it seems I'll have to stand corrected as Becky wraps her mouth around the hot dog and eats the whole thing in three bites. I gape, somewhere between disgusted and awed.

'You got enough in there?'

When she's done laughing, she accepts the napkin I hand her

and wipes mustard from the side of her mouth. 'You'd be amazed how much I can fit in here.'

For a moment, I can do nothing but stare at those damn perfect lips and talk my member back into its cage. Then she winks, knowing full well she sent my mind to the gutter. 'Come on, I don't want to miss the game.'

'Your banter leaves a lot to be desired, Cupcake.' I subtly adjust my jeans as I follow behind her, deciding I'll eat my food when we reach our seats.

She follows me up concrete steps toward our seats. When she finally turns to take in the view of the stadium, her eyes sparkle, her jaw loosens, and she sighs, as if being here is some kind of accomplishment. She looks happy. Content. Alluring. Watching her could become a new guilty pleasure of mine. Who am I kidding; it already has.

The game is starting as we make our way past a row of people and take our seats. The Yankees pitcher is announced over the PA system. I'm trying my damndest to watch the game instead of thinking about the press of Becky's thigh against mine. But she blows my concentration when she leans in to my ear and I catch that sweet scent I've come to know, then her hot breath comes with her words, caressing my neck.

I swallow hard.

I'm starting to think maybe I should just take her to bed. Get this over and done with. Then walk away.

'What's that thing they say in *Top Gun*?'

I drag my mind from the gutter, again. 'You mean when Goose says, "It's bottom of the ninth; the score is tied, it's time for the big one"?'

I spend the next twenty minutes explaining the quote. How the scoring works. The positions of the team. By the end of the game, she's hurling insults and screaming when the bases are loaded. Not that I'd ever admit it to Sarah or Marty, but she's the most fun guest I've ever had at a game.

'Enjoy that?' I ask when we're squashed like canned sardines into the subway again.

The smile she gives me is worth every second of the torture I'm enduring on this ride. 'Thanks, Drew. I know you're busy and everything. Watching a game was way better than taking a tour.'

'It's really no trouble.' And I mean it. Oddly.

With two stops to go, more bodies file into the already-packed car, and I feel her move against me. Her slender frame rubs against my waist. I jerk my attention to her, our eyes locking. I swear if the heat between us keeps ramping up with every look and touch, me and my big-city attitude are going to go down in flames.

The chug of the train breaks the tension but rocks her unsteadily into me. Instinctively, I wrap an arm around her waist to support her.

She looks at me, apologetically, but it's me who should be sorry. Sorry that I can't bring myself to move my arm from her waist, sorry that I must be giving off every signal on the planet that I want this woman, because I do. Badly. So damn sorry that I'm not the kind of man who does long term, and I can't risk hurting her by doing what I really want to do and waving her out of my apartment hours later.

Not to mention, Edmond would kill me. Maybe he'd even bend the ear of the other partners who love a good steak in the exact opposite direction of supporting me getting my name on the door. The reward just doesn't balance the risk either way.

When she drops her gaze to the floor, her head comes under my chin. She's so close, I'm breathing her in. Defenseless. When we chug out of the next stop, whether she does it reflexively or not, her hand moves around my waist, and we're locked together, forced together, in an unintentional embrace. Yet, neither one of us shifts as the train moves toward our stop.

Exiting the station doesn't just mean I get fresh air; it means breathing space from my own irrational thoughts and from being pinned up against a woman who is quickly starting to drive me crazy.

We stop walking outside Lexington Tower. The orange glow from inside the building casts a light across Becky's cheeks. Her lips look so kissable, it's madness. That's what I'm thinking when she cuts into my thoughts. 'Do you want to grab a beer? Maybe a late burger? There's an Irish bar just around the—'

'Sorry, Becky, I can't.'

*I can't be near you for a second longer without taking you to my bed and screwing you until you're screaming my name.*

'I need to check on things in the office. Wait here and I'll go grab my wallet to pay you back for—'

She presses a finger to my lips. 'Stop. It's fine, Drew. We're two friends who caught a baseball game together. You don't need to do the excuse thing, and you don't need to pay me back. You can pay next time.' She pats a hand against my chest and says, 'I'll see you when I see you, then. Have a good rest of your night.' Then she heads toward Paddy's Irish bar, her tight ass in those tiny shorts teasing me as she goes.

I ride the elevator to my office, staring out at Manhattan's lights as the car climbs. I'm wondering whether I should have gone to Paddy's because I can't remember the last time I didn't want a night to end as much as this. She's beautiful, no doubt about it. But she's also smart and wickedly funny. That's a combination not often found in women I know.

My thoughts immediately change when I notice Sarah sitting behind her desk, then I hear my phone ringing in my pocket. She looks up as I retrieve the phone and cancel her call.

'What are you still doing here?'

'We have a problem.'

'What kind of—'

'Drew, what the hell kind of advice did you give me?' Malcolm Eddy cuts me off, storming like a double-chinned bull out of my office.

My body instantly reacts, my shoulders drawing back and my chest rising. 'You need to lower your tone and get the hell out of my space.'

Wisely, he takes a step back. I move past him into my office. He follows, closing the door behind him.

'Talk,' I tell him, in no mood to be 'human'. We stand feet apart, facing each other.

'Your advice was a load of shit.'

'Hold up! You came in here asking about patents, trademarks and copyright. I told you how the protections work. There was no shit in there.'

'You told me copyright attaches to an author without registration.'

'It does. I also said registration gives you greater protection because it creates a presumption in favor of the author.'

'A presumption! You didn't tell me to register.'

I understand without his needing to go on. I put my hands into my jeans pockets to stop myself accidentally flipping the incompetent dick the bird. 'Let me guess. You decided to take on an intellectual property case that you know nothing about. You were slow off the mark registering your client's rights, and someone beat you to it, trying to claim that they are the real author. About sum things up?'

He stays silent.

'Who's the client?' I ask.

'Astrana.'

'Shit. Our biggest real estate client.'

'Our.' He snorts. 'Suddenly you give a shit about the firm when you're less than four weeks from a vote on whether you make named partner.'

'Wrong. I've always given a shit about this firm. Give me the case and I'll fix it.'

He sniggers and rubs a knuckle under his nose. I refrain from asking if it smells like he's been shoving it up his asshole. *Be human, Drew.*

'See, there it is. You don't give a damn about the firm. You want to make a move on my client, like you always do.'

'You know something, Malcolm; I've never taken a client from a partner at this firm who didn't beg me to do so. Now, if you don't want my help, show yourself the hell out of my office.'

I'm still seething as he marches out of the office.

Sarah moves into his spot. 'That wasn't exactly a lesson in how to buy votes.'

'He had it coming. He'll be back with his tail between his legs tomorrow.'

'Maybe. But you need more than that to get your name on the door.'

She's right. I drag a hand roughly over my face. When I open my eyes, I catch sight of my wallet on my desk. The wallet I forgot on my non-date with the most 'human' person I know.

\* \* \*

Paddy's is still busy when I arrive. Not like a weekend night but busy enough to have some atmosphere. A couple of guys are playing live music on the stage, just their raspy voices and guitars. I can hear their Irish accents in their words. They're good. Real good.

A group of women in tailored skirts and blouses are dancing. I guess they had a rough day and need to blow off some steam. I can understand that. Other clusters of people stand and sit around high tables. Feet are tapping, heads bobbing.

The place looks like a typical Irish bar: green, leather upholstery, mahogany bar frame and tables, gold trimmings. I don't see Becky. My irritation at Malcolm Eddy is suddenly subdued, replaced by disappointment. Maybe she had one drink and left. Maybe she decided not to come.

A broad, inked man wraps his hands around four beers and moves away from the bar. As he does, I see Becky, sitting on a stool, turning a bottle of Bud in her hand. Her hair falls back from around her shoulders as she laughs at something the bartender says.

Has she looked this gorgeous all day?

I make my way toward her and place a hand on the small of her back, glaring at the young bartender like an animal claiming its prey. It's undeniably territorial, even though I know I have no right to behave like that. That's how men with girlfriends, fiancées and wives behave. It's not how men like me behave. Women are never around long enough for me to be territorial. And that's how I like it. How it needs to be. Look what happened today. I took a few hours off and the shit hit the fan. That's why men like me, and Marty, we focus on the job.

As I'm thinking that, she blindsides me, flashing me the kind of smile Julia Roberts would flash: big, perfect, hypnotizing. 'You changed your mind.'

I clear my throat and with it my head. 'Kind of. I need your help.'

She pats a barstool beside her and I order a bottle of Bud to match hers. 'What can I help you with?'

I explain my position at Statham Turner. I tell her about the vote for named partner in four weeks. And, for the first time feeling a little ashamed by it, I tell her that half the partnership hates me. When I'm done, I drain my beer and ask the bartender for two more. The whole time, Becky stays quiet. I silently hope that she doesn't see me the way the real estate team does. And I silently admit to myself that I give a crap about what she thinks of me.

'Okay, I've got it all. I think. But why do you need my help? I don't have the first clue about being a lawyer, or attorney, as you freaky people say.' I raise a brow while taking a swig of beer.

'Freaky people?'

She shrugs, amusing me.

'I need your help because you're... you.' What I want to say is, *Because you have a way with people, with me.* What I actually say is, 'You're human and friendly. You can mix with people in one of the finest restaurants in New York and be equally comfortable stuffing an entire hot dog in your mouth, or sitting in an Irish bar drinking beer.'

'A girl can have roots and wings.'

Her words make me pause, my hand holding my bottle midway between the bar and my mouth. I'm familiar with those words. Very familiar.

'So?' She bites her bottom lip, and it takes every ounce of willpower in my body not to lean forward and take it between my own teeth. 'You said he thought you were out to steal his client, right? And he wanted to do this work himself, even though he's not really clued up enough on that type of law to do it. So, my guess is, you do work that maybe the guys on the forty-sixth floor don't think you should do sometimes?' Her words end on a cautious question.

'It's different. Real estate work is easy. I could do that stuff with my eyes closed.'

She takes an exaggerated breath and sits back on her stool, looking self-satisfied, like she just won the biggest case of her career. Well, okay, not quite that smug.

'You think I should hand over some cases?'

She shrugs. 'You wanted my advice. Give them something that

isn't just important to them but that shows a concession on your part. A change in your ways. If you really want to have your name on the door, you'll need to start spreading the wealth. I don't mean to speak out of turn, but since you asked... You need to consider yourself less and firm more.'

'Ah, British Becky, what are you doing to me?'

As soon as the words are out of my mouth, I focus on the top shelf of the bar. Those words have so many meanings.

# 9

## DREW

I hate every goddamn second of this, and it hasn't even begun. I knock on Malcolm Eddy's office door. He doesn't look pleased to see me, nor does he beckon me in. But he does lean back in his chair and rest his hands on the arms. I recognize that as an invitation.

I close his door behind me. I don't need support staff in earshot of what's going down this morning. If I could turn the volume of my own ears to mute, I would.

'Malcolm.' Even his name sounds strained as it leaves me. 'I'm sorry. Maybe I should have been more forceful in telling you to register rights.' *If you'd told me the facts, I would have been.* 'I'd like to help you put things right. It's my bag. I can fix this for you. But I understand your reservations. That's why I'm giving you this, if you have time to take it on.'

I hand over a file from one of my medium-size clients. 'My client is interested in buying a commercial plot of land to build a warehouse. It's your territory, not mine. So, I was thinking we could trade. Share our expertise.'

He takes the file from me and looks inside. 'This is a decent client.'

*All my clients are decent, dumbass.*

He stands from his desk and waves the file at me in the way he might point a finger.

God, I'd like to rip his hand right off.

'I know you're doing this to win my vote, Drew.'

I hold up my hands. 'Malcolm, I want your vote. No doubt about it. And hopefully you recognize that my billables mean making me named partner over Patrick would be the best thing for this firm. But right now, all I'm trying to show you is that you were right.' The words physically burn like acid in my throat. 'Sometimes I put myself before the firm. This file is my way of telling you that from here on, I promise to put the firm first. Always. That means placing work with the best partner to service the client and, in this case, that's you.'

He stares at me, then drops my file to his desk and puts his hands on his hips. 'I'll think about it.'

*Goddamned motherfu—* 'I appreciate it.'

I walk away, silently fuming. Back in my office, I pace the floor, trying to contain my anger. Just as I'm beginning to find a bearable level of proverbial red mist, Malcolm appears, holding a bundle of documents.

'The case. It's yours. I respect that you came up to my office, and I respect your apology. Don't prove me wrong.'

I take the bundle from him in my left hand and hold out my right. He shakes it and switches his miserable mug into a condescending smile. As he leaves, he calls over his shoulder, 'And a free dinner might not hurt, Harrington.'

What a dickhead.

'Uh, what was that?' Sarah stands in her familiar pose: one leg straight, the other pointed out to the side. Her hands are on her hips. Her Hollywood pout is in place.

'Just making sure we get our name on the door.'

\* \* \*

I'm dialing Becky's number before it really registers that I want to speak to her.

'Drew. Hi.' Her voice is mumbled, as if she's holding the phone between her ear and shoulder. Then I hear a sound, as if she's sucking her finger.

'Are you making cupcakes?'

'Bugger off, Drew. I don't make cupcakes. But I am making cheesecake.'

'What kind of cheesecake?'

'Not that you'll care, Dessert Hater, but it's chocolate orange.'

'That sounds kind of plain for you.'

'That's because you haven't tasted my chocolate orange cheese-cake before.'

'I'm going to concede because I know it will be fantastic. I thought you weren't working this week.'

'I'm not. I'm in my apartment, but my next bucket-list item is the Empire State Building, and since you told me I must go up there at night, I have nothing better to do right now.'

'Huh. Well, I'm glad you listened for a change.'

She giggles, and I give myself a second to indulge in the sound. 'Becky, I'm calling to thank you for your advice last night.'

'Did you give the other guy a case?'

'I did. He smiled like a chubby kid eating one of your cakes.'

She's laughing again. Heartily this time. It warms me from the inside out. 'Well, Drew Harrington, budding master of the universe, I'm pleased you listened for a change.'

Now it is my turn to laugh. God, this feels good. Being around her makes me feel good. I should get back to work but I don't want her to go yet. 'What's next on your list?'

'After the Empire State? South Beach Boardwalk. Staten Island.'

'When are you doing that?'

'I don't know. This weekend, maybe. Do you want to come?'

'To Staten Island? This weekend?'

'Ahh, yep.'

I remember Millie's insistence that I go to Mom and Dad's for Aunt Nellie's sixtieth barbeque. Aunt Kathleen's farts. Uncle Geoffrey's snoring at the dinner table. Uncle Jack's incessant whining about being the chef, even though he cremates the meat every time. It would be torture, but it's been a long time, and Millie looked so disappointed when I said I'd think about it.

I take a deep breath before I suggest the most boneheaded thing in the world. 'Well, you know my family lives out there. They want me to go this weekend. How about you get me through the torture of that, and I'll show you South Beach properly?'

'Ah, family? I, erm, I'm not sure, Drew. It's just... I just...'

I'm an idiot. 'Sorry. That was a stupid idea. Forget it. I have to go, Becky. Have a great time tonight.'

'Drew—'

I hang up the phone and look at my Omega, wondering whether it's legitimately late enough for scotch. What the hell was I thinking? Take her to meet my family?

Screw it. 11 a.m. is plenty late enough.

I take a crystal decanter from the bar table in the corner of my office – hey, this man works long hours. Before my glass of scotch reaches my lips, it is snatched away.

'Far too early,' Sarah says. 'What's going on?' She opens my mini fridge and hands me a bottle of sparkling water.

'Can't a man just want a drink?' I ask, moving to sit on the leather sofa.

'A man, yes. You, at this hour, no. Spill.'

'Sarah, there's nothing to spill.'

'It's Becky, isn't it? She's gotten under your skin.'

I don't reply. I stare at the abstract aluminum art on my wall.

'I had brunch with her on Saturday, and I've got to tell you, she's great. Normal. There's a lot to be said for normal in this city.'

I know exactly what Sarah means. But Becky isn't normal. She's far from normal. There isn't a stereotype I could fit her into. She breaks every mold. She's smart, funny, incredible looking. And there's no pretense with her. That's definitely uncommon in the city.

'I've never known you to want anything more than a one-night stand with any woman besides your mother, your sister and me, all of which would be very wrong, for the record. Yet, you can't stay away from Becky.' She's calling me out and I don't like it. To even consider Becky as more than a one-night stand rocks me to the core.

'I took her to the game because I was being nice. Not romantic. Not looking for anything. I was just... Damn it, Sarah, you told me to take her.'

'No, I didn't.'

'Well, you told me she needed a friend. Same thing. And I've got work to do. So...'

I move across my office and open my laptop, dropping heavily into my desk chair and keeping my focus on anything other than Sarah.

She stands. 'Fine. I'm just calling it how I see it, Drew. But I think you like her. And I think you're afraid because you've never really allowed yourself to like anyone before.'

'You need to go take a pill or something, Sarah.'

'Maybe I do. I must be crazy to have stood by you all these years.' She moves huffily to my door. With her hand braced on the handle, she tells me, 'It doesn't always have to be about work, Drew. You're entitled to a life too.'

I lift my head to look at her. 'No, Sarah, it is about work. It's about making a life for myself that a lot of people aren't fortunate enough to be able to. And right now, there's a hell of a lot going on in this firm.'

The sharp attitude I saw just moments ago is replaced by something I like even less. Pity. 'I overstepped. I'm sorry. Just... don't waste precious time if you like her. God knows life can be too short.'

Now it's my turn to pity her. Her husband, one of my best buddies, died in his early thirties and I held her when it happened. I don't force her to try to see anyone else, even though it's been five years. But I hear her pain now, and I'm an asshat for bringing it to the front of her mind.

She dips her head as we tell each other in a look that we understand each other.

'I invited her to Staten Island for the weekend.'

'And?'

'She was going to say no. I don't even know why I asked her. I just thought, she could see the boardwalk and...'

'You want her to go with you to see your family. As I said, you like her.'

With an I-told-you-so smirk, Sarah goes back to her desk, and at least between us, the world is right again.

\* \* \*

I've spent the day putting out fires and fixing Malcolm's case. A few calls were all it took to reach a settlement. It turns out Malcolm was panicking over some flaky kid, who was looking to make a quick buck by riding on someone else's idea.

I send one of the associates out of my office with instructions to draft a settlement agreement and check my watch. Done for the day at 9 p.m. Not bad at all.

As I let my head hang over the back of my desk chair, I think about what Sarah said earlier. Life is too short. She's right. It's been a while since I've seen my folks and, regardless of the mess I made with British Becky, I should go to see them this weekend.

I pick up my cell phone from my desk and drop my sister a message to tell her I'll be there – Aunt Kathleen's farts and all.

When I look up from my phone, Marty is making his way past the glass wall of my office and to my door.

'Hey, are you done for the day? I thought we could grab a drink, since I've heard on the grapevine that Malcolm Eddy is likely to side with us over Patrick.'

'As a matter of fact, I am done.' I push back my chair and stand. 'Give me two minutes. I'll meet you at the elevator.'

I grab my wallet and pull on my jacket over my shirt. While I'm shutting down my computer, my cell chimes. Expecting it to be my sister sending some kind of abuse, I read while on the move. But what shows on my screen stops me dead in my tracks.

A picture of Becky loads. What I notice first is her intentionally sad face. Her bottom lip sticks out beyond the top. But she doesn't have sad eyes. Her blue irises betray her happiness. That's when I notice the background of the image. She's standing at the top of the Empire State Building. The Chrysler Building is lit up like Christmas behind her. And she's holding... yes... she's holding a cheesecake and a spoon.

The phone bleeps again. Words follow the image:

You were being friendly. I panicked. I'm an idiot. I'm sorry. For what it's worth, I'm punishing myself by eating until I become the size of a house.

I let out an amused breath. Even the size of a house, I think she'd still be attractive.

'You coming?' I hear Marty call.

I'm watching the bubbles on my screen that tell me she's typing. 'Just a sec.'

P.S. you were so right. The view from up here at night is breathtaking. I never want to come down.

She's still there.

I get to the elevator as the doors are opening to our floor. 'Sorry, Marty, change of plan. There's something I need to take care of.'

'Take care of what? Work?' Marty is asking as we step into the car.

'Just something,' I tell him, as I scroll through the contacts in my phone.

\* \* \*

I'm met at the eighty-sixth floor of the Empire State Building by Alicia. One good thing about being a true New Yorker and a well-known city attorney is that you get familiar with all the best people to know.

Alicia tucks her blonde hair behind her ear and bats her eyelids at me. It worked once, but I won't be visiting her bed again. 'Hey, Drew.'

'Hey. How are you, Alicia? You look good.'

She rolls her eyes, pretending she doesn't know how to take a compliment. She does.

'Thanks for doing this; I owe you one.'

'No problem. It's quiet out on the deck right now. The bottle of champagne is in a bucket, and this is your glass.' I take a flute full of golden bubbles from her. 'She's right out there.'

I follow the direction of Alicia's hand toward the observatory deck. As I step outside, Becky is being handed a glass of champagne by a waiter. She looks completely confused and downright adorable.

When she's alone, staring at the glass in her hand and looking around her, I approach from behind. 'I received a call from the district attorney's office. Apparently, some tourist smuggled a cheesecake to the top of the Empire State Building.'

The chug of her shoulders tells me she's laughing before I reach her side. I stand next to her, both of us looking out at the view of Manhattan against the night sky.

'I forget how beautiful it is up here,' I tell her. She glances at me. 'It's criminal not to enjoy a good bottle of champagne with a view like this.'

She looks to her feet, then lifts her head to show me that mind-blowing smile. 'I thought I was the one supposed to be apologizing.'

'Well, since I've developed a sweet tooth, I couldn't resist that cheesecake.'

'You seem to make all my experiences just a little bit more special, don't you, Drew Harrington?'

Suddenly feeling nervous for absolutely no reason, I put my free hand in the pocket of my pants and look away from her to the horizon. 'Well, don't tell anyone, or you'll ruin my reputation for being a hardass.'

'Your secret's safe with me. Hold this for me?'

She hands me her glass, and I watch her go to a bag she must have left on the ground, now next to a champagne bucket. She comes back holding a cheesecake. As she does, a live saxophonist begins to play the sounds of Kenny G. We lean back against a railing, taking turns working our way through the bottle of champagne and bites of cheesecake.

Up here, high above the city, with her, with a killer cheesecake, I don't have a care in the world. I can't remember the last time I felt like this.

'I'm sorry about earlier, on the phone.'

I take the cheesecake and fork from her. 'Don't worry about it. I don't know why I mentioned it. I just happen to be going to Staten Island this weekend, and I thought maybe I could show you the boardwalk.' I put a spoonful of utterly delicious chocolate orange cheesecake in my mouth. Without swallowing, I tell her, 'It's not worth getting fat about.'

'Oh my gosh, that's disgusting,' she says through a chuckle.

'So was the thought of you sitting up here eating an entire cheesecake by yourself, Chubs.'

She snorts, actually snorts, and it's the funniest thing I've heard in a long time.

'I wouldn't have eaten the whole thing, you know.' She takes a breath and closes her eyes, lifting her face to the sky. She looks relaxed. Peaceful. Angelic even. 'The saxophone is beautiful.' The saxophone is nice, for sure. But what is truly beautiful is her skin, glowing under the twinkling city lights, her long hair flowing down her back. While her eyes are closed, I let myself indulge in the sight of her. The way her bottom lip is more plump than the top and begging to be nipped between my teeth.

'When I left the UK, I left a nine-year relationship.'

Her words are barely more than a whisper above the saxophone, but they bring me back to the here and now. I think of an appropriate response as I will my semi to disappear. I want to keep her talking and letting me in. For some reason, I want to understand this woman.

She inhales deeply. So deeply, her chest rises. 'I feel like I've only just found out who I really am.' She opens her eyes and turns her head to look at me. 'I panicked earlier because I'm not here, in New York, looking for a relationship, and family just sounded relationship-y. Although, I understand it wasn't intended to be, obviously.' She squeezes her eyes shut and shakes her head. 'You must think I'm crazy.'

'I don't.'

When she opens her eyes, they're staring right into mine. I have forgotten entirely what we were talking about.

'This job came up in New York and I wanted to get away. I wanted to get off my doorstep and leave behind... I just wanted to be allowed to be myself.'

'I get that.' I do. Entirely. I've worked hard to make a life for myself that is completely different from my childhood, different from my parents' struggles to bring up a family of five. 'I know the feeling.'

'I just don't want to lose the self I've found. I'm just not looking for a relationship, Drew. Not that I'm a one-night-stand kind of girl either.'

'You're babbling, British Becky. You don't need to defend yourself. Believe me, I know you're not a one-night-stand kind of girl.'

She bites down on her lip and nods.

'I'm really not anything other than a one-night-stand kind of guy, so this works quite well, wouldn't you say?'

She smirks. 'We're completely incompatible.'

'Exactly. I like spending time with you, Becky. You make things... better, somehow too. So, what do you say we hang out sometimes and we don't worry about the stuff that makes life complicated?'

'Sounds good.'

We resume our position, both leaning back against the railing. I meant what I said. I enjoy her company, and I'm not looking for a relationship either. But I can't pretend her words haven't cut me. Why? I have no idea.

We watch the city and listen to the smooth sound of the sax, in silence. Comfortable silence. It's not until we're out of the clouds and back on the sidewalk that I ask the burning question I've been wondering about. 'What happened? With you and the guy?'

Her exhale puffs out her cheeks. 'Long answer. I was seventeen when we got together. I wasn't the most confident person in the world. He represented safety, I guess. He cared for me and looked out for me. I was naïve. I didn't realize that he, the town I grew up in, family, everything stopped me from ever working out who I really am. Short answer: babies.'

'Babies?'

She shakes her head quickly. 'Oh, I don't have them. You could say we split because we were in different places about the idea. I mean, that's kind of why we split. I should have walked away a long time before I did.'

I don't know why I keep pressing for more, but I do. 'You wanted kids and he didn't?'

She stops abruptly, making me stop and face her. 'Men. You all assume we women want to clean your dishes, do your ironing and have your babies, don't you?' She's scowling and there's definitely a lot of meaning behind her words.

I hold up my hands. 'I stand corrected.' But I want more. 'So, it was you who didn't want them?'

She eyes me for some time, as if trying to read my mind. Then she nods slowly. 'He did. I didn't. Not then.'

I've never given serious thought to whether I want kids. I love my niece and nephew, but I've always had bigger things happening. I've never seen myself taking the step that comes first: the getting-a-wife part. But the scary as hell thing is, I'm looking into the eyes of this woman I hardly know, and for the first time ever, I can imagine it all. The house in the suburbs, children in the yard, lazy Sundays with my family. I can see my unborn child in her arms. And it scares me to death.

'But I've come to appreciate since I've been here...' She swallows deeply, and the way she looks at me now, the way I think I'm looking at her, it's like she knows everything there is to know about me, and it's all okay. 'I just couldn't imagine having children with him.'

My arms are aching by my sides because I want to take her cheeks in my palms and press my lips against hers so damn much.

But she isn't looking for a guy.

And me, one-night guy, I am definitely not the man for her anyway.

I throw out an arm and turn to face the road, finally able to breathe. A yellow cab comes to a stop. 'Come on. I'll ride with you.'

Fortunately, Becky's block isn't too far away because the silence between us this time isn't comfortable. It's awkward as hell.

When she tells the driver to stop, I'm relieved. I need a cold shower and something hard and amber colored, on the rocks.

I step out of the cab so she can climb out on my side. When she's on the sidewalk, she tries to give me money, which I turn down. 'Okay, well, the next one is on me. Thanks for tonight, Drew. I had a great time.'

'You're welcome. Thanks for the cheesecake.'

'And the gym hours?'

'Right.' Just like that, the tension between us fades, and we're back to being buddies. 'Listen, the offer still stands. If you want to come to Staten Island this weekend. I'm going anyway. And now that we've established we are completely platonic...'

She's laughing and shaking her head as she walks to the door of her building. 'Okay.'

'Okay?'

'Okay, New York Drew.'

# 10

## BECKY

*Nine years ago*

I'm the last person to leave my nanna's graveside. Her friends have left, Aunt Lizzie has gone, and the priest who performed the service is heading back inside before the ominous gray sky bursts.

She'd been sick for a while. Nothing specific, really. Infections she couldn't shake, pneumonia, flu. The hospital says Nanna really just died of old age.

It started with bronchitis three years ago. I wished I could have moved into her house or brought her to live with us but I was just too young to care for her alone. Aunt Lizzie – my dad's sister – was visiting once a week, taking a five-hour round-trip train ride. But we weren't enough.

Reluctantly, we found Nanna a nursing home. It wasn't a sad, melancholy kind of place. It was more like a hotel that happened to have caregivers on site. She had some nice friends there, and I visited her at least three times a week after school.

It didn't come cheap, and Nanna hated that. She wanted to leave what little money she had to Aunt Lizzie and me. But there was no chance I was putting her in some skanky home, just so I could get her inheritance.

I dry the last of my tears on a tissue that's now so overused, it has become a ball of paper strands. I press my fingertips to my lips, then blow them in the direction of Nanna's temporary headstone. 'I love you, Nanna.' The words make more tears fall. I wipe them away and walk the long path out of the cemetery toward the bus stop.

The number ten bus pulls up just as I arrive. I pay the driver and take a seat at the back of the bus, where I am less likely to be seen or spoken to.

The bus drops me about a kilometer away from my house. The gray sky has now turned to rain and continues to darken as dusk descends. By the time I'm back, my hair is wet and sticking to my skin. My wool coat, which was one of Nanna's and is really too big for me, is saturated.

I slip inside and hang up my coat on the old, wooden stand by the door. I slip off my flat, black shoes and stack them neatly on the shoe rack, despite the fact tens of pairs are scattered around the hallway floor.

'Rebecca, is that you?'

I follow my mum's voice to the lounge. She's standing in front of the wall mirror that hangs above the old, stone fireplace, fixing gold hoops into her ears. She speaks to my reflection. 'Dave and I are going to the pub quiz at The Heath. Your brothers and sisters are out, so it's just you for dinner. The oven is still broken but there might be something in the freezer you can microwave. Of course, now that your money's coming from Meg, we can afford a new cooker. I'm so excited to replace the kitchen. If there's anything left over, we might be able to get a new tub for the bathroom.'

She turns to face me now.

'How do I look?'

I consider her wet-look leggings, leopard-print blouse and ridiculously clunky heels.

'Nanna said that money was for me to go to university.'

She plants her hands on her hips. 'Yes, well, your nanna isn't around anymore. We need to fix things in the house, Rebecca, and I don't see you contributing any other way, do you?'

*Besides the money that was left from my dad's estate, that I never saw, you mean?*

'But—'

'Sweetie, it's a nice dream that Meg had for you, but it's not like you're going to be a lawyer or a doctor now, is it?'

'I was going to do a culinary course.' I can feel my eyes stinging for the millionth time today.

'Well, if you want to cook, all the more reason to have a nice kitchen to do it in. You don't need a degree to read a recipe, Rebecca. It would be a waste of money, and I don't think Meg would have wanted that, do you?' She walks by me, not saying another word on the subject. 'Dave! Let's go. I told Rhonda we'd be at the pub by seven.'

*But that money is for my education, just like the money my father left.*

I've so often wondered how different things would have been if my father had taken me to live with him, if he'd never died, if I had been allowed to live with Nanna.

Nanna used to tell me about my father. *He was a very good businessman and a good person*, she'd say. She only told me one time what happened between him and my mother and she would never repeat it.

'He made one mistake, Rebecca,' she told me. 'He and his wife were having some problems, and your mother was in a bar one night when he was looking to drown his sorrows.'

She made a point of telling me that I was not a mistake, that he loved me very much. Nanna said he had tried to do the right thing and stay with my mother when I was born, but my mother had a number of men on the go and she drank a lot; Nanna couched that in better terms, but I knew the truth. I lived the truth.

'Your dad wanted to take you with him when he moved back in with his wife,' Nanna told me. But she said my mother wasn't interested in him taking me; she was more interested in the money he would send every month. I never had reason to question the truth of that statement.

My father died in a road accident when I was one. I don't remember him. I do know that his wife sent some money to my mother from his estate. I have never seen a penny of it.

When I hear the front door close, I wander into the kitchen. It really is a dump. The cupboards are held together mostly by nails. The work surfaces are cracked and bubbled at the seams.

I wish I could throw myself on the floor and kick and scream and demand that someone hear my voice.

I open the freezer and see ice for Dave's gin and tonics, a can of beer he must have forgotten to take out, and a small cheese pizza. I close the door and head upstairs to my bedroom. I lie back on the bed, not bothering to turn on the light. Not bothering to take off my dirty clothes. And I sob, for no one's ears except my own.

At some point, I must have cried myself to sleep because it is almost 10 p.m. when I wake. And I wake with a new resolve. I'm going to leave home. I don't know where I'll go. Perhaps Aunt Lizzie's. I'm seventeen. It's not like I can't fend for myself. I just need somewhere to stay. Somewhere far away from here.

I drag a bag out from under my bed and start to stuff clothes inside. I grab the toiletries I absolutely need, like a toothbrush and toothpaste. Locating the tin I keep hidden in the bottom of my clothes drawer, away from my brothers and sisters, I count the money I have saved inside from making coffee on Saturday mornings. Forty-six pounds and twenty-one pence.

Before I leave, I glance one last time around my tiny bedroom. I don't feel sad. I feel relieved to be going.

My coat does little to shield me from the blustering wind and rain until I reach the bus stop where I got off just hours ago. I'm still wearing my black, skater-boy dress and thick, wool tights.

I ride the bus to the nearest station and go inside, still with no idea where I am headed. I remember the name of Aunt Lizzie's town in Yorkshire, but the information stand is already closed for the night. The entire station is deserted but for the driver who just closed down the bus I came in on.

'Excuse me. Excuse me. Can you tell me how to get to York on the bus?' If I get to York, I'll be closer to Aunt Lizzie. I can work out the rest from there.

'York? Treacle, that's a long way. You need a coach.'

'Where would I pick up the coach?'

'There's a station on the other side of town, but you won't be able to book a ticket now.'

I jump, startled by the sound of a breaking bottle. Two drunk-looking men start to have an argument.

'Okay, then can I take buses from here and keep switching?'

The driver scrutinizes me and the big bag I'm carrying. 'I'm sure you can but not tonight. The station is almost closed. Why don't you go home and, if you still want to get to York tomorrow, someone at the information desk will be able to help you then.'

He heads out to the car park, and I slump down onto a metal bench. The cold penetrates my wet clothes and makes me shiver. The arguing men start moving away from the station, and my heart rate calms a tad.

I take the money from my pocket and wonder how far it can really get me. As I do, I realize, I don't have anywhere else to go.

I'm not going back there. I won't.

A loud group of people burst from the doors of a pub across the road from the station, laughing and joking.

Well, if beer makes people happy, I'll take it.

I lug my bag to The Lion's Head and take a spot on a stool in one corner of the bar; I'm underage, only seventeen, and I don't want to be called out on it. It seems like the pub is starting to empty, but people are still being served, and a group of men are still playing pool.

'What can I get you, love?'

I try not to seem sheepish when the middle-aged man leans his big hands on the bar and towers over me. 'Erm, a bottle of lager, please.'

His eyes narrow, as if he's debating my age, but he backs away and takes a bottle of Heineken from the small fridge.

'Will you be having another or do you want to pay now?'

I look around the grungy bar. It's bigger than my bedroom. My mum and Dave aren't here. It's dry. 'I'll be having another.'

He nods and leaves me to wallow alone.

By the time I finish my third bottle, my head is feeling a little fuzzy. I like it. It's better than thinking about my nanna or being ignored and told I'm worthless by my own mother.

'Mind if I sit here?'

I raise my head to see a man who had been playing pool. He has stubble on his face and muscly arms beneath his Rolling Stones T-shirt. He's older than me. Maybe twenty-five. Maybe older. I shake my head, and he sits.

'You look like you've had a rough day.'

I scoff. 'You could say that.'

'You going somewhere?' He points to my bag on the floor.

'It was my nanna's funeral today. She was the only person who has ever given a crap about me, and now she's gone. So, I'm going somewhere, anywhere away from home. I just don't know where.' The words come quicker than usual, and it's not like me to blurt something like that to a complete stranger.

The man gestures to the barman, and within seconds, two bottles of Heineken are placed in front of us. The man raises his bottle. 'Cheers to shitty days.'

'Are we supposed to be happy about it?' I ask after choking down a gulp from the new bottle.

'No. But we live and learn. I'm Mike.'

I hold out my hand. 'Hi, Mike. I'm Rebecca.'

'Where are you staying tonight, Rebecca?'

I shrug.

'Would you like to stay with me?'

My heart starts to hammer with panic as I take in his expression and realize he's serious.

'I'm not a serial killer or anything. I live nearby. You can stay with me tonight, and we can work out what you're going to do tomorrow.'

'I... I don't know.'

'Look, I'm offering a warm place with a bed for the night. What are you going to do otherwise? Sleep on the streets in the rain?'

He has a point. I take the biggest drink of my beer yet, and he smiles. It's a nice smile. The kind that makes me think he really might not be a serial killer.

We have another two beers. Mike tells me about his job working on construction sites as a brick layer. He asks me if I have any hobbies. Nobody asks me whether I have hobbies. When I tell him cooking, he says, 'You could stay with me longer than one night then. Beans on toast is as good as it gets for me.'

'That's really sad,' I tell him. Only it comes out like, 'Thasss reeeally shad.'

'Okay, princess, let's get you home.'

*Princess*. That makes me think of Nanna, and for the first time that I've thought about her today, I'm smiling. Mike pays the man behind the bar, not asking me for any money, then picks up my bag.

He's going to take care of me.

* * *

'Well, this is it.' I step through the door he's holding open and see a double bed that's unmade. The duvet is in a ball at the bottom of the mattress. There's no base sheet. He has a chest of drawers with sprays and hair gel on top. There's one small wardrobe, and the doors are open. He puts my bag on the floor by the bed and turns on a lamp.

'Come here.' I go to him, anxious and feeling a little queasy from the drinks. 'Let's get you out of this wet coat.'

He unbuttons my coat at the neck and unties it at the middle, then slides it down my arms to the floor. I can hardly catch a breath as I watch him.

'What are you doing?' My voice trembles.

He reaches up to cup my face. 'You're really pretty, Rebecca.'

No one has called me pretty, not in a long time. I close my eyes and lean into his palm. It feels nice to be touched. To be wanted.

His hands move around my shoulders, and he draws the zip of my dress down my back. 'Take it off, Rebecca.'

I'm not sure I want to, but I don't want him to stop touching me and talking to me the way he is, so I do it, letting it pool around my flat shoes.

'You're gorgeous,' he says, taking hold of my breasts over my white cotton bra. My heart is beating so hard, it might burst from my chest, and my mouth is dry.

He slips his hands into my tights and cups me. It doesn't feel right. I don't really know him. But his finger slips through my lips to a place only I have touched before and it feels so good, I want more.

He takes off my tights and knickers, then turns me and takes off my bra, leaving me completely naked. 'Now lie on the bed, Rebecca.'

I do as he says, walking backward and sliding up the bed. He takes off his clothes, then fumbles around for something from his top drawer.

I gasp when he tears the foil of the condom. He rolls it on quickly. I'm relieved he doesn't ask me because I wouldn't have a clue what to do.

He crawls up the bed, between my legs, forcing them farther apart.

'Have you done this before, Rebecca?'

I shake my head, unable to find my voice.

'You're going to be so good at it. I can tell.'

I force myself to smile at his words. I hope I am good. I have no idea what I'm doing, and I'm so nervous, my body is locked tight like a brick.

'So pretty.' He strokes my hair back from my face. 'I'm going to take care of you, Rebecca.'

'I'd like you to take care of me.'

# 11

---

## DREW

Thanks to a last-minute screw-up by one of the associates, I'm running late. I check my watch, as if I didn't check it just two minutes ago. I'm seriously pushing it to make the Staten Island ferry on time.

I throw my leather weekend bag over my shoulder, adjust my jeans over my boots and try, once again, to leave the office.

'Sarah, can you keep trying to reach Becky? Tell her not to get on the ferry until she sees me.'

'Sure thing. Have a great weekend. Your mom is going to be so happy to see you.'

I respond to Sarah's maternal beam with an exasperated sigh, but truthfully, I am looking forward to seeing my family.

My direct line rings as I start walking by Sarah's desk. I turn back and glare at my phone through the window-wall. 'For fuck's sake.'

It's pointless, but I check my watch again.

'I've got it,' Sarah says, shooing me away with her hands. 'I'm sorry, Mr Harrington is in a meeting at the moment.'

I mouth thanks and actually run to the elevator. I promised Becky we would make this ferry. I promised my mom would be there in time for dinner. I may not commit to doing things for others often, but if there is one thing I am, it's a man of my word. I bounce my foot as the elevator stops at every floor on the way down Lexington Tower. There are a lot of things to love about being in the gods section of a high-rise. Painfully long descents to the ground floor are not one of them.

My driver is waiting outside in his staple black suit and white shirt and takes my bag from me. I tell him the plan while looking at my watch, again. I swear time is speeding up.

'We'll get you there, Drew. Sit back and relax.'

I try Becky's cell again, but she doesn't pick up. *Where are you?* I have visions of her standing on the ferry, alone, without a clue what to do at the other end, and me waving from the terminal.

We pull up at the dock on Whitehall Street with a minute to spare. I run into the terminal building and spin in circles, trying to find her.

'Drew!'

I eventually locate her voice. She's standing on the upper level. Her hair is curled at the ends and draped across her shoulders. The shirt that's tucked into her skinny jeans is draped off one shoulder. She looks like an ad for Ralph Lauren or something: casual yet incredibly appealing.

'Hurry!'

I snap back into action and bound up the stairs where we both run onto the ferry together. She's laughing and breathless when we reach the outside deck of the boat.

'That was close,' she tells me, her hands finding their way to my chest.

I work out, I'm a fit guy, but all that running has me panting. 'Don't you ever answer your phone?'

She takes her hands away and dips one into the purse that's across her shoulder. 'Oops. Sorry.'

'You'll be the death of me,' I tell her, mildly annoyed at how funny she finds the situation. Mostly, enjoying the sound of her laughter. I notice the bag by her side for the first time and take it from the floor. A voice comes over the speaker to announce departure.

'Come on, we'll get a better view up here.'

I lead her to the front of the ferry. Despite the number of rush-hour commuters, I find us a spot with a view and plant our bags by the safety rail.

'Get your camera ready. You'll get a great shot of the Statue of Liberty.'

Giddily, she takes a digital camera from her weekend bag, then leans her forearms on the safety rail, mirroring my pose. The wind blows her hair back from her shoulders as she takes in the surroundings. I take in her. Only her.

It's a good thing she has sworn off men because, right now, I'm not sure how much more self-restraint I have.

Once she's taken about a million pictures – I would exaggerate but there's really no need to – she comes back to stand beside me. 'So, Mr Tour Guide, tell me something about Staten Island.'

'My family lives there.'

She nudges into me. I notice goosebumps on her bare shoulder and take off my jacket to wrap it around her. When she opens her mouth to protest, I place a finger over her lips. I freeze at the softness of her skin. She seems to be locked in this moment with me, until she opens her mouth wide and bites down on my fingertip, taking me by surprise.

'I know your family lives there,' she says, both of us now scowling. 'Tell me something I *don't* know.'

I go back to leaning across the railing, which is now a hell of a lot cooler against my uncovered forearms in only a black T-shirt. 'Don't you have one of those tour books you can read?'

She shoves my shoulder again. 'Be quiet.'

'If I'm quiet I can't tell you anything.'

'Quit being a smart arse.'

'All right, all right. Something historical. Let me see. Well, the South Beach Boardwalk you're so desperate to see is also known as the FDR Boardwalk, named after Franklin Roosevelt.' I talk her through the history of the island and New York Bay until we dock, surprising myself with the number of useless facts I've retained over the years.

We hang back until the main crowd has dissipated, then I carry both our bags out to the parking lot.

'Drew, in case I forget to tell you, I had a lovely weekend. Thank you.'

I'm about to ask her if she stole that line from *Pretty Woman* when I see two small bodies hurtling toward us. I drop the bags and tell her, 'Hold that thought.' Then the bodies are throwing themselves at me.

Annalise hits me first, despite being younger than my nephew. 'Uncle Drew.'

'Drew-bew-smew.' Timmy bounds into my legs.

'Hey, kiddos.' I fling my niece onto my hip, blowing her wispy, blonde curls from my face, and I ruffle my nephew's hair. 'Guys, this is Becky.'

'Hi, Becky,' Timmy says.

Almost sing-song, Annalise says, 'Hi, Becky. Are you Uncle Drew's girlfriend?'

'Ooh, erm, no. Just his friend.'

She gives me a mock look of horror. Whether it's being here with Becky, or having my niece and nephew around me, the scene makes me laugh from the pit of my stomach.

I set Annalise down on the ground and tell both kids to take Becky's hands while we cross the parking lot. I carry the bags. Annalise is chattering away to Becky, who is her usual smiley self. Timmy, on the other hand, is talking to me.

'Hey, Uncle Drew, Great Aunt Kathleen farted so loud after lunch, it woke up Great Uncle Geoffrey. Great Uncle Geoffrey had been snoring really loud. Grandpa was picking his nose too and Nanna caught him and she said...'

Christ. So it begins.

Glancing to Becky, I mouth, 'You okay?'

She smiles and nods, then turns her attention back to Annalise.

I spot my dad's red truck, then him standing beside it. His signature checked shirt is tucked into his signature stonewash jeans. His hair is gray-white, but he's clinging to most of it. He's not quite as tall as me but still a big guy, and somehow, my mother's love of cooking hasn't taken its toll on his waistline too much.

'Hi, son.'

I plant a bag on the ground and offer my right hand. 'Pop. How you doing?'

'Not so well as you by the looks of it.' He casts his eyes across my shoulder to Becky and the kids.

'Pop, you know the deal.'

Ignoring me, he moves to Becky.

'You must be the Becky I've heard so much about.' Quite an exaggeration.

'If Drew said it, I'm sure it's all lies,' she jokes. 'You must be Drew's dad.'

'That's right. Bill.'

She leans in to kiss his cheek, and the way my dad flaps is comical.

'She's European, Pop. They can't help kissing everyone.'

'Well, lucky for you, son; that's all I'll say. Come on, Becky.'

As she follows him to the truck, where he uncharacteristically holds open the rear door for her, Becky socks my arm with her fist. It really doesn't hurt all that much, but I feel the intent.

When we're in and belted up, I cast a glance from the front passenger seat to see Becky wedged between Annalise and Timmy. The sight of her knees pulled up to her chest tickles me.

'Now then, is Becky short for Rebecca?' my dad asks.

'It is.'

'And does Rebecca have a last name?'

'Fletcher. Rebecca Fletcher.'

'He's an ex-cop,' I tell her. 'He'll run a search for you on the database as soon as we get back.'

'Very Jack Byrnes. You'll find me squeaky clean, Bill, I promise.'

I snort at her reference to *Meet the Fockers*. My dad really is a bit Robert De Niro, without the suave and the paycheck.

'How old are you?' Annalise fires.

'I'm twenty-seven. How old are you?'

'Nearly five.'

'So four then?' Becky teases.

'No. Nearly five.'

She wisely concedes the point.

* * *

The sun has set by the time we reach the house. A gentle, pink glow is cast against the clouds. Despite all my efforts, I've never been able to convince my parents to let me help them find a bigger, better place. They live in the same three-bedroom house we lived in when I was growing up. It's just another white house among the many white houses on the street. Except the tree on the front lawn of my parents' house is decorated with twinkling tea lights. Its leaves rustle in the light breeze coming in off the bay behind us, cool but not chilling.

There's definitely something warm, nostalgic even, about the place, but that doesn't stop my sudden strike of nervousness as we pull into the driveway. This is not what Becky would expect of a hotshot attorney from the city. High-rises and big, expensive apartments, like mine: that's what she'd expect.

What was I thinking, bringing her here?

*No. We're friends*, I remind myself. With friends, anything goes.

I step out of the truck as quickly as I can, in a bid to open the rear door, but Timmy beats me to it, jumping down to the driveway. I'm left lingering by the door, waiting for Becky's reaction as she slides out of the backseat. She swivels, taking in everything about the house. She says nothing. She just gives me a slow, soft smile.

Still feeling anxious, I scoot by her. 'I'll get the bags.'

'Oh wait.' She unzips her bag and takes out a plastic container. 'Bribes,' she whispers.

We follow the others, at a slower pace than the hyper kids, straight through the house to the kitchen. Not without Becky taking in the multitude of family pictures hanging on the walls. I may need to do a sweep and approve these before she sees my plump, early teenage years.

I silently curse my mom for having an obsession with hanging pictures of Millie, Jake and me.

In the kitchen, Becky is folded straight into my mother's arms. 'You must be Becky. Let me see you. Oh my. Gorgeous.'

Becky's cheeks flush pink. For a sassy, witty woman, she's easily affected by a compliment. It's charming.

'Thank you, Mrs Harrington.'

'Oh lord, would you listen to that accent. And it's Maggie to you.' She turns to me. 'Hello, stranger.'

'Hey, Mom.' I let her wrap her arms around me, and I squeeze her a little harder than I probably should. I take in the scent of the lavender shampoo she's used for years and the powdery smell of her skin. I've missed her; I just didn't appreciate how much until this very moment. No amount of Skype calls can replace the familiarity of her hold.

When we pull apart from one another, she pats my cheeks, then pinches my face between her hands. She turns to Becky, still gripping me. 'Thank you for bringing my son home.'

'Oh no, he was desperate to come home, Maggie. He just invited me along for the ride.'

My mother gives me a look that says, *Yeah, yeah*, and gets back to setting cutlery out in piles on the old farmhouse-style kitchen table.

'You must be special, Becky,' announces a new voice, 'because the last woman Drew brought here, besides Sarah, who doesn't really count because she's like his right arm, was Jaci Cuttle in his senior year of high school. Hi, I'm Millie, Drew's sister.'

Millie swoops in from the garden, carrying empty beer bottles and glasses to be refilled. Her usual Converse, which today are red, match her jeans. She calls them her 'Mommy shoes': reliable and comfortable.

'Hi. I'm Becky, obviously.'

The way her words come out, babbled, I'd guess my family has her flustered. As if she's found an emergency exit from the roller-coaster line she really didn't want to be in, she lifts the box that she had taken from her bag outside.

'I brought dessert.' She hands over the plastic container. Now I understand the bribes comment. Nice diversion, Cupcake.

My mother opens the box on the counter. Inside is a selection of Becky's restaurant cakes. She has decorated them just as she would if they were being served in Edmond's place.

'These are exquisite,' my mother tells her. 'They must have cost you a small fortune. You shouldn't have. I'm just grilling tonight.'

'Oh, no, they didn't cost anything but the price of some flour and sugar. I'm a patisserie chef. I made them myself.'

My mother and sister look at the cakes and back at Becky.

'You made these?' Millie asks.

Pride fills my chest. 'Wait until you taste them. The purple one is incredible.'

'That's Drew's favorite,' Becky says, smiling at me. We share the briefest moment, and in it, I love that she knows something about me that no one else does. 'Plus, I hear it's a special birthday barbeque. I couldn't turn up without a birthday cake.'

'Well, it's very sweet of you. Son, why don't you take your bags upstairs, and I'll show Becky around the house and introduce her to the family.'

The anxiousness I felt as we arrived is back. Becky's opinion matters to me. I realize it matters a lot, and I'm worried what it might be.

'Which room will Becky sleep in?' I ask, trying to mask the apprehension I'm feeling.

'Your room, of course,' my mother says.

My room. They've really never changed it since I left for college, despite my quarterly visits.

'I'll be sleeping on the sofa,' I say for Becky's ears.

'You don't have to do that. This is your home. I'll take the sofa.'

'You're both adults,' Millie says. Well, I thought my words were for Becky's ears... 'Can't you just share the double?' Knowingly trying to cause trouble, Millie leaves the kitchen for the outdoor deck. I scowl when she sticks out her tongue across her shoulder.

I take the bags upstairs and find myself standing in the middle of my unchanged bedroom. Everything is blue, from the walls to the wooden desk and the lamp that sits on top of it. Even the rim of the corkboard that's covered in high school pictures is blue. Mortified, I unpin a few of the more tragic pictures; mostly Brooks and I flipping the bird or pulling shirtless poses for the camera. One, a particularly cringe-worthy image of me topless with a tie knotted around my forehead, is first to be stuffed into the drawer of my desk.

Then I look around the room at the multitude of certificates and trophies that I've won for sports and academic honors. Some less embarrassing. Others, like the 'No.1' trophy for the state spelling bee in eighth grade, more embarrassing. I contemplate hiding everything before my reputation is obliterated. I could even pretend Millie's bedroom is mine. Pink beats the heck out of this old crap.

'Your home is beautiful.'

Becky and Mom are at my bedroom door, and there's no time for me to fix anything. So much for Drew Clooney-Harrington. More like Alfalfa from *The Little Rascals*.

Becky glances from my look of dread to the walls of the room. Her gaze lands on a giant poster of Melanie Finlay. The model – who was seriously hot when I was eighteen – is naked, but for the whipped cream covering her three important parts.

Becky brings her fingertips to her lips. 'Cute.'

'I can only apologize. Mom, we really need to talk about you redecorating this room.'

My mother wafts a hand dismissively. 'I'm just pleased you can finally understand how traumatic it is for a mother to have a randy teenage son. I'll see you both downstairs. I need to check that Uncle Jack isn't making charcoal of my meat.'

When we're alone, Becky turns to me, her fingertips still pressed across her lips, failing to disguise her mocking grin.

'Come on. I was eighteen.'

'Melanie Finlay though, seriously?'

'As if you didn't have the Backstreet Boys pinned up all over your bedroom.'

'You're such a loser, Drew Harrington. I'd bet the real estate partners would vote for you in a minute if they could see what a freak you are.'

Now she's laughing, hard, and I can't help joining in. She's so damn beautiful when she laughs.

Killing that thought, I make for the door. 'If you want to clean up, the bathroom is along the hall.'

'Thank you. And thanks for bringing me here, Drew. I know you don't invite people here often.' She steps toward me. So close, she's looking up at me in her flat shoes. 'I also think I know why. And, for the record, I don't think you should worry. This home, your family, you should cherish them.'

I swallow hard. How does this woman see through me like my skin is made of glass?

'This place is amazing. I adore it. It's so full of... love. And your family is incredibly sweet.'

Now I feel ridiculous and guilty in equal measure. I should have known she'd react this way. God, everything about this woman is good. So much better than me.

Her gaze drops to my lips, my own eyes falling to hers. I want to kiss her. Every bone in my body wants me to press my lips to hers. To feel that soft, plump flesh.

Friends. Friends. Friends. Friends. Her long-term relationship. My bid for named partner. And Edmond's words that haven't left me – *she's been through enough*. His warning was unequivocal and so unlike my placid friend. He meant it.

'You think my family is sweet because you haven't met Uncle Jack yet.'

Her eyes flicker. She smiles. This time, it doesn't fill her cheeks. 'Actually, I have. He's great, although I'm not sure he's the best choice of chef. I think it's possible your Aunt Kathleen did a little bottom wind when she shook my hand too.'

And on that note, I drag myself away from her and outside to the yard.

Everyone is sitting on plastic furniture around the small lawn and on the deck. Between the row of houses running parallel to ours, we can see the coastline, now lit only by street lights.

The barbeque is loaded with meat. Salads, potatoes and sauces fill the outside dining table. Wine and beer are flowing. My mother and Millie are telling Aunt Kathleen and Aunt Nellie all about Becky's patisserie skills. Uncle Jack, Uncle Frank and my dad are standing around the barbeque, Uncle Jack in an apron that shows a naked man sporting a ripped torso. Uncle Geoffrey looks as if he's fighting to stay awake, his bottle of beer leaning to one side in his hand. My brother-in-law, Eddie, is appeasing Annalise and Timmy, playing ball on the lawn. He holds up his beer in acknowledgment.

My mother catches my eye and gives me a certain kind of look.

'Stop it. Right now,' I tell her, my voice not sounding as determined as I mean it to. And I do mean it to sound very determined.

Ignoring her, I spend some time chatting with my aunts and uncles. When Becky comes out back, I pull up a chair for her next to mine. We eat and talk through the night, laughing and joking. After midnight, the aunts and uncles leave, the kids are asleep, my dad is also asleep, or passed out from beer and sugar, since he took out the majority of Becky's cakes himself.

'Well, let's get these two to bed,' Millie says, nudging Eddie, who is holding both sleeping kids on his lap.

'Us too,' my mother says through a yawn. 'Wake up, Bill, you old man.'

My dad snorts, or snores. His legs kick out reflexively when my mother tips back his chair. 'Jesus, woman. Are you trying to kill me?'

After we say our goodnights, Becky and I clear the remaining glasses and empty bottles away. When I bring the trash bag outside, she is standing on the deck. Her long hair blows in the gentle breeze, her arms are folded across her chest, her head is tipped back.

'It's a beautiful night. The moon is so pretty and I can see the stars. I haven't seen this much from the city.'

I ditch the trash and move to stand beside her. 'There's a lot less artificial light here. Do you want another drink?'

She shuffles an inch so her shoulder is pressed to my arm. I have no idea whether it's an intentional move, but her touch warms me, even through my shirt.

'That would be nice.'

I bring us each a glass of red wine and move two reclining lawn chairs to the edge of the deck. Mostly, we sit in silence, staring at the stars.

'If you had one wish, only one in the entire world, what would it be?' she asks.

'One wish?' I turn my head so we're looking at one another.

*In this moment, I'd wish I could give you more than one night. I'd wish you weren't running from a long-term relationship. I'd wish that we could spend one night together and still be friends the next day.*

'I'm not sure. What would you wish?'

She stares at me, her expression unreadable. I wonder if she had any of the same thoughts as me. Eventually, her eyes wrinkle as her lips tip upward. 'I'm not sure.'

She moves the hand that isn't holding her wineglass and rubs her opposite arm.

'Let me get a blanket,' I say, happy to break the intensity of the moment. Trying not to wonder what she was just thinking.

I open the storage unit on the decking, which usually has blankets inside but tonight is empty.

'Damn it, they're usually in here.'

'That's okay. I'll be fine.'

I stand behind her and notice the small bumps on her skin. 'You have goosebumps.'

I take a seat in my lounge chair and recline a little more. 'Come here.'

Without hesitation, she climbs onto my seat and nestles her head in my shoulder. Maybe it's the wine. Maybe it's the night sky. Maybe it's being here that brings home how lonely the city can be sometimes. Whatever the reason, I'm more than happy to have Becky in my arms.

At some point, we must have fallen asleep because I wake as dawn is breaking. I'm cold but not unbearably so. Becky is snuggled tight into my chest and her face is nothing short of divine. Her eyelids are closed. Her cheeks are relaxed. Her hair has fallen across her shoulder and rests on her chest. Knowing she's asleep, I don't fight the urge to press my mouth to her skin. I hold her tighter and bring my lips to her temple.

I lie awake, wondering if it would be so bad if I tried more than one night with this woman.

The problem is, I'm starting to think the risk of losing her is worse than the possibility of being distracted by her.

And she is looking for a friend. Only a friend.

For now, I rest my cheek on her head and let myself drift again.

\* \* \*

'Rise and shine!'

I open my eyes, and Becky darts upright on my lap at the sound of my dad's too-loud-for-this-time-of-day voice.

'I'd bet you two could use a hot drink,' he says, holding out two cups of coffee. 'Your mother put the machine on especially.'

Becky twists on my lap as she takes hold of a mug. I take the other from him but with my free arm, I stop Becky from leaving my lap. I sense her eyes on me but I decide to ignore them.

'Christ, Pops, what are you wearing?'

He looks down over his blue striped, two-piece pajama set. 'Ah, I knew it.' He looks at Becky and shakes his head. 'Maggie said they looked good on me.'

'Christ.'

Becky slaps my chest with her free hand. 'I think they look dapper, Bill.'

He holds the lapels of the ridiculous cotton shirt. 'Dapper? You think so?'

'I do.'

He walks away with extra swagger in his stride.

I nip Becky's hip in my hand until she gives me her attention. 'You realize he'll continue to wear those things now, don't you?'

She shrugs and leans into me as she takes a sip of coffee. I could freak out right now. I'm sitting with this friend, who I brought home to my family, and I've held her in my lap as she slept all night.

But I don't need to do anything because, as if she just had the same moment of clarity, Becky freaks out. She jumps away from me as fast as the coffee in her hands will allow without spilling.

'Right. Well. I. Erm. I should shower.'

'Not so fast. I've got bacon in the pan. You like bacon, Becky, don't you?' my mother says, coming onto the deck with a spatula in her hand, a thin bathrobe wrapped around her own red pajamas: almost as offensive as my dad's.

'Erm, yes, yep, bacon. Wonderful.'

She takes the chair next to mine and bores holes in me with her eyes when I smirk. Feisty Becky is kind of hot.

While we're waiting for breakfast, Eddie comes back from an early morning, pacifying drive with my niece and nephew. The kids immediately dive on me, then Becky, then my dad. They make as much noise as is humanly possible, only pausing when they each have a bacon roll in their mouths.

After breakfast, Becky escapes upstairs to shower. I've seen her blush more during breakfast than in the two weeks I've known her. I feel like I've known her all my life. Yet there's still so much I don't know. So much I want to know.

I help Millie gather the dirty plates and mugs, and we head into the kitchen to clean up. I fill the sink with hot water – my parents never let me buy them a dishwasher – and Millie grabs a towel to dry. She's the only member of my family not sporting outrageous nightwear, instead wearing sweatpants and a T-shirt.

'She makes you happy.'

I keep my eyes on the plates in the sink, not needing her to clarify her meaning. 'She's a great woman. She's fun.'

Millie raises a brow as she takes a soapy plate from me. 'Just fun? Are you sleeping together?'

'Seriously, Mill?'

'Well, are you?'

'No, as a matter of fact. She just got out of a long-term relationship, and she doesn't want anything serious.'

'And you?'

I shake my head and puff out a breath, scrubbing the next plate needlessly hard. 'I've got a lot going on at work.'

Millie tsks. 'Will you still be saying that when you're in the grave from overworking yourself? Look, I get it. You worked hard to get where you are. Fine. But it's like Mom says, you can have roots *and* wings. You have a little too much in the wings department. Maybe some roots might help balance your life.'

I stare at my sister, replaying her words in my mind. Remembering Becky's words. *Roots and wings*. But roots don't exactly fit with named partner of a Manhattan law firm.

'Even if I—' No, I won't go there. 'She doesn't want a relationship, and neither do I, Mill. Just leave it.'

Even as I say the words, I wonder how much I believe them and how much I am trying to fight what I'm starting to feel for the blonde from the bagel truck.

The sound of Becky clearing her throat draws my attention to the kitchen doorway. Even though I said the words and I meant them, even though I know she doesn't want a relationship, the look she gives me for a fleeting moment is like the road being wrenched out from under my wheels. She obviously overheard my conversation with Millie.

I fight against my own dry throat. 'You ready?'

'Yep. Ready.'

There's no emotion behind those words and the way she looks at me as I pass her to go to shower is nothing... emptiness.

*  *  *

'I'm actually on South Beach Boardwalk. This is so cool.'

The awkwardness of this morning is gone as Becky tugs off her flat shoes and runs down the sand to the water's edge. I pull off my boots, turn up the ends of my jeans, and follow after her. We stand in the water, people coming and going around us. Kids play in the sand. People eat ice cream. Kites are flying. All under the brightness of a cloudless sky, not that that does anything to warm the chilly Atlantic around my toes.

'Another thing off your list. What happens when there's nothing left?'

'I guess I'll have to find another reason to make you stick around.'

As soon as she's said the words, she starts walking along the shoreline, leaving me wondering whether there was an undertone to that statement or not.

I catch up to her, and we head onto the boardwalk, where I buy us waffles and ice cream from a cart. Becky douses hers in chocolate sauce – the woman really does have a sweet tooth – then we take a seat on a bench to eat.

'Your family is really great, Drew. The way you all look out for each other and take an interest in each other. God, you actually listen to each other and have fun. It's something very special.'

I nod, guilt resting in my stomach.

'Is there a reason you don't see them often?'

'I speak to them every week,' I say, sounding a little too defensive. 'I'm busy.' I sigh. 'My parents gave me everything they had when I was growing up, so I could get a good education. I don't ever want that to go to waste.'

'That's why you work so hard.'

I stare at waves rocking gently against the sand in front of us. 'Mostly. I saw what it was like to struggle, and I don't want that for myself. Or...'

'Your family.'

I want to tell her that I'm not a family man. That I'm not that kind of guy and I just don't have it in me. But the words come to my tongue and get swept like a wave, silently out to sea.

'Maybe if my family had been more supportive and hadn't wanted to just marry me off like in the Dark Ages, I'd be like you too.'

'You work at one of the best restaurants in the world, Becky. I'd say you did pretty well for yourself.'

What I meant as a compliment doesn't seem to have been taken well at all. She drifts somewhere, lost in a world I'm not invited to as she stares out to sea. I count the seconds until her next breath. When it comes, she closes her eyes and her shoulders fall as her chest fills. Her body seems to go rigid. Then she slowly comes back, relaxing into the bench.

'For your information, the posters I pinned around my bedroom as a teenager weren't of the Backstreet Boys. I was a major Boyzone fan. Then Westlife.'

I smile, grateful for the turn of conversation, but a small part of me wonders where Becky just went in her head. If she wanted to talk, she would; that's what I decide.

'Boyzone and Westlife. And they are?'

Her jaw falls open. 'No way!'

And just like that, she's back to the Becky I've come to know. She breaks into a rendition of some song I've never heard – completely pitchy. I'm laughing so hard that my ribs are aching, as she does hand movements to match the words.

'Becky, that's horrendous.'

'The dancing, or the singing?'

'Can I say both?'

She chuckles. 'That's probably fair.' She takes another giant bite of waffle that has me shaking my head in disbelief. Where does she put it? 'So, Mr I'm-So-Good-At-Everything, what kind of music did you like growing up?'

'A bit of everything. Rock, mostly. It depended on whose pants I was trying to get into.'

'You really have no shame. What was the first concert you went to see?'

'I used to go to gigs, not concerts, for a start. I was actually in a band in high school, so I guess my first gig would have been some band in school, maybe.'

'You've never been to an actual concert, with a known band?'

I fight against my lips, which are curling already because I know how ridiculous the truth is.

Becky swivels, lifting one knee onto the bench. 'Oh my God, is it that bad? Who? Tell me.'

'*NSYNC.'

She actually folds over, she's laughing so much.

'Come on, it's not so bad. Millie wanted to go, and I said I'd go with her.' When she's composed, she sits back on the bench, our arms touching. 'You realize I'm never telling you anything again?'

'Drew, honestly, there's a good chance I wouldn't want you to if all the answers are *NSYNC.'

We fall silent for a moment; then I start humming the tune to *NSYNC's 'This I Promise You,' which sets her off like she's been on laughing gas... again.

As she laughs, my cell phone rings in the inside pocket of my jacket. I take it out but don't recognize the number. I should answer. But for the first time since I can remember, there's something more important. I silence the call and put the phone back in my pocket.

# 12

---

## DREW

Back at the house, Becky is roped into showing my mom, Millie and the kids how to bake 'real' cakes. After the salty, humid air, we both need showers first. I tell Becky to shower before me and take a seat on the sofa with my dad and Eddie to watch the last five minutes of the current quarter of college football: actually a rerun from last season but a game I didn't see live. It's nice, doing nothing, at home. My mind isn't thinking of anything other than the touchdown I'm watching. It's a rare moment and one that I don't want to overthink. If I do, I know I will somehow bring it back to Becky. Something about her influence. The way she affects me. That I probably wouldn't have come this weekend if she wasn't around.

Yep, that's where I wasn't going.

My quiet time ruined, I push up from the sofa and make my way upstairs. I hear the shower water running, so I dip into my bedroom to grab a change of clothes and a towel. Not without my mind wandering to Becky's naked body under the hot water. I'd bet she looks hot naked. That ass. What I'd give to put my hands on that fine behind.

'Drew, I'm going to put in a load of whites, do you have anything?' my mom shouts up the stairs, zapping my lascivious thoughts.

I peel my white T-shirt over my head and take off my socks, then pad out to the landing in my jeans, and throw the laundry down the stairs where my mom is there to catch it. I come back into my room, and my attention is pulled straight to the poster of Melanie Finlay.

Christ, I'm twelve again. Now all I need is to rub one out over Becky and develop a zit.

I put my towel down and pull Melanie Finlay off the wall. I ball her up and try to throw her, and my raging testosterone, in the waste basket. Once this weekend is over, I'm putting some distance between Becky and me. Not forever. Just long enough to stop thinking about her naked. Imagining how my hands would feel roaming over h—

'Oh my God!'

I turn sharply to face the door, where Becky is standing with wet hair, covered only in a towel, which really doesn't cover much of her at all.

My eyes refuse to stay on her face, and my already semi-hard Prince Harrington jolts as I trace a line from her lips, across her bare chest, around her towel-covered hips, down those toned legs. I've never been more thankful for the heavy hold of denim around my fly.

'Sorry, I was just grabbing some clothes.' The break in my voice betrays how much my body is desperately fighting against my mind. I'm in my parents' house and my body is screaming at me... *Let me take her to bed, please!* The combination of my nervous system breaking down and my semi leaves me rooted to the floor, staring at Becky, whose cheeks are the color of red hot se—

'Ah, Jesus.' I drag my hands over my face. Of all times, my cell starts to ring. It's sitting on the desk right by where she's standing. I take a step toward it and falter. I end up in some kind of dance with Becky, both of us stepping to one side, then the other. I place my hands on her shoulders to make sure we pass each other, but the heat that radiates between us when our skin touches has me stupid again.

We're so close, I wonder if she can hear my heart pounding in my chest. If she was anyone else, she would be on the bed right now, under me.

I squeeze my eyes shut and the phone stops ringing. With my eyes closed, I navigate around her. I blindly fumble my way to the doorway, when I realize I have left my towel behind. Opening one eye, I move past her again and grab it from the bed.

There was heat between us. Blazing heat. Like a goddamn inferno. I felt it. My body definitely felt it. But now, her hand is pressed to her mouth, disguising what I know is a smirk because those damn irresistible eyes are glistening with amusement.

'If we're going to continue this platonic thing, you're going to have to wear more clothes,' I grumble as I stomp into the hallway, as if my uncontrollable testosterone levels are entirely her fault.

'I could say the same for you!' she calls out.

I slam and lock the bathroom door. I'm still feeling like thunder when I step under the hot spray, which does nothing to cool my man piece. She's in my head. Sex is in my head. I brace my hands on the tiles in front of me and watch as water falls from my body to the floor.

This is a test. Like the Garden of Eden. Becky is the goddamned apple, and she looks so appetizing. But biting the fruit will cost the grand prize of Statham Harrington Law Firm.

As the glass around me steams, I wonder what she's thinking right now. Whether seeing me in only a pair of jeans had anything close to the effect on her that seeing her in a small towel has had on me. Her hair messy and wet. God, how I'd like to get wet in the shower with her and give her hair a reason to be messed up.

Without conscious thought, my palm covers what is now a full-blown stand to attention from Prince Harrington.

*Don't do it, buddy. Kill the thought.*

I can't.

I'm like a bug to a light.

I know I'm crossing a line I don't want to cross.

But what if she has stripped out of that towel? What if she's lying back on my bed right now, crossing the line with me?

If she is, we relieve tension together and forget it. Move on. That's all.

When I exit the Garden of Eden, I dry off in the bathroom and slip into a clean pair of jeans and a black T-shirt.

I head back to my bedroom, a little disappointed when I find an empty room, rather than Becky naked on the bed.

No, that's a good thing. Back to Drew and Becky, who have agreed to just stay as friends. Who shouldn't be thinking about each other that way. Who, I'm realizing, both seem to have mental issues. Who, at least for my part, are better versions of themselves when they are together.

Yep, back to Drew and Becky. Who absolutely will not be sleeping together. I head downstairs with wet hair and bare feet, feeling more at home than I have in years. My dad and Eddie are still watching the football, both gripping bottles of beer as if their lives depend on them. Timmy is now asleep on Eddie's lap – how I like the kids best. Joking!

They update me on the score, and I watch the next play, then I follow voices into the kitchen.

I find all the women in the house at work, beating what I

imagine is cake batter in large bowls. Annalise has a smaller bowl. Her One Direction T-shirt is covered in flour. She is standing on a chair by Becky, still only just tall enough to stir a spoon into her bowl on top of the counter.

Michael Bublé is playing through docking speakers, and I recognize Becky's cell phone in the stand. I may have to give her some grief about Bublé later.

On second thought, that will probably lead to her giving me grief about *NSYNC. Better not.

I lean against the doorframe and watch the scene. Becky is wearing leggings and an oversized shirt that falls off her shoulder. Her blonde locks are tied in a messy knot on top of her head, still damp from the shower. She's put a small amount of makeup around her eyes, but otherwise, she looks fresh and young...

...and extremely bed-able.

Ah, British Becky, you are torturing me.

Annalise catches me and flashes a huge, teeth-baring grin. She rubs flour from her nose, or rather, deposits more on the end, as she says, 'Uncle Drew, we're making cupcakes.'

My lips burst into a beam that turns to a short laugh when Becky looks right at me and shrugs.

'I think I'll leave you ladies to it. I'm just going to grab a beer.'

I take three bottles of Bud from the fridge and move to the bench by Becky, gesturing to the drawer that is home to the bottle opener.

'Can I just—' She steps back, clumsily bumping into my shoulder.

'Oh, yeah, sure.'

I flick the tops off the bottles and put the opener back in the drawer. Our eyes meet, and there's something about her expression that I like. A spark. A flame. It makes me wonder whether she did take care of herself on my bed while I was showering.

As if she's asking herself the same question, her lips part. I immediately feel the heat between us again. Then I put out the fire with my equivalent of water: guilt. She doesn't want or need this. Neither of us does.

I'm going to take my beer and walk away. Then I notice the globule of cake batter on her cheek.

'You have, ah...' I indicate on my own cheek with my finger the spot where she needs to wipe. She rubs her hand across the wrong cheek.

'I've got it.' I put a bottle down on the counter and run my thumb over the batter.

Her lips part again as she watches me suck it from my thumb. Watching the effect that small move has on her, my eyes narrow, and the look I give her now is intended to ask, *Did you do what I think you did in my bedroom?*

When I take a seat in front of the TV, I'm not thinking about the football at all. I'm thinking about the one thing I absolutely should not be thinking about.

* * *

By the time the smell of my mother's to-die-for lasagna is drifting into the den, the heavens have opened. Rain is bouncing so hard outside, it blows under the canopy that shelters the outdoor dining table.

I help Millie bring things in from the deck and set the indoor table. I bring two plastic chairs from outside and dry them down before placing them inside. Another thing I've tried to replace that my folks won't have.

As the rest of us take our seats – the kids being designated the plastic chairs – Millie and Becky help Mom serve up plates of mammoth pasta portions. I watch Becky move around, completely at ease, almost as if she's genuinely enjoying being here, as simple and suburban as it is. Once again, I feel ridiculous for being so nervous about her reaction to my slightly crazy family and the modest home I grew up in.

Last up, Becky puts two plates of garlic bread in the middle of the table. I pull out the chair next to me for her to sit. The tight packing of chairs around the table means her leg is pressed against mine. I set about getting us both a slice of garlic bread, pretending I'm completely unaware of the contact.

We eat and talk in that same position. It feels... natural. Right somehow.

Terrifying.

'It's a treat to have you all around the table,' Mom says after placing her knife and fork together on her now empty plate. 'It's just a shame Jake couldn't be here.'

I refrain from saying he's probably perfectly content banging some English chick and living the high life in London.

'Say, Becky, whereabouts in England are you from?' my dad asks.

'A place called Kent.' When my dad looks blank, she adds, 'It's not too far from London.'

'Well, when you're home, you should look up our Jake.'

I swallow the gulp of wine in my mouth, trying not to choke, and I glance from my dad to Becky and back again. Not once had it occurred to me that she might not stay in New York. Not really. It hadn't dawned on me that her home is still in England, thousands of miles and an ocean away. I wait for her to say she won't be going home. That she'll stay here forever.

But she doesn't.

'I'll do that,' she says, smiling meekly and undeniably avoiding looking at me. Irrational sickness churns low in my stomach. I've known her five minutes. We're friends. Yet, I can't stand the thought of my life without her in it.

If ever I needed confirmation that I wouldn't want to mess up our friendship and lose her through a one-night stand, this would be it. Damn it, I even feel guilty for getting off over her earlier. I rub a hand roughly across my dry mouth, then pick up my wine, and drain the glass. What does it matter? She could leave the city any time, then I won't have her friendship, and we never even had one night of tearing off each other's clothes, of screwing so hard and for so long, there's only sweat keeping our flesh apart.

I reach for the bottle of wine on the table and refill my glass, immediately taking a mouthful.

I catch Millie staring at me from across the table. My sister has always been able to read me. Right now, she can probably see the nonsensical panic that is infiltrating every cell in my body.

Am I panicking because Becky could leave? Or am I panicking because I realize that I don't want her to leave my life?

'How long do you think you'll stay here, Becky?' Eddie asks, completely numb to the shift in the air around the table, oblivious to how much I would like this conversation to end.

Yet I look at Becky beside me, because if she is going to answer this question, I want to know the answer. Her face is unreadable as she meets my gaze.

I silently will her to say indefinitely. *Say it.*

Her attention falls to the base of her wineglass as her fingers slide it back and forth on the table linen. 'I left the UK in a bit of a hurry and with a few things to take care of back there.'

I feel my jaw lock. Angry at myself for caring so much. It's irrational. I'm not an irrational guy. My hand grips my wineglass, too tightly. Whether it's intentional or not, Becky's thigh presses a little harder against mine, making me look at her.

'But I have no plans to go anywhere any time soon.'

She'll never know how much those words affect me. I can't honestly believe it myself.

The conversation shifts. Everyone wants to know more about Becky, especially where she trained to be a chef. And although she answers, Becky seems less comfortable when she's the center of attention. I listen to her responses but don't have anything to offer. I'm too preoccupied with what is happening in my own head.

I use clearing the table as an excuse to take a breather. Not from my family, or Becky, but from my own damn thoughts.

Not even the cupcakes for dessert can distract me.

As I'm peeling the last of the paper casing from the cocoa cake, Becky leans into me. 'Is everything okay?' she asks softly.

Is everything okay? Besides the fact I'm falling head over heels for a woman I shouldn't want and can't have? Besides the fact she just said she'll be going back to the UK? Besides the fact I have no idea why she left the UK in a hurry in the first place and that there are so many things I'm still dying to discover about this mysterious and exceptionally beautiful woman?

'Perfect. You?'

She nods quickly. 'Great.'

That's the last thing we say to each other before it's time to call it a night.

\* \* \*

When I come to the bedroom for sheets and a pillow after brushing my teeth, Becky's standing by the window in a short nightie, the room lit only by moonlight that shines against the silk. Her slender hourglass figure is kissed by the fabric, every curve shown in her silhouette. Her hair flows down her back in waves.

She turns when she hears me come into the room. 'Are you sure you won't take the bed? It's your room.'

'No, you're a guest. I'm just going to grab some sheets.'

There's no need to go to her, but it's as if an invisible force is drawing me nearer. Knowing what I would do to any other woman wearing something like that, standing in my bedroom, looking and smelling the height of temptation. Me half naked in only boxers and practically feeling the heat radiating between us when we're inches apart.

'You're quite a hit with my family.'

She lifts her chin to look at me. The moon's blue shine dances across the ocean view behind her. She's a vision. A portrait. Everything about what I'm looking at is truly incredible.

I feel her slow breath and smell the fresh mint. I want to reach out and touch her face. I want to hold her cheeks and taste her lips, to wrap my tongue around hers.

Maybe. Just maybe.

She turns away from me to look back out of the window, pressing her fingertips to her lips and her other hand to her stomach. 'They're great, Drew.'

I know my own reluctance. I know she wants to be single at the moment. But I don't know how she has the strength to fight this. God, I would like to have the same strength. I step closer to her, far enough away not to be touching her, close enough to feel the charge between us.

I plug for something more. More information to understand this woman. 'Does it make you miss your family?' I ask.

At first, she's still. I wait. Then she shakes her head. 'No. We aren't all close like your family. I guess that's part of the reason I could never...'

'Go on.'

'Never mind.' She sighs and folds her arms across her chest. 'This view is beautiful.'

I cast my eyes over her again, greedily taking her in. 'It really is.

Thanks for coming this weekend. I probably wouldn't have if it hadn't been for you.'

'Thank you for bringing me.'

'Another thing ticked off your list. When the list is completed, will you go back to the UK?'

She turns to face me, perhaps not realizing how close I'm standing to her. Her chest lightly grazes mine. The feel of her against my bare skin shoots electricity through my veins. She looks up at me through lowered lids.

'There's still a lot left on my list.' She digs her teeth into her bottom lip, and I have to have it. I have to kiss those lips and run my hands over that silk nightie. I lift my palm toward her cheek.

It's as if something snaps inside her. She grabs my hand. 'Well, you know how to make all these experiences better. You're the best friend I've found in New York, Drew.'

Ouch. Friend zone. Right where I'm supposed to be, in fact.

I swallow the out-of-control hormones that have my throat feeling like it's been grated. 'Well, goodnight, Becky.'

'Yep, sleep well.'

''Night.'

'Goodnight.'

'Yeah. 'Night.'

'Goodnight, Drew.'

'Becky.'

I grab sheets and a spare pillow from the wardrobe and bolt to the sanctity of the sofa downstairs.

Lying back, staring at the ceiling, I can't help thinking about how it felt when she was pressed against me. And somehow I just know: she wants me. God knows I want her.

I fight against the desire for my hand to be down my boxers. She may be upstairs wearing a silk nightie. She may have a devastating body. But this is my parents' sofa. I'm a grown man. Giving in to lust could result in me losing Becky altogether, and that would be a horrible idea.

But my hand moves down to my boxers anyway.

Ah crap. Where have thirty-five years of self-control gone?

I flip onto my side and tuck both hands up under my pillow. The next step is handcuffing them to the kitchen sink.

# 13

## DREW

I'm roused by the sound of cupboard doors being opened and shut and china being moved around. I pad through the den and into the kitchen, stretching my arms above my head as I yawn. Surprised, given my last thoughts before sleep, that I haven't woken up stiff.

Millie and Mom are making breakfast. 'Morning, big bro. Do you want toast?'

'At this stage, I'm unsure how much more food I can eat this weekend, but I could definitely use coffee.'

Millie pours me a cup and hands it to me. She reaches up to plant a kiss on my cheek, as I lean back against the kitchen cabinet.

'Okay, I'm going to see if the kids have drawn all over Eddie's face with my lipstick again,' she says.

'She needs to discipline those children,' my mom replies. The humor in her voice tells me she wouldn't manage it in Millie's shoes either, not when the kids flash their big, puppy-dog eyes. Then she says, 'I'm pleased we're alone,' and moves to the junk drawer by the refrigerator. She takes out a white envelope, which she hands to me.

I put down my coffee and open the envelope. Inside is a check for five thousand dollars.

'What's this?'

'Jake put five thousand dollars into my bank account. I told him not to, but you know what he's like. He wants to start paying us back for his college tuition now he's working and all.' She turns from me and begins to butter some toast.

'I see.' I put the check back into the envelope, fold it, and move behind my mom to tuck it into the pocket of her robe. 'You should keep it. Use it to redecorate my bedroom or for whatever you like.'

'It's not our money, Drew. It's yours.'

I rest back against the counter and resume the hold on my mug. 'Well, I'd like you to keep it.'

She slams the knife she is using against the work surface. Her spine straightens, her shoulders stiffen and rise, and she speaks with her focus on the counter in front of her. 'And I've told you that you've earned every dime of your money and you should keep it. Now, your father and I agreed to let you pay for Jake's tuition, and we agreed to keep your secret. We won't accept him paying us back money that we never gave him.' She turns to face me, her eyes full of tears. 'Do you hear me?'

Pride. That's what has her eyes wet. Jake was never planned. Our parents were taken by surprise when he came along ten years after me. When it came to college, our parents had already spent everything they had saved, putting me through Columbia and helping Millie and Eddie set up home.

'I wish that we could have paid for him, Drew.'

When her voice breaks, I cross the room and pull her against my chest, wrapping my arms around her. 'All right. I'll take it. I'll take the money. I'm sorry.'

I press my lips to her hair, and she grips me tighter. When she pulls away, she presses her fingers to the corners of her eyes, then takes hold of my face in her palms. 'You're a good man, son.'

'If there's any goodness in me, it's because you raised me.'

'Charmer,' she says, tapping the tip of my nose. Then she turns to the doorway. 'Oh, Becky, good morning, sweetie. Would you like toast, coffee?'

'Coffee would be wonderful, thank you, Maggie.'

She is back in leggings and a shirt, her hair knotted on top of her head, her face makeup free. Her fresh look reminds me that she is only twenty-seven.

'Did you sleep well?' I ask.

'Once I got to sleep.'

She struggled too. Was she also fighting to keep her right hand out of her underwear? I decide not to ask.

\* \* \*

After breakfast, Becky and I agree, under the duress of high-pitched begging, to take Annalise and Timmy to the park.

We sit on a bench and watch them playing on the small jungle gym and slide. The air between us doesn't feel as easy or comfortable as usual. I know it's because I've crossed so many lines this weekend. Those transgressions have been mostly in my head, I think, but I'm sitting here now wondering where her head is in all of this. Did I imagine the looks, the touches?

'Can we swing, Uncle Drew?' Annalise asks, bounding toward us.

'Sure.'

I lift Annalise into one of two swings. Timmy is man enough to climb onto his own. Becky and I stand behind the two swings, me behind Annalise, her behind Timmy.

'Hold on tight. Don't let go,' I instruct them.

'I'm not stupid, Uncle Drew,' Annalise chastises me.

Becky sniggers and bites down on her lip.

'Not a word,' I tell her.

'I was only going to say it looks like you have a lot of authority there, Uncle Drew.'

I scowl at her and push the swing.

The kids scream and giggle, begging to go higher.

'So, this morning, I didn't mean to eavesdrop or anything, but I overheard that you paid for your brother to go to college.'

'You heard that, huh?'

'I think it's an incredible thing for you to have done.'

'It was the least I could do. Jake doesn't know about it. Neither does Millie for that matter. And I'd appreciate it if you—'

'Hey, of course. I would never share your secrets, Drew.'

'Higher! Higher!' Timmy shouts. Becky pushes him higher after telling him to keep tight hold of the chains.

'Millie never went to college. We don't discuss it. She always said she wanted a family, and she got a job working for a construction company right out of high school. She and Eddie met when they were twelve or something crazy. He got a job with the state police. They just got on with things. They got married and moved out to New Jersey. Thing is, I've always suspected she knew our parents couldn't afford for both her and me to go to college and she decided not to go. It kills me to think she sacrificed what she wanted for me.'

'Well, I've only known her all of two days, but I'd say your sister seems perfectly happy to me. She's got a great husband, two gorgeous kids. Some people don't want more than that from life.'

'Maybe. Anyway, when it came around to Jake going to college, it would have cost my folks everything they had managed to save. They would have spent their retirement pot.'

'So you paid for him.'

'After a lot of fighting and back and forth, my parents saw sense. They never let me help them out with anything else. My dad once returned a winter coat I bought him because he saw the designer label and said he'd only ruin something expensive. I think it's pride more than anything. And hell, I can understand that.'

'It's where you get it from, tough guy.' She curls one side of her lips affectionately. For a fleeting moment, I consider whether pride is something stopping me from making a move on Becky. But it's so many things.

'You're probably right,' I tell her. 'So we agreed to keep it between us. Jake thinks they paid for his education, and it's only coming up now because he's working for a big hedge-fund company, and he can afford to start paying them back.'

I bring Annalise to a stop and Becky follows suit with Timmy, both kids moaning huffily.

'We can come to the park again next time,' I try to reason to little avail. 'Becky and I need to get back to the city and your mom wants to take you home.'

Annalise flashes me those fatal, puppy-dog eyes. 'Do you promise next time?'

I ruffle her curly locks. 'I promise, kiddo.'

We start walking back to the truck – borrowed from Pops – the kids running ahead. Suddenly, Becky grabs my hand and tugs me so hard I'm forced to turn and face her. Before I know what's happening, she crashes her mouth against mine.

Stunned, I don't respond at first. Then I realize this woman, who drives me crazy, is pressing those soft lips I've been desperate to feel against mine. The animal instinct inside me comes out like a tiger through flames: hot, fierce. My body takes over. My fingers fist in her hair. My free hand roams her back over her thin sweater. She groans when my tongue parts her lips, tasting the decadent mix of sweetness and coffee all at once. She tastes even better than I imagined. I pull her into me. She pushes herself closer, making me forget we're in the middle of a children's park.

'Ew!' Timmy's voice breaks the spell.

Becky pulls back first. She covers her mouth with her hands. 'I'm so sorry. I shouldn't have done that. I don't know what came over me.'

Her chest is rising and falling quickly, matching my own panting breaths. I need a moment to come back to the here and now. I need a moment to tell my member to get the hell down. I want desperately to take her to my bed. Hell, I'd like to strip her naked right now, right here, anywhere.

I draw a hand back through my hair. 'You're right. You're right. That shouldn't have happened.'

*But damn if I didn't want it to.*

I won't hurt this woman. I can't. She's too... good, perfect.

Christ, where is my head?

*Up your ass, Drew. Your head is up your pig-headed ass. You don't want to screw her and hurt her by dropping her the next day, but you don't want a relationship with her either.*

Walk away.

'We should...' Becky gestures in the direction of the park exit and starts walking.

'We should.'

We drive back to the house in excruciating silence. I also think we may have scarred the kids with that kiss. It was... intense. It was hot. So hot. I subtly adjust my position behind the wheel, and think of something, anything, to stop the war raging in my boxer briefs. I settle on my late grandfather. A peculiar choice, granted, but one that works nonetheless.

Back at the house, I hold open the door as the kids run inside first, then Becky walks by me.

'Thanks,' she says, her cheeks scarlet.

'Nanna, Nanna! Uncle Drew kissed Becky!' I hear Annalise shout in the kitchen.

'No, Becky kissed Uncle Drew,' Timmy retorts.

*Atta boy!*

If possible, Becky's cheeks glow even brighter red. The fact that she looks adorable and like she just ran over someone's dog all at once makes me catch her hand in the hallway and kick the door closed behind me.

'Hey, look at me.' When she doesn't, I lift her chin with the knuckle of my index finger. 'I said look at me.'

'Don't. Don't try to control me. That's exactly what I don't want.'

When her eyes glaze over, I know she means it. But I have no idea why.

*What do you keep locked away?*

'I'm sorry. I'm not trying to do that. I just want to make sure we're okay.'

She closes her eyes on a sigh. I don't go anywhere, waiting for her to open them again. 'We're good. I'm sorry about the park.'

'Don't be. I haven't been kissed like that in a while.'

In fact, I'm not sure I've ever been kissed like that. So it rocks me to the core and completely takes over my senses.

She bites her lip, and I have to pull it from her teeth with my thumb before I bite it myself.

Distance. We need distance.

'It's not enough that you've damaged my kids irreparably?' Millie sticks out her tongue when Becky and I snap our gaze to her.

Becky laughs nervously. 'Sorry about that. My fault entirely.'

She really thinks that? She has no idea.

## 14

### DREW

If my life had a headline right now, it would be this:

> The award for the most awkward ferry crossing from Staten Island to Manhattan ever goes to Drew and Becky: Drecky.

Then there would be a picture of us looking like deer caught in headlights on an open country road. The caption would read:

> Congratulations guys, you messed up big time, and one kiss was all it took.

This is why men and women can't be friends.

When we dock, I carry Becky's bag out to the street, despite her protest – which is, incidentally, the most she has spoken to me in the last few hours. I hail a cab and put our bags in the trunk while she gives the driver her address.

You could be fooled into thinking it was an August day with extreme humidity in the back of the cab. The tension radiating between us is almost unbearable. What I can't figure out is whether she's angry with herself for kissing me, or angry that we got stopped in the act.

Honestly, I don't know which camp I'm in myself. I know it shouldn't have happened. I've been talking myself out of doing the very same thing to her – and worse – since the day we met. But it did happen. And now I can't stop thinking about the feel of her lips. The slip of her tongue against mine. The way she gripped my back, digging in her nails. How she pressed herself into me. She wanted me then and I'm damn sure I want her now.

I also need this mid-afternoon traffic to disperse because my willpower is waning fast. I want nothing more than to reach over and pull her onto my lap. I want to tear off those jeans, maybe find some sexy lace panties underneath. I want her to straddle me, right here in this car, and...

'So.' The word leaves my mouth louder than I intended, making Becky jump and dart her attention from passersby to me. 'What's next for Becky Does New York?'

'What? Oh, the list? Right.' She's flustered. So much so, I'd be willing to bet her mind had just been in the gutter, right there with mine. 'Ah, some eateries. I can't remember which ones. My vacation is over, though. I'm back to work tomorrow so the list will have to be parked. For now.'

I wonder whether that was a complete brush off, or whether she's on my wavelength and also thinks that if we are going to make this friend thing work, we need some space.

We pull up outside her block, and I grab her bag from the trunk. I hand it to her on the sidewalk, and we're left facing one another. I try to focus on saying something sensible. Closing the weekend. But my gaze drops to her pink lips, and all I can think about is how much I want to taste her again. There. Everywhere.

'I really enjoyed meeting your family. It wasn't so scary after all. And you made the boardwalk... special.'

'Are we...' I move my hand back and forth between us. 'Are we okay?'

'Yeah. We're good.'

'Good.'

'Well, I'll see you when I see you.'

I push my hands into the pockets of my jeans for something to do with them that isn't grabbing her by the nape and pulling her to me.

'Guess so.'

I watch her leave until she's beyond the glass doors. I'm still ogling her pert behind as she waits for the elevator to reach the lobby. She never looks back, and I'm left standing on the sidewalk, pining after her like an obsessed idiot.

The sound of my cell phone ringing in the back pocket saves me from beating myself up. I take out the phone as I climb back into the cab. As I do, the battery dies.

'For fuck's sake.'

Dropping my head back on the seat, I will the thought of Becky, naked and straddling me, to leave my mind.

'Trouble in paradise?' the cab driver asks, eyeing me through his rearview mirror.

'Never even made as far as paradise.'

And damn, do I want to bite that apple.

After paying the driver, I take the elevator to my penthouse apartment. It seems bare, with no kids running around, without the smell of cakes baking, without Becky.

I dump my bag and find a charger for my cell, then flop back onto the sofa, my hands tucked behind my head. I even surprise myself when I begin to wonder, would a relationship be all that bad? I managed to have a weekend away. That's unheard of. What's more, the world didn't fall apart.

But it's not just me. Becky doesn't want a relationship.

Does she?

She wants me, I know that much. She wants me as much as I want her. I see it in her eyes. I felt it in that kiss. Jesus, that kiss. If a kiss was that hot, I can only imagine how incredible the sex would be.

I remember her response to my innocent touch when I lifted her chin. She was afraid to be controlled. Is that what she's been running from? Did she have her wings clipped by the man she used to be with?

I can't imagine her being that woman. She's no wilting flower. She's feisty. Sassy. She's got confidence. Her attitude is sexier than everything else about her, believe it or not. And she's funny. No one makes me laugh like her.

I moan in frustration. That woman has no idea just what she can do to a man. This man. She has me contemplating things I've never wanted. She actually has me wondering whether I could fight for named partner *and* have her in my life. She ties my stomach in knots at just the thought that I could lose her. I've known her a matter of weeks, and the mere idea of it already kills me.

There's not a thing about Becky that I don't want to call mine. I run my fingers over my lips, remembering how they had ignited against hers. Remembering how urgent my need to have her was. How she took me out of my head, made me forget everything except how much I wanted to make her mine.

She doesn't want a relationship. And I thought I would hurt her with one night. But we're currently sitting in separate apartments after a great weekend together. We've already screwed this up.

My body is aching at just the thought of what I'm contemplating: going over to her place right now and stripping her down. Forgetting about all the what-ifs and taking her to bed.

'Screw it.'

I kick up from the sofa, pull my jacket over my T-shirt, grab my keys and leave. I hail a cab with only one thing on my mind: her.

* * *

After working a little charm on another resident who was entering the building, I'm standing outside Becky's apartment door, with no idea what I'm going to say. I knock hard and try to find the words that will help her understand what I'm thinking. The thing is, I don't understand what I'm thinking.

She opens the door and I imagine I look just as startled as she does. 'Drew.' My name leaves her on an intake of breath. Her pupils dilate. And I think, I hope, she's in the same headspace as me.

I brace my hands on either side of the door. 'Tell me again that that kiss shouldn't have happened, and I'll walk away.' My heart is pounding so hard, I can feel my pulse in my head. This may be the dumbest thing I've ever done.

She just stares at me, blankly, and I wish I was a mind reader.

'Becky, I don't understand this, but I do know that I want you. I want you so much, it's driving me crazy.'

She continues to stare, her lips parted slightly. I have to do something.

'The sensible thing would be to walk away, for both of us. I know that. But... what do you say to thinking about sensible in the morning?'

She finally drops her hands from the door. Her eyelids seem to become heavy. Her chest rises and falls faster than just seconds ago. It's now I notice she's wearing an oversized check shirt. Only an oversized check shirt. And my breaths match hers in an instant.

I move into the apartment, and she takes a step back, not exactly inviting me in but doing nothing to stop it either. I kick the door shut behind me.

'This is a bad idea,' she whispers, her voice trembling.

Nodding my agreement, I step closer to her. 'I know.'

I'm not sure who moves first but our mouths crash together. Her hands fist in my hair as our bodies collide. It's messy. Hurried and frantic. But I swear nothing ever felt or tasted so good. She's a mix of the taste I remember, some kind of unique sweetness that's just her, and wine. A deep, smooth red. I wrap my fingers in her hair and force my lips to break from hers.

'You're drinking wine.'

I rest my forehead against hers and feel her push back, as if she's frustrated. As if she wants more of what I stopped.

'Yes. I thought wine would help. There was something I didn't want to think about.' She bites my bottom lip. 'But I couldn't stop thinking about it.'

I fight against her to take her lip in my teeth, a low, rumbling growl leaving my chest.

She groans and drops her head back, exposing her neck to me. I waste no time tasting her skin. She grinds her pelvis against mine and pushes my jacket over my shoulders to the floor.

I kick off my shoes. Everything I've been trying to resist since the first time I saw her takes me over.

She smiles at me, but it isn't a sweet, innocent grin; it's wicked, lustful. She begins to unbutton her shirt, torturously, button by button. She lets it fall to the floor, leaving her in only a black lace thong. She has never looked more beautiful.

But as her cheeks flush, she glances down and I know I'm losing her, her mind and body in different places. The self-assurance she showed a split second ago fades. I hold her cheek and lift her gaze back to me.

'Don't look down, Becky. You're stunning.'

I press my mouth to her neck. Kiss her sternum.

'Tomorrow,' I tell her. 'We'll figure it out tomorrow.'

Her response is a heavy pant and an arching back. 'Kiss me.' Her words leave her as a whisper.

*Gladly.*

\* \* \*

When I'm back in my jeans and she in her shirt, Becky pours me a glass of the red wine she has open. I stand by her in the kitchen and finally take in the open-plan apartment. The white walls would be cold, but Becky has filled the place with candles and colored cushions. Not so many that it's stifling but enough to be warm, cozy even. I subtly search for photographs but all I see are pictures from New York, and few at that.

'You don't have pictures of your family and friends.'

She hands me a glass of wine. 'I'm not really a sentimental person.' She shrugs and sips her drink. The conversation is over, but I get the feeling that's not true at all. I want to know what she keeps tucked away in her mind, but tonight, I just want to enjoy being with her.

We take our wine to the sofa. Before it becomes awkward, I wrap an arm around her and pull her to my side, giving her no option about where to sit. She takes my hand in hers and entwines our fingers. 'I'm pleased you came over.'

'Me too.'

She puts her glass on the coffee table and slides over to where she can trace shapes with her fingers on my chest and across my abs. 'How come you look like this? What do you do?'

'I box with one of my friends, Brooks. And run. I rock climb but not as often as I should. I like most sports, so if the guys get a game going and I can make it, I do.'

'It's good,' she says with a chuckle.

'So, tell me, how did you come to train with Edmond?'

'Well, it's kind of a bizarre story.' She stops drawing shapes and rests her head against my chest, her hand on my stomach. 'I was working in a café, making coffee and cakes. My nanna taught me how to bake. Her cakes were the best. And, like I've said, my family didn't really have big aspirations for me. So, I ended up working in a local café. It was a chain, and one day I got a call saying they needed help in one of the London branches because the manager was on long-term sick leave. Some people thought it was a ridiculous idea for me to go... I mean, the commute. It didn't sit easily at home. I thought it was a chance to get... into the city. And, you know, management experience.' I feel her body tense as she speaks and stumbles over her words, as if this story isn't as easy to say as it ought to be. 'I spent half my wages in train fare commuting to the city, but it was... I don't know, nice to be out of the town I lived in.'

She reaches for her wine and takes a sip, avoiding my gaze. I tug her free hand, encouraging her back to my hold.

'You were working in the café...'

'Well, one day this man came in for coffee. It was Edmond. I recognized him from the TV show he did, you know, *Sweet Tooth*? I served him coffee, and he ate one of my cakes. He chatted to me about baking. I quizzed him on everything I could think of, asking about techniques.' She looks up at me and smiles. 'It probably sounds crazy to you, but it was one of the best moments of my life. He asked me questions. I learned something new. Anyway, a week later, he came back into the café and asked if I would be interested in training in his London restaurant. I practically snapped his hand off.'

Her mood shifts from excited to somber in an instant. She looks down and runs her fingers across the line of hair down my navel.

'It caused a few arguments at home, but ultimately, I started working for him. I mean, he was based in New York, but I would see him occasionally, and the other chefs in the restaurant are amazing too.'

'Why did it cause arguments?'

She sighs and continues to focus on my stomach. 'Just the commute, I guess.'

A wave of protectiveness comes over me, almost instinctively, and I have no idea why. 'Tell me about your family.'

'There's not much to tell. My two half-brothers are brick layers. One of my stepsisters is a hairdresser. The other is a stay-at-home mum. Do you want a top up?'

She stands, but I grab her by the hips, toppling her forward so she's hovering over me, her hands on my shoulders. Finally, her mood seems to lift. I tuck her hair behind her ears.

'I want something, but it's not wine.'

'Is that right?' She flashes me a coy smile and I'm grateful she's come back to me.

I want to keep that smile this time. 'That's right.'

# 15

## DREW

I shift onto my side and when my arm wraps around nothing but mattress, I wake properly. I force my eyes open to the brightness of Becky's white bedroom walls. I look around for a clock but, seeing nothing, I flop onto my back and stare at the ceiling, replaying last night. I won't lie. I love sex. Damn, sometimes I think I live for money and sex. But last night was something else. I know Becky hasn't been with a lot of men, yet the things she made me feel, physically and emotionally... God, it was the best night I've ever had with a woman.

I listen for her and hear nothing, so I pad into the bathroom across the hallway. I take a leak and still don't hear her. As I head toward the kitchen, my foot slides across a piece of paper on the wood flooring. I bend to pick up the note:

*I had to go*

A yard in front is another piece of paper, torn from the same sheet:

*to work*

Another as I enter the kitchen.

*Help yourself*

Then one on the kitchen counter.

*to coffee*

I follow the arrow to the refrigerator. Tucked under a magnet is another torn message:

*and breakfast*

She went to work. Of course she had to go to work, but it doesn't stop me from feeling a little bereft.

This has never happened.

I stand in the kitchen with a handful of notes, looking for another. Something that will tell me what she's thinking this morning. Did she have the best sex she's ever had?

Nothing. Zip.

Jack.

Just closed Becky who doesn't tell me what is really going on in her mind. Usually, I'm the one leaving women in my apartment and telling them to help themselves to coffee. This is new. And I have a small taste of how shitty I make women feel.

I notice the filter machine is already full and still turned on to keep the coffee warm. She at least thought to make me coffee.

I hunt around the cupboards for a mug. Only now do I catch sight of the clock on the wall above the stove.

'Fuck!'

I run back to the bedroom and throw on my clothes.

I'm hopping out of the apartment, trying to put on my boots and get my arms into my jacket at the same time. A total waste of energy and time. I eventually stop and do both in the stairwell.

'It's ten fucking a.m., Becky!' I curse at the roof.

I reach for my cell as I run down the stairs, forgetting that I was in such a rush to get here last night that I left it charging. Damn it, I can't even go straight to the office.

I climb into a cab, only to sit in Manhattan's infuriating traffic: row upon row of yellow cabs and pedestrians running between them.

'Shit and balls!'

I need to get a message to Sarah and tell her to cancel anything I have on my calendar this morning. Without my phone, I don't even have a clue what that might be.

It's nearly eleven by the time I get to my apartment. Half the working day is done. Inside, I head straight for my phone.

The thing is off the charts with messages, emails and missed calls. I hit dial for Sarah.

'Sarah, it's me.'

'Drew, thank God. Where are you?'

'Becky didn't put an alarm on. She just... argh, never mind.'

'Whoa! Hold up. You slept with Becky?'

'Sarah, not now. I need to shower and get to the office. Send the car for me.'

'Dre—'

I have half a mind to call Becky and scream at her for leaving me in bed without an alarm. How damned irresponsible could she be?

Deciding against wasting yet more of my working day, I shower, shave, pull on a suit, and thank the lord my driver is waiting down on the street.

\* \* \*

As I round the corner toward my office, I'm accosted by the associate whose screw-up made me late for the ferry on Friday night. Comparatively, that was a small timing issue, but he's an associate, and I shouldn't be caused to be late because he's dog crap. I still him with a glare that tells him exactly where he can shove his apology.

'Nicky, Drew doesn't have time for this today, okay.' Sarah ushers him away with a patronizing brush of her hand, then falls into stride with me. 'You have a problem.'

'You know, some days, Sarah, could you open with something else?'

'Okay.' She leans toward my ear. 'How about this... You slept with Becky?'

I stop on the spot and take the cardboard coffee cup she's holding.

'Is this for me?'

'Yes.'

'Thanks.' We move again, this time with my first caffeine hit of the morning seeping into my bloodstream. Small mercies.

'We really do have a problem, though.'

We move into my office and she closes the door behind her, which means we really do have a problem and it isn't just Sarah being melodramatic. 'Give it to me.'

'Jerome Yearwood.'

I open my laptop and scan the papers that people have scattered around my desk. 'What about him?'

'Charles Wickman is trying to bring a case against him for fraud.'

I slam the pile of papers in my hand down on the desk. 'Fraud over what?'

'Haven't you seen any of your emails?'

'No, I... Just tell me, please.'

'Well, the big problem is that Wickman went to Jerome and threatened to freeze his assets until the case is over, which obviously poses problems for Jerome's clubs and hotels. But the biggest problem is that he's launching his new rooftop bar this weekend.'

'Wickman went directly to Jerome? That son of a bitch.'

'That's not the worst part. Jerome said he couldn't reach you this weekend, and he's worried about being served today, so he's gone to Felman Richardson to represent him.'

'He's done what? Felman Richardson? That firm is a sack of shit.'

'We know that, but to Jerome, they answered their phone when you didn't.'

I drain my coffee and crush the cup in my hand before nailing it into my waste basket.

'One fucking night.' I knew I couldn't have both.

'I take it you're referring to Becky?'

'Not now, all right. Get me Jerome on the phone.'

'Please?'

'Sarah, don't push me this morning. Please.'

As she stomps out of the room, Marty stomps in. I hold up a hand before he speaks. 'I know. I'm fixing it. Jerome won't leave us. Charles Wickman will get what's coming to him.'

'Where the hell have you been, Drew? You were completely off the grid. Jerome is a lot of money to us.'

'I'll fix it, Marty.'

'Make sure you do. Of all the times to start messing up, Drew, three weeks before the partnership vote is not it.'

I stand and ball my fists at my sides. *Damn you, Becky.*

'I know. I'll make it right.'

Sarah pops her head around the side of the door. 'Drew, Jerome is on the line.'

'Put him through.'

I pick up the receiver to a barrage of abuse from Jerome.

'Jerome, listen, it's not okay that I wasn't there for you this weekend. It's never happened in the six years I've been your attorney, and it won't happen again.'

More abuse. I clench my free fist, digging my nails into my skin to stop myself from retaliating. Taking crap is not something I'm good at. Groveling is something I'm even worse at. All because I took a goddamn weekend off to impress some girl who I didn't even wake up with this morning.

'Jerome, I'm hearing every single word. You're right. Like I said, it won't happen again but trust me, you don't want to go with Felman Richardson. You know that, and I know that. So let me hang up and fix this for you. Your club will be opening this weekend as planned. I'll be there on Friday night, drinking your most expensive champagne, and we'll toast at Charles Wickman's expense.'

'I'm not one for second chances, Drew. I needed you this weekend, and you let me down.'

I clench my teeth. If the man makes me forfeit anymore of my dignity, he can go to hell. 'I know, Jerome. I'll fix this for you.'

'You've got an hour to tell me this is over.'

'I'll be in touch.'

I hang up and put my hand on the first thing I find: a paperweight. I launch the thing at the wall of my office.

Why didn't she put on an alarm, goddamn it?

'All this for nothing.' The words grate through my teeth.

'Hey, are you okay?'

I regard Sarah, standing on the threshold of my office.

'I'm fine. I need to pay Charles Wickman a visit.'

She plants her hands on the hips of her white dress. 'I think you need to calm down before you go anywhere.'

'I'll calm down on the drive.'

'I'll say one thing, then I'll move out of your way. Charles Wickman is a class A dick, but whatever is going on with you and Becky isn't his fault.'

'This has nothing to do with her.'

It has everything to do with her.

\* \* \*

Agatha, the receptionist in the SEC building, rises from behind her old rosewood desk, taking off her glasses as she does. 'Now listen here, Drew Harrington. I don't come to your place of work and barge into your office. I've told you to make an appointment to see Charles.'

'Agatha, I like you, I do, but right now, you can either buzz me through or I'll smash the damn door down.'

As I'm contemplating whether I'm angry enough to do just that, Charles Wickman steps out of the door to the side of the desk.

'Your office, now.' I storm toward him, leaving him no other option. As soon as he follows me into his small box of an office, I ram him up against the door, slamming it shut in the process.

I grip the collar of his shirt and watch as fear fills his eyes. 'I am so fucking fed up with your bullshit, Charles.'

'Take your hands off me before I have you locked up.'

I release my grip but not before ramming him back into the door again. 'What kind of shit are you trying to pull with Jerome? I've read the file. You've got nothing on him. This is about me beating you in court two weeks ago. You've gone after me, not him, and you know it.'

'No, I have reason to believe there may have been fraudulent activity within—'

'Bullshit. It's some bogus tip from one of his competitors. He's a big client of mine, and that's why you followed up. Let me tell you something. You go to one of my clients again and you threaten to freeze his assets when you know you have no goddamn case to do so, and I won't be the one getting locked up.'

I cross the room, moving away from the dickwad to stop me from punching him in the face.

'If you think you have something on Jerome, you bring it to me, his attorney.'

His lips curl and I swear I'm going to smack the smug bastard.

'From what I hear, you're no longer his attorney. Felman Richardson, isn't it?'

'See, you've got that wrong too, Charles. Just like you get everything wrong. I am his attorney. You know why? Because I'm the best goddamn attorney he could have, and he knows it. So, I'll say it again. If you take issue with one of my clients, you come to me. And until you've got something concrete, you back the fuck off Jerome.'

\* \* \*

My count for the day: lost and regained a client, pinned the attorney for the SEC to a wall by his throat, made an associate cry.

I glance at my cell, which is staring up at me from my desk and add to my count: woke from the best night I've ever spent with a woman, rejected her call and ignored her text message asking if we can talk.

Sighing, I close the lid of my laptop and move from my desk to the bar table in the corner of my office. Given the place is almost deserted, I pour myself a scotch and take a seat in the corner of the sofa.

I recognize Sarah's footsteps without looking, the way the thin heels of her shoes click against the floor. 'Do you mind if I join you?'

'Help yourself.'

She silently pours herself a scotch and comes to sit in the opposite corner of the sofa, crossing her legs and adjusting her wrap-dress across her knee. 'I thought men were supposed to be happy when they've, you know, had their happy ending, blown their load, emptied their loins.'

I raise one brow and turn my gaze from the rain drops peppering my windows to Sarah.

'Emptied their loins? Seriously?'

She shrugs, her face full of humor.

'Shouldn't you be home by now?' I ask.

'Well, I had a call from Agatha. She filled me in on your visit to Wickman, and I thought maybe you would like a drink with a friend.'

I raise my glass. 'To my finest professional hour.'

She raises hers in mock toast. 'To clarify, are you referring to nearly beating an SEC official to a pulp or making Nicky cry?'

'I'll admit one was inappropriate, but I'm secretly proud of the other.'

She smirks. 'I'm going to take a guess at which way around that applies. Wickman is a dick.'

'True. But the kid has to learn a few lessons.'

We sip the orange liquor, for my part, enjoying the smooth heat against my throat. Sarah makes a popping sound with her lips as she swills the remaining contents of her glass. I brace myself for what she's evidently about to say.

'So, are you mad at yourself, or Becky?'

Her. For not putting on an alarm this morning. For driving me crazy with need. For making me want her so bad, I did the thing

I've promised myself I'll never do: put my work, my position, at risk.

Me. For letting those things happen. For not being strong enough to stay the hell away from her. For taking my eye off the ball and constantly screwing up since she's been around.

Me, for not knowing where to go from here. Me, for knowing I'm going to hurt her because I need to draw a line under the whole thing and move on.

Her. For not giving me any goddamn clue about what she would have said to me this morning if we'd woken up together.

I drain my drink and rest my empty glass on the sofa arm, turning the crystal with my fingers.

'Both.'

'What happened?'

'We crossed the line. Argh, men and women can't be friends. Maybe I should be pissed at you for making me befriend her. You and your poor-British-girl-in-Manhattan routine.'

'Oh, no, Drew. I didn't force you to do anything, and I certainly didn't tell you to go to bed with her.' She takes my glass from me and tops us both up, then comes back to sit. 'You like her,' she says, definitively.

Like her? Understatement.

'Are we going to talk about relationships? If so, I'm not sure I should be taking advice from someone who lives like a nun.'

She chokes a laugh through a mouthful of scotch. 'Point taken.'

We resume a companionable silence. I lied. Men and women *can* be friends, but it's a rare and precious thing when it really works out.

'I'll say one thing, though. Then I'll leave you to wallow.'

'It's never just one thing with you, Sarah.'

She raises one shoulder to her ear. 'Maybe you're seeing her as a distraction, rather than what she really might be. A part of life you've been missing out on because you're too proud to shift any of your focus from this place.'

I take it back. It's not precious, it's annoying.

She pats my thigh as she stands and leaves me sitting alone, where I've spent numerous nights. The thing is, it was me who woke up in bed on my own. I was the one who went to Becky and stupidly thought a relationship might even be a possibility. But it was she who maintained she wouldn't have one.

I'm not ignoring her. I'm giving her exactly what she wants.

The next mouthful of liquor burns, tightening my chest.

Or maybe it's not the liquor at all.

# 16

## DREW

Not even the scotch I drank too much of last night could knock me out. I lay awake, staring at the ceiling and intermittently checking my phone. Ironic, given not checking in with my phone was the cause of a fecal mountain yesterday. I actually don't know why I was checking my phone. I just thought she'd try to call again, or text.

She hasn't.

Now, I've got my earbuds plugged in to Kings of Leon as I run to Brooks's gym. I couldn't sleep last night, but now the lack of it has left me sluggish. I need something to wake me up, and I need something to stop me from overthinking this whole Becky thing.

It was one night. Like every other night with a woman. Nothing more. It can't be more. Yesterday proved why. I'm making named partner. I've worked for it. My parents gave me everything to get here. I'm not throwing it away chasing after someone who doesn't even want to be in a relationship.

I'm also not risking a solid friendship with Edmond.

I won't. Career, family and friends. That's the definition of who I am.

The heavy glass doors of Brooks's gym open into the café bistro:

a recent addition. He's been working his butt off to build up his brand of personal training and the gym. I have to admit, I'm proud of the guy. He came from nothing and worked with the one thing he has in abundance: motivation. It's finally paying off.

'Drew, hey!'

I pull a plug from my ear as Dianna – I'm pretty sure she's Dianna – leaves the counter where her fruit salad is being prepared and moves in front of me.

'Are you working out?'

I raise my brows instead of stating the obvious.

'Right.' She laughs, way overzealously, and twists her wet hair around her hand. Despite having obviously just showered, she's sporting a face full of makeup and a clean pair of yoga pants, teamed with a sports bra. To be fair, she looks hot, if not also a little ridiculous. 'I haven't seen you in a while. We should get together.'

I've fallen for that figure and easy access twice in the past. But today, I only have the energy to pound a treadmill. Mentally, I'm drained, and playing cock tease with Dianna is not high on a list of things I want to do.

'Yeah, perhaps,' I say.

'I'll call you.'

Putting my music back into my ear, I tell her, 'Sure thing.'

I hold up a hand at two other guys I recognize as I make my way into the changing rooms to dump my backpack.

Maybe someone like Dianna is exactly what I need to get back to being myself. Winning and getting laid. That's what I do best.

I crank up the volume of my music when I hit the treadmill and ramp up my speed to a hard run. When my forty minutes are up, I'm not thinking about women. My gray T-shirt is saturated, and I'm pumped. I want more.

I head into the boxing room, which is surrounded by mirrors, with speed bags lining one side and punch bags hanging from the ceiling. I incline my head at Brooks when I see him holding pads for someone in the central training ring, then sit on a bench to strap my hands.

Imagining Charles Wickman's face and considering how much I've lost my mind in the last couple of weeks, from forgetting my wallet to almost losing a big-money client, I hammer the punch bag. If there was a dry spot on my pants and T-shirt before, there isn't now. Brooks has the music banging in the room, and I land every punch in time to the beat.

By the time Brooks steps behind my bag to hold it still, I'm firing on all cylinders.

'Give me more, Harrington. Give me a left right left. Nice. Again. Now a two, two, one. You're killin' it, man.'

Once Brooks is through with me, my endorphin fire has gone out. All the salt and water that can leave my body have done so. The feeling I had twenty minutes earlier, like I was king of the world, has disappeared.

Brooks throws me a chilled bottle of water as I slide my back down a wall and come to sit on the cushioned floor, my elbows resting on my knees.

'You good, man?' Brooks asks, coming to sit next to me, mirroring my position, his inked arms bulging beneath his T-shirt.

I nod as I glug water. 'Fine.'

'Got anything to do with the Brit, Edmond was grilling you about?'

'Do you have to do that?'

'You mean call it like it is?'

'Argh. I've known her two weeks, Brooks. It can't be that big of a deal.'

'It's as big of a deal as you feel it is, no matter how long you've known her.'

I ponder those words. If that's true, it's a big deal. The biggest.

'Brooks, I came here because I don't want to think.'

He clamps his hands together, then pushes up in one fluid move to stand. 'If you really want to forget, stand up and we'll go a round.'

'No, I'm done.'

'Only if you feel done.'

'Does that psycho-talk work on anyone?'

'You tell me.'

'Ah, Christ.' I drag my ass up and head to the ring to hammer the nails into my coffin.

By the time I'm done, I'd rather be going to bed than the office. I shower and put on a three-piece that I keep in a locker at the gym.

* * *

When I get to Lexington Tower, I'm ravenous. Marty is talking to Fabio at the truck as he waits for his breakfast and a coffee so I head over there.

'Did you get everything straightened out with Jerome yesterday?' Marty asks.

'Of course I did. Fabio, I'll have the usual.'

The three of us start talking sports, Fabio chiming in intermittently as he fixes my bagel. Despite the crowded street and the fact that I'm focused on Marty, I sense her in my peripheral vision. I turn to see Becky twisting back and forth on the street corner, clearly contemplating whether to continue coming to the cart or run for the hills.

'What do you say, Drew?'

'About what?' I ask Fabio, never taking my eyes off her.

'The new pitcher.'

She looks perfect. Her hair in a messy knot on the top of her head, her cheeks flushed. Her fitted shirt shows me every curve I know is beneath. But all I feel is a building sense of rage. My nostrils flare, and I grind my teeth. If we weren't in the street, I'd give her a piece of my mind.

She seems to finally make the decision to come toward us. I'm not doing this again. I won't start my days or end my days thinking of her. I won't screw up my career because of her.

Fabio hands me my bagel, and I waste no time taking it from him and turning my back on Becky.

# 17

DREW

The week has passed in much the same way as it started. I've hardly slept. I'm constantly hungry from putting my body through the mill with Brooks. Yet, when it comes to eating, nothing seems appealing. And I'm more distracted than ever, which ticks me off. If I'm not thinking about her, I'm checking my phone to see if she's called. She hasn't. Not even a message.

She got under my skin. Messed with my structure, my routine.

There's one difference between today and earlier in the week. I'm still angry, no doubt about it, but I miss her. I know how insane that sounds. Regardless, it's true. I miss her attitude. How she laughs at her own quips. Her silly British sayings. I miss her smile. And I'm damn sure I miss the feel of her skin against mine.

The last thing I want to do is spend my Friday night at Jerome's club opening, but I have no choice, and maybe I could use the change of scene.

I stop staring at the blank email on my screen when there's a tap on my office door.

'Malcolm. What can I do for you?'

Malcolm Eddy sits on the chair on the opposite side of my desk.

His hazy eyes tell me he's back from a boozy Friday lunch. His breath tells me that booze was a heavy red. He makes himself comfortable, tugging up his pinstripe slacks an inch and unfastening the button of his tailored jacket.

'I wanted to thank you, Drew. I received a call earlier from my guy at Astrana. He admitted that he liked your style in the intellectual property case. He told me he brought a new piece of work to you.'

I rest back in my chair and bring my fingertips together, braced for a fight.

'He also said you told him that all work should come through me as the client partner. Well, I appreciate it. I think maybe you do have the best interests of this firm at heart.'

I release my steeple. 'I said it. I meant it.'

He purses his lips as he stands. 'I also just had lunch with Patrick.' My ears prick up. That sleazy bastard is trying to buy votes with an overpriced steak. 'He took me for steak.'

I knew it.

'I've got to tell you, it was the best steak I've had in the city. But do you know what I was thinking the whole time he was schmoozing me and trying to convince me to vote for him? I was thinking, "Have you got no dignity?" I don't like you much, Drew, but I respect that you didn't try to buy me like that. You did something good for the firm and that gets my vote every time. I would rather be led by a bastard with substance than a pretentious bastard.'

At that I have to laugh, and it feels freakin' good too. 'I'm sure there was a compliment in there somewhere, Malcolm.'

'There was. I'll be on your side when it matters, Drew.'

'I appreciate that.'

He dips his head once, sternly, and leaves. If I've got Malcolm in the bag, I've got this. I'm almost certain of it. The other real estate guys will follow his lead.

Sarah struts into the office, her eyes dancing. 'Did I just hear what I thought I heard?'

'If you heard the bell ringing on Patrick's fight for named partner, I'd say you heard right.'

'I guess Becky and her ideas did you some good after all.'

Just like that, she swipes the smile from my smug lips.

'I guess she did.'

In a signature move, she plants her hands on the hips of her cobalt dress and says, 'Maybe it doesn't have to be all or nothing between you two.'

\* \* \*

As I step onto the sidewalk and my driver pulls back into the street, I catch sight of Kit and his wife, Madge. They are holding hands as they walk into the glass tower that now hosts Jerome's new rooftop bar, Black Velvet. I speed up my pace to catch them as Kit pushes the revolving door and motions for Madge to step in ahead of him.

'Kit. Madge.' On the inside of the building, I shake Kit's hand and kiss Madge on the cheek. 'It's been too long, Madge. You look amazing.'

She rolls her eyes but needlessly straightens her black dress. 'It feels strange to be out of shirts and sweatpants covered in baby puke.'

I take her hand, encouraging her to twirl under my arm. 'I can see why Kit wants to keep you locked up.'

She's gone all out. Her hair is curled and resting on her shoulders. I'd guess she had it styled in a salon earlier today. She has a full face of makeup, for the most part subtle, with fiery red lips.

'Are you hitting on my wife?'

I drop an arm over Madge's shoulders, not much below the height of mine in her high heels, and we head to the elevator.

'Always.'

'You're such a smooth talker,' Madge tells me, leaning her head against my black, button-down shirt. 'I hear you're going to get your name on the door at the firm.'

I let her go, and she moves to Kit's side in the elevator while I hit the button for the rooftop.

'That's the plan.'

'I'm proud of you, Sparky.'

My lips curl at her use of the name she used to call me in college. Back when there was a group of us who would play pool and drink beers most nights. When Kit was too busy chasing every girl on campus to see the best one was sitting right under his nose.

We step out of the elevator onto white marble floors. I run my hands around my shirt to make sure it's still tucked into my gray slacks. We're met by two women in black suits: pencil skirts so tight, they might be sprayed on.

We follow the women through black and chrome double doors that open into the bar. Chill anthems are playing, rather than heavy beats. The sound is classy and slick, like all of Jerome's places. It's a dark space, lit by blue-white lighting that catches the crystal chandeliers. Drapes made of crystal hang floor to ceiling around the padded booths that line the periphery of the space, all facing the wall of windows that slide open onto the roof terrace. Directly in view is the Chrysler Building, bursting with light. The first thought that comes to me is, *Jerome has done it again, the place is amazing*. My second thought is, *Becky would be awed by this view*.

I spot Jerome in one of his shiny suits, looking as dapper as ever and turning on the charm with a woman who looks like Press. I point Kit and Madge in the direction of the booth Jerome reserved for me and hold up a hand across the room when I spot Marty,

Sarah, and Brooks already sitting around a bucket full of champagne bottles.

After spending ten minutes blowing smoke up Jerome's rear – some of which is warranted – I head over to the others. Edmond has now joined the group. As I reach the booth, a waitress switches out an empty bottle of Dom Pérignon for a full. She bumps into me as she backs away from the table and offers fluttering lashes with her apology.

'Don't worry about it,' I tell her. She waits a beat too long before remembering she was leaving.

'Jeez, how does he do that?' Kit asks, shaking his head.

'Some men are born great and get greater, Kit,' I tell him, brushing my shoulder for effect.

'And some men get fatter,' Brooks says, patting Kit's stomach. 'When are you going to get your lazy ass into my gym?'

'Brooks, I keep telling him. I could find myself a Harrison Ford if he isn't careful,' Madge says, completely straight faced.

'I like my food. Right, Edmond? And I like a drink. I don't see any of you guys drinking water.' Kit downs his champagne. 'Plus, Madge can joke all she wants about Harrison Ford. I know she loves something to grab hold of.' He does some scary action that involves wiggling brows and plants a kiss on Madge's cheek.

'It's a good thing I love you. I'm not sure we could find another home for you.' She reaches across the oval table and places her hand in Brooks's. 'Baby steps, Brooks. We'll keep wearing him down.'

'You know, I could always think of other ways to work out, Madge,' Kit says, again with the wiggly eyebrow thing.

'Yeah, that's worked out so well in the past,' she says. 'We bore devils.'

Laughing, I tell Sarah to scoot around so I can join them in the booth.

I drop a kiss on her cheek when I sit. 'You look a million, as always.'

'You don't brush up so bad yourself.' She rubs the collar of my shirt between her fingers. 'Is this Marco's latest?'

'Who's Marco?' Madge asks. 'Your stylist guy?'

'Christ, Madge, make it sound a little more masculine. I don't have a stylist. He's more of a personal shopper because I can't stand crowds and lines.' I pour myself a glass of champagne from the bucket and sit back with one arm resting along the rim of the booth.

'Well, whichever, can Kit have his number?'

I literally choke on my Dom. 'Are you going to give the man a break tonight?'

'Where's the fun in that?' Marty asks.

We work down another two bottles of champagne, the banter in the group in full swing. I hadn't been in the mood for a big night but this is the kind of partying I love. Good friends, good music, good drinks, a barrel load of laughs. This is actually what I need.

Between restroom and cigarette breaks, we end up shuffling our seating order around the booth. When Edmond comes back from his latest smoke, I wind up sitting next to him. As soon as he catches my eye, I know my night of not thinking about Becky has come to an end. At the same time, I admit to myself that I've been avoiding this conversation all night.

We both rest back against the black velvet of the booth. 'It's none of my business, Drew, but I told you to stay away from her.'

'It takes two people, Edmond.'

'I understand that, and I don't want to give you a rough time. Just appreciate that she came here to leave mess behind. She doesn't need to run into it in Manhattan too.'

'I'm not trying to bring a storm down on her.'

'Well, intentional or not, she's hurting. She hasn't even accepted my pappardelle for dinner the last two nights. My pappardelle is good, Drew, the best in fact, and Becky doesn't often turn down food.'

Despite my annoyance that I am somehow being told I'm to blame for whatever situation we've got ourselves into, his comment entertains me. 'Yeah, missing meals doesn't sound like Becky.'

He pats a hand roughly on my shoulder. 'That's all I'll say on the subject, my friend. Top up?'

'Sure.' I slide my glass toward him and rub a hand over my chin, contemplating our conversation. She's hurting. Yeah, well, me too.

Another table shuffle has me sitting opposite Marty and Brooks, and the conversation switches to ice hockey and how we should get a game together soon. A safe space. We're laughing about our last game, which was a friendly knock around with the puck, until Kit got his nose broken. That brings everyone in on the conversation again. I'm starting to feel for the guy but Kit gives out as many jokes as he gets.

I drop my head back, laughing heartily, until my attention is grabbed by the next two people to walk into the club. Like a magnet, I'm drawn in, my eyes fixed on Becky. Her blonde hair falls in waves down her back, glossy under the lights. Her short, silver-blue sequined dress finishes high on her chest but the back droops low. Silver heels elongate those killer legs. She has on more makeup than usual. Her eyes are smoky, dark, sultry. Her lips are red and utterly inviting.

Before my body finds the ability to react, Edmond has called her over to the table. She rests a hand against the arm of the man she walked in with – the bartender from Paddy's – and says something into his ear before he moves toward the bar.

Well, that didn't take long, did it?

At the sight of her with another man, the rage burning through every cell in my body overwhelms the nausea in my gut.

Edmond stands to greet her, throwing me a glare as he does. 'I'm glad you could make it.'

Sarah steals her attention next. 'Becky, I told you you'd look amazing in that dress.'

I watch her embarrassment show on her face as she glances down. 'I don't know. I feel like it's a bit much, to be honest.'

Madge laughs. 'Oh my God, listen to that gorgeous accent. Hey, I'm Madge and it's not too much, at all.'

Kit kicks my foot under the table and says, not subtly at all, 'That is British Becky?'

If I could shoot daggers with my eyes, I'd have just stabbed him.

I can sense Brooks and Marty watching me too. The whole thing has me rolling my stiff jaw.

'Scoot over, everyone,' Sarah says. 'Come sit down, Becky.'

Becky looks at me, holding on to her clutch with both hands. Does she expect me to invite her? No chance.

'Becky came here with someone else, Sarah,' I bite out. 'I'm sure there's somewhere she should be.' I say the words without looking away from Becky. She's clearly taken aback. Maybe it was harsh but it's true. She came here with another guy. Good luck to her.

When she eventually speaks, it is just to me, and I can barely hear her above the music. 'I came here alone. I bumped into him on the way in. He's just a friend.'

'You seem to have a lot of friends, until you...' As irate as I am, I check myself before finishing that sentence with *fuck them*.

She shakes her head, everything about her expression screaming her incredulity. 'I can't believe you're mad at me.'

She swallows hard, and her eyes glaze. I want to go to her and wrap her in my arms. But I don't. I stay right where I am and stare back at her, as defiant as I wish I felt. She looks at Sarah, then Edmond.

'Thank you for inviting me, guys. You were right; this place is great.'

'Becky, please, sit with us,' Sarah says.

'No, really, I was just dropping in to say hi and take a look at the view.' Her eyes clear and she rolls them, flippantly gesturing toward the rooftop. 'I have a touristy thing for views.'

I watch her walk out to the rooftop, with the growing knowledge that I'm a dick. When I see her rub the back of her hand under her nose, I have 110 per cent confirmation.

The table is silent, waiting for my reaction.

Sarah is first to speak. 'Drew, you can't just—'

I drag a hand through my hair. 'I know. All right. I know.'

Edmond stands to let me out as I push up from the booth.

I find her outside, her elbows resting on the balcony edge as she takes in the view. She has a drink in her hands but the Irish guy is nowhere to be seen. She's like a perfect portrait. I wish I could capture her in this moment and keep her.

'I'm sorry I upset you.' She doesn't turn but the shift in her shoulders tells me she heard me. 'I was out of order in there. But it doesn't change the fact that I am pissed at you.'

She pushes off the railing so hard to face me that her drink sloshes out of her glass. I brace myself for a tongue-lashing, but when her eyes meet mine, she looks down at her feet, and the inferno seems to go out.

'Don't do that, Becky. Don't look down. If you have something to say to me, you say it.'

When she doesn't respond, I reach out and lift her chin. Whether it's my words or my touch, her temper comes back full throttle.

'I've told you not to do that. Don't try to control me, Drew.' She slaps away my hand, making me step back, holding up both arms.

'And yes, I'm bloody angry with you. You haven't even spoken to me since we slept together.'

'Ha. You're the one who left, without giving any indication of how you felt. You're the one who didn't even put a freakin' alarm on and almost cost me a client.'

'Are you joking? You're mad at me because you're not grown up enough to put your own alarm on?'

'Yes!' I shout the word and appreciate how ridiculous I sound. 'It's not just that. It's you. You mess with my head. I've never screwed up so many times in a year as I have since I met you. You're a distraction, and I don't have time for it.'

She snorts. 'You're a real piece of work. I was just your friend, Drew. You kept showing up places and doing nice things. I enjoy being around you. I've never met anyone like you. You're the first...'

'The first what?'

'You're the first time I've felt happy in this city. You're the first time it's felt like more than just a place I work. The first time it's felt like somewhere I want to call home.'

I step closer to her and this time, she doesn't cast her eyes down, she looks up at me. 'Becky, you're the one who doesn't want a relationship. You said so.'

'So did you.'

'I know that. And I meant it then.' I raise my hand to her hair without conscious thought and tuck it behind her ear. 'I wouldn't know the first thing about being in a relationship, Becky. And now really isn't a good time for me to start finding out.'

I fill my lungs, trying to establish in a nanosecond whether my next words are the right thing to say.

'But I realized this week that I miss you when you aren't around. And I can't stand the thought of you being with someone like that Irish goof ball.'

She laughs and sniffs at the same time. 'He's a good guy, and he really is just a friend.'

'I know what you do with your friends,' I say. Smiling to let her know it's a joke this time. Thankfully, she takes it as such. 'You're more of a distraction to me when you're not around, Becky. So, I'd like you to be around.'

'I want to be around you too, but I... I can't be in a relationship right now. There are things...' She sighs, and I know she won't finish that sentence.

I take the glass from her hands and place it on the bar table closest to us. I take her cheeks in my palms, and I'm staring down at those red lips, wanting desperately to take her to bed.

'Then how about we spend time together? We keep having fun. And we don't label it; we don't make it a thing. We don't go nuts at each other for working late or not being available. We just do whatever comes naturally to us and leave it at that?'

'I don't know, Drew. I... The timing is not good: horrible, in fact. But I don't think I have the strength to stay away from you. And... what feels natural to me...' She bites her bottom lip and one side of my mouth lifts.

'I know. Me too. So, maybe we're friends who fool around sometimes. At least for now.'

Her lips curl. 'You New York folk are weird. This all sounds a bit *Sex and the City* to me.'

I take a step back from her. 'Whoa! You want to have sex with me? Slow down, Samantha.'

She throws her head back on a laugh, her neck elongated, her eyes bright. She's exquisite.

I grab her hand and pull her to me. 'Are we good?'

'We're good.'

'Want to go inside and meet my friends?'

She nods. 'I'd like that.'

'Come on then.' With my hand around hers, I start to leave the rooftop, but she pulls me back.

'First though, I want to do something that feels natural to me.' She rises onto her tiptoes and presses her mouth to mine. I take hold of her nape and part her lips with my tongue until she groans. Her hands roam my back, and her fingertips dig into my hips.

Reluctantly, I break our connection and lean down to her ear.

'I'm pretty sure it's going to feel natural to me to take you home tonight. This dress.' I run my fingers down her spine. Pimples rise on her skin under my touch. 'These heels.' I slide a hand up her thigh, stopping just under the hem of her dress. I kiss her once more and lead her back to the booth.

At the table, I introduce Becky properly and the others pretend we didn't act out something from Oprah on the balcony. It takes less than a minute for the guys to start regaling Becky with stories of my college days. Needless to say, they don't paint me in the best light. The recurring themes seem to be booze, women – the few crash and burns, because why would they want to brag about my conquests – and sporting disasters.

'I was also a cool guy,' I tell Becky, unable to hide my own amusement. I casually drop an arm around her shoulders without thinking. I contemplate moving it but when she leans into my side, I decide to leave it there.

'So, Becky, I hear you're ripe to steal Edmond's kitchen,' Kit says. 'Edmond says you're the best raw talent he's seen in a long time.'

She tilts her head to one side, toward me, and tucks her hair behind her ear. I lean in to her temple and whisper. 'You need to learn how to take a compliment.'

'Well, that's kind of him,' she says, smiling at Edmond. 'But he's my knight in shining armor. When a man has rescued you as many times as Edmond has me, you don't thank him by taking his spot.'

The look Edmond gives her is so warm and fond that my liking for him increases tenfold.

'You did everything for yourself,' he says.

I'm also struck by something that I would like to think is curiosity but that may even be jealousy. I want to know more about Becky. I want to understand what gives her the strength to fight the feelings between us. And, yeah, I want to be the one to rescue her from whatever she needed rescuing from.

When did that happen?

When 2 a.m. rolls around, Madge and Kit declare they are 'pooped', in Madge's words. Edmond also calls time to get home to his wife and kids. As we're saying our goodbyes, a redhead I recognize from a few other occasions comes up to Marty, pushing herself subtly – but not so subtly that I miss it – against his arm. I manage to count to six in my head before they move to the dance floor, which is now full. Like all of Jerome's clubs, he keeps the door count low enough that it's not like a sweat shop when he brings in his top DJs for a set late in the night – or morning.

Sarah, Brooks, Becky and I order another bottle of champagne. I don't mind admitting I'm starting to feel that buzz and with it, an increasing desire to be touching Becky. The hand she dropped to my thigh five minutes ago tells me she's feeling it too. The tension between us is mounting, and I'd like to take her to bed. The longer we wait this out. Touching. Drinking. The more intense it's going to be when I finally get her there.

'Say, Brooks, when was the last time you showed me your moves?' Sarah asks.

Brooks's usual stoicism is nowhere to be found – that's a combination of booze and Sarah. 'You want to see my snake hips?'

'Bet your sweet ass I do,' she tells him.

She stands and pulls Brooks by an imaginary tie around his neck, backing onto the dance floor. It's great to see them so happy.

When they are out of earshot, Becky asks, 'Are they...?'

'Sarah and Brooks? No, just good friends. They both have stuff to figure out. Do you want to dance?'

'Sure.'

Taking her hand, I lead her onto the dance floor. The track changes to a trippy, danced-up version of Lana Del Ray's 'Diet Mountain Dew.' In the middle of the floor, I tug her to me, our bodies so close, they're almost touching. She's rigid as she glances around us.

'Relax,' I say against her earlobe.

'I'm sorry, it's just, I haven't been allowed in a club for a long time, let alone dancing.'

'Allowed?'

She jerks her head back to look at me. 'I just mean it's been a while.'

This issue she has with being controlled. Not being 'allowed' to do things. I think I'm starting to get a picture of Becky's life before New York. I could be calling it wrong. Maybe the champagne is making me think I know things I don't. But there are Edmond's words again: *she's been through enough*. And if holding her didn't feel so right, if I hadn't consumed a skin-full of booze, I might remember all of the reasons this could get complicated.

Right or wrong, I encourage her to move into me and tell her, 'I'll never try to control you, Becky. I want you to be whoever you want to be.'

Her chest seems to deflate, as if she has been holding her breath, or more, for too long. She gives the faintest of nods, uncertain, I think. Then she takes my hand and twirls under my arm, suddenly happy, free, and absolutely smokin'.

We dance through a few tracks, more because I am enjoying watching her than because I love dancing. But we are shouting at each other, trying to be heard above the heavy bass. Eventually, it becomes so frustrating that I ask her if she wants to come back to my place, making a sign for home with my hands.

I'm fairly sure she shouts yes and then something along the lines of no funny business. Smirking, I tell her, 'Not unless you make the first move.'

She must get the gist – I'm game if she is – because she shoots me a jovial scowl.

I take her hand and find Sarah and Brooks, who are still dancing. 'We're going,' I yell above the music.

Sarah kisses my cheek and gives me a drunken wink. Brooks grabs my hand, pulls me into him and thumps me on the back, harder than he would if he were sober. 'I'm not going to see you in the gym tomorrow morning, am I?' he asks.

I lean into his ear. 'I really hope not, buddy.'

'She's a good girl, man. I like her.' His s's are severely slurred. 'Never seen you fight for a chick like that. She's good for you.'

'You're wasted.'

'That. I. Am.'

'Are you two going to get home okay?'

'We'll be fiiiine. Go,' Sarah says, nudging my chest away from them.

\* \* \*

I've never been more grateful for the location of my apartment. Ten minutes in a cab was all I could take. Being so close to Becky, her perfume, her slender thighs tempting me from beneath her dress, I was dying in there.

The fresh air – as fresh as city air gets – is welcome when I step into the street. I move around the car to open Becky's door, but she's already climbing out by the time I get there. She blows out so hard, it puffs her cheeks, then she sucks in air just as hard and straightens her shoulders, pulling her fingers through the front of her hair.

'Rough ride?' I ask.

She just stares at me, like she's staring into the depths of me. Once again, I'm left wishing I could read her mind. Just the smallest insight to tell me I'm not crazy for being absolutely blindsided by this woman, tackled sideways and knocked on my ass by the spiral she's got my head in.

I acknowledge the building concierge and lead Becky to the elevator, which we ride up to the top floor.

Letting us into my apartment, I nudge the door closed with my foot. Becky stands on the spot at the entrance to the open plan space and looks around in silence. The sensory lights cast a low glow over the wood floors of the space. I pick up the master remote and flick on the electric hearth and living room lamp.

As I knew she would, she moves straight to the wall of windows and gazes out across Central Park. She works her way around the room slowly, until she's looking toward the city's skyscrapers. Eventually, her fingertips slide down the windows, and she turns to face me, her back to the view.

'Are you flipping kidding me? You told me to go and sit at the top of the Empire State Building and pay tourist prices for the view when you have this?'

I chuckle. 'When you put it like that, it sounds a little harsh.'

'Who are you, Drew Harrington?' She turns back to the glass and puts her fingertips on the panes again. I move toward her, unhurriedly, not wanting her to move and spoil the image of this entrancing woman, in a magnificent dress, set against the backdrop of the city I love. 'I mean, I knew you had a good job, but this is incredible.'

Despite what my impulses are screaming at me, I don't want to make a move, not if she's not into it. We are just back on good terms.

So, I stand beside her and point out the highlights of the skyline. Manhattan really is stunning but it's not a patch on the woman standing next to me.

'Do you want a drink?' I ask.

'Coffee would be good,' she says, finally tearing her attention from the view.

Bizarrely, I'm okay with sitting up talking into the morning if that's all she wants tonight.

## 18

### DREW

The noise of my apartment door closing rouses me. It takes me a second to process the sound, then I'm jumping out of bed and running into the living room. I realize, as my member bounces around in my loose-fitting lounge bottoms, semi-hard from whatever dream I was just enjoying, that I'm not worried I'm being burgled. No, the pounding in my chest is because I thought she left, again.

I come to a halt when I see Becky walking into my kitchen holding a brown paper bag in her arms. She has on her sequined dress and those killer heels from last night. Her hair is loose and wavy, hanging across one shoulder. Her face is fresh, makeup-less, and she doesn't look half as tired as I feel.

She sets the bag down on the counter with my keys. 'Well, that is right up there in the top three most mortifying things I've done in my life.'

I bring my hand to my mouth, feigning casually rubbing my day-old stubble, to hide my amusement.

'I guess that's what they call the walk of shame, right?'

Now I chuckle. 'I think you have to have actually done the deed, as opposed to falling asleep on the guy's sofa and being carried to bed, in order for it to be a conventional walk of shame. I think you just got a walk of embarrassment, without the fun part.'

'Sounds like me.' She rolls her eyes playfully.

'Where have you been?'

'To get things for breakfast. You really should keep some provisions in your fridge. I mean, do you always eat out?'

'Mm, no. Sometimes I order in.'

She shakes her head, but I catch her amused look before she turns away from me. She busies herself around the space, putting things away and pouring two cups of coffee, while I grab a shirt from the bedroom and come back into the kitchen. I sit on a stool at the breakfast bar and sip my coffee, all the while unable to tear my eyes off her, riveted by her simple moves.

'Okay, we're all set. It won't be long,' she says triumphantly, leaning back against the counter, holding her mug in two hands.

'It's kind of nice having a woman in my place.'

'You mean in your kitchen.' She picks up a spatula and wiggles it at me, uttering a caution. Then she sips her drink and asks somewhat sheepishly, 'Have you, erm, ever lived with anyone?'

'No. Is that ridiculous at thirty-five? Don't answer that. I've just had bigger things to focus on, and women, as we've established, can be a bit of a distraction.'

Her lips curl behind her coffee before she sips. 'Well, I kind of like being here too.'

'Stay today. I'd really like to hang out.'

She raises a brow. 'Hang out, huh? Well, I have no clothes, as you can see.'

'Baby, you won't need clothes for what I have in mind.'

She throws her head back on a laugh. 'Okay, Romeo. Whilst I would love to say yes to indulging your bachelor fantasies, I'm working today.'

'Then we'd better make the most of this morning.'

She gives me a cheeky, lopsided grin. 'Do you have no shame?'

'Nope. Especially not on a hangover.' Thankfully, she laughs with me, though I'm not entirely joking. One word from her and I would ravage her in that dress. My member is still chastising me for not closing the deal last night after that intense cab ride. In fact, being kind to myself, I suggest, 'Why don't you go and pull something from my closet to wear? I'll keep an eye on this stuff.'

'This stuff is eggs Benedict, and if you mess it up, there'll be bloody murder.'

She ruffles my hair as she walks by. I'm happy we had our talk last night because waking up like this with her is a hell of a lot better than waking up to an empty apartment. The only thing better would have been waking up sated and next to her.

She comes back in a white T-shirt. Only a white T-shirt. I look to the heavens because I need the big man's help here.

I watch her bare legs move as she plates our breakfast and comes to sit on the stool next to me to eat, pulling one knee into her chest.

She asks about my friends. She starts with Kit and Madge, then Brooks and Marty. I suspect she ends up where she really wanted to start: with Sarah.

'You two are really close, huh?'

'We've known each other for years.'

'Have you... ever... you know?'

'Sarah and I? No. Never. I was actually good friends with her husband before her. He was a great guy.'

'Sarah's married?'

'He died in a motorbike accident.'

'Wow, that's awful. She never told me.'

I shrug. 'I guess some things are hard to talk about, especially when you're getting to know someone. I think sometimes it's easier for her to be single than widowed.'

I could try for an eternity and still fail to read the look Becky gives me now. She eventually casts her attention down to her hands in her lap. 'I can understand that. Sometimes, with these things, it's all about timing, don't you think?'

I watch her twist her fingers around each other, waiting for more, but it doesn't come. Whatever she holds inside is painful, that much I can take an easy stab at.

'Timing and the right pair of ears listening.'

She looks up to me and the somber air of just moments ago is gone. 'Well, I've finished my breakfast.'

I guess today won't be the day she lets me in. I gesture to my empty plate. 'Would you look at that. Me too.'

'If you have no objections, I think I'll take a shower.'

I shove my plate aside. 'The hell I do.' I lunge from my stool and hoist her over my shoulder. 'You won't ever have to ask me twice, Becky.' She squeals with laughter as we run to the bathroom. It's a sound I am rapidly coming to love.

* * *

Becky left around three to go home and change before her shift at the restaurant. It was strange to feel a sense of loss once she'd gone, as if she'd taken one of my limbs with her. My apartment seemed empty, lifeless and gray, even though nothing had changed. It was quiet, so quiet it started to get on my nerves. Usually, I like my apartment to be filled with silence, or music, but definitely not voices. Not when I spend so many hours a day in an office full of people. Today, it was too quiet.

I was grateful for Jake's Facetime call from London around five. He was getting ready to go out for the night. That's my kid brother.

He keeps the hours he likes, trading in stocks and shares during market hours, or until he's made enough money for the day. Then he's done. His free time is his, and he likes to fill it with drink and women. I can understand that.

After his call, I made myself coffee and avocado on toast, courtesy of the shopping Becky did. I wandered around my penthouse. I put on some music and thought about Becky. That's what I'm doing now. Sitting on the sofa, overthinking. How amazing we are in bed together. How well we get along; we can talk and she makes me laugh as not many people can. How nice it was to have her in my apartment, making us breakfast in my kitchen. I don't get bored of her company.

I know I'm starting to let her in. I can feel her slowly penetrating my walls, slowly working her way into my mind and my heart. I'd be lying if I said she didn't already have some kind of hold over me. The only thing I'm not sure of is whether it's a little more than friendship or a hell of a lot more.

The problem is, I can't tell if I have any hold on her. She smiles and laughs when she's with me. I know we make each other happy. But there's something in her distant looks, and in the way she stops short of telling me things, the way she did when we were talking about Sarah's husband. I'm letting her in, no matter how scary it is to do so, yet her defenses are up.

We promised each other we weren't going to do this. To overanalyze whatever is going on between us. Just take it slow. Natural. But I'm afraid I'm going to let a woman in, let her put my heart in a vise, mess with everything I've worked so long and hard for, and she doesn't feel the same.

'This isn't healthy,' I say into the empty room, exasperated with my clouded head, with myself.

I finally leave the sofa and go in search of my laptop. Booting it up, I deal with low-hanging fruit in my inbox, then work on a few ongoing cases.

By the time I'm done, it's after nine. See, there's no need to over-think. This works well. We see each other. Have a great time together. She goes to the restaurant, and I get my work done. I can do this; friends with benefits that isn't detrimental to my partnership.

At nine thirty, I get a text message from Marty, telling me he's headed out if I want to meet him for drinks. I contemplate it for only a matter of seconds before I determine I don't want to go out and try to pick up women, not when I could have one amazing woman.

I tell him I'm not up for it tonight and receive a barrage of insults in return, not unkindly meant, I'm sure.

Becky won't be done until late tonight. Maybe even the morning. I pull on my sweatpants and take to the streets, pounding the sidewalk until sweat is running from every follicle of my skin.

It's after eleven when I get back to my apartment. The most ridiculous buzz takes me over. She'll be done soon.

After showering, I run some product through my hair and pull on a pair of jeans, my staple plain T-shirt, black today, and my leather jacket, then take my Aston Martin out for a drive. The whole time I'm out, my excitement is building. My stomach is tying itself in knots.

What in the hell is wrong with me? I'm a grown man, for Christ's sake, not a kid going to see Santa Claus.

I pull up to the sidewalk outside Edmond's place shortly before midnight. Through the glass windows, I can see there are only a few tables of diners left, and none of them are eating. Becky must be done for the night.

I get out of the car and lean back against it, my hands in my pockets, despite the warm breeze. I once read somewhere that men put their hands in their pockets when they're thinking about sex. Well, I most certainly am. I've been thinking about sex with Becky since I last had sex with Becky. That's pretty much all I've thought about for 70 per cent of my day.

Saving me from my own rogue thoughts, I see Becky leave the kitchen and make her way through the restaurant to the outside door. It's a shame the sexy mini-dress has gone, but the figure-hugging jeans and shirt she has on do just as much for me. She's talking to two men who are vaguely familiar to me from times I've been seated at a table by the open kitchen.

She stops still outside the restaurant doors when she sees me. The change from shock to happiness on her face actually makes my insides leap.

'Good evening, Mr Harrington,' she says, her British accent in full tilt, her eyes alight.

'Becky.'

The two others say their goodbyes and she comes toward me, carrying a large bag. There's already charged energy between us, and we're standing a yard apart. She takes a step toward my black Aston Martin and runs her fingers along the roof.

'Nice wheels.'

'I like to get it out every now and again.'

'Are you here to take me for a ride?'

I chuckle. 'The ride of your life, babe.'

Laughing, she hands me the bag she's been carrying. 'Well, it's a good thing I brought clothes for tomorrow this time.'

I raise a brow as I take the bag from her. 'I wasn't aware you Brits are quite so presumptuous.'

'Hopeful. And, of course, do tell me if I read this situation incorrectly.'

Shaking my head with a grin, I walk around the car and hold

open the passenger door, dropping her bag into the back almost-seat.

When I pull out into the road, she's still looking around the interior and touching everything on the dash. 'I've never been in a car like this. I feel like a Bond girl. Can we drive a while, James?'

'Why yes, Vesper. Where do you want to go?'

'For the record, if that was an attempt at James Bond's English accent, it was terrible. To answer your question, I have absolutely no idea.'

She has me laughing, again. I wonder if I have a quota of happiness in a year because she's probably used it up in less than three weeks. I drive us out toward Long Island. Becky takes in everything we pass: people, buildings, street names. The way she views everything has me seeing the city in a different light, even seeing it for the first time. It reminds me how great the place can be.

When we reach Long Island, she's sitting back in her seat. I feel, rather than see, that her focus is on me. 'I know I shouldn't say it, but you look really sexy driving a car like this.'

I glance at her from the corner of my eye. She gets more brazen, more open, every time we're together. I goddamn love it.

'Hell yes, I'm in.' I swerve off the road as quickly and safely as I can, feeling like a randy teenager on prom night.

# 19

## DREW

Waking up with Becky in my arms, or catching her looking down at me when she's been watching me sleep, are officially my new favorite things to do. That's what I'm thinking as I'm waiting in the courthouse for my hearing to begin.

Since we declared whatever is going on with us as something we won't overthink or label, life has been pretty damn good. For two weeks, we've spent almost every night together. It's easy. It's hot. And it feels... right.

If she's working the night at the restaurant, I pick her up. If she isn't, she's waiting at my place for me, generally with something cooking, sometimes already in underwear on my bed, showing me what I could have been enjoying instead of working late.

The thing is, every day, I fall deeper for her. I know what we said: friends with benefits or whatever. But that's not how it feels. When we're together, I can't get enough of her. When we're not, I think about her. And I'm managing work fine, mostly, except the occasional desire to stay in bed with her rather than get to the office. Who am I kidding? That's every morning, but I mean the mornings when I let lust take over my willpower.

I can do it. I can have roots and wings. Now, I want both.

The problem with that is Becky is still holding back. She drifts to a distant place sometimes, at the smallest provocation. Yesterday, I joked that I liked having a woman in my life to cook, and it was like she went into lockdown. I admit it wasn't the best joke, but she knew it was a joke Christ, I'd tell her not to cook at all if it meant she wouldn't put up her walls. It's times like that, I know she still doesn't want a relationship.

So where in the hell does that leave me?

'Drew.'

I follow the voice along the courthouse corridor to Ben Granger, my client. He's a young guy in his early twenties, and he's an absolute tech genius. I told him in no uncertain terms he had to wear a suit, rather than his usual college style get-up, for the hearing. He's done it, and the kid cleans up all right. His ordinarily messy hair, which looks like some dude took a pair of shears to it, is tamed with product and combed. He looks like someone a judge might actually take seriously, as opposed to booting right out of the courtroom.

'Ben, how are you feeling?'

'Nervous.' His fingers tell me as much as they tremble when he reaches out to shake my hand. I don't generally get affectionate toward my clients but I feel for this guy. That's new to me.

'You have no reason to be nervous.' I move my hand to his shoulder. 'Trust me. I've got this. You're on the winning side.'

He nods too quickly, as if he's spent the morning on a caffeine drip. 'I trust you.'

We're called into session. I take my spot at one of two wooden tables opposite the judge's bench in the courtroom. The attorney for the other side, the Goliath of software companies, Codaware Technology, stands behind an adjacent table. Ben – or David, if you will – takes a seat beside me, and I pour him a glass of water, genuinely wondering whether the kid will be able to maintain consciousness for the entire hearing. His face is gray-white and his breaths are coming quick and shallow.

The CEO of Codaware looks across with a supercilious grin at Ben's state. A big company like that preying on a kid and his invention; I've half a mind to jump over there and beat the shit out of the guy.

Meet sentimental Drew. I'm just getting to know him myself.

I bend to Ben's ear. 'Hey, you need to try to calm down, buddy. Can you do that for me?'

He nods.

'They stole your idea, Ben. What did I tell you? You're David. Codaware is Goliath. I'm going to get back what they took from you. I just need you to hang in here for a few hours. Okay? Good man.'

Judge Matterson is announced to the room. When he's seated at the bench, the twenty or so members of the public and press take a seat behind me. I spot Marty as he slips into the room and comes to sit on the bench closest to me. It's something we do sometimes: watch each other in court. We might learn something, or we might razz each other later for some jackass statement or blip.

'Mr Harrington, are you ready to give your opening statement?'

I straighten my jacket. 'Yes, Your Honor.'

I step from behind the table, where I can get the attention of the room and, more importantly, the judge and jury.

'Ladies and gentlemen, today, you will learn how the industry giant, Codaware Technology, stole from my client. You will hear that Benjamin Granger, at just twenty-two years of age, could be a pioneer of technology for generations to come. How he could do great things for the industry and society. But not if we let bullies like Codaware steal from the young men and women we hope will lead our future.' I pause, giving the jurors a chance to consider my words, then I soften my tone, looking for the sympathy vote. 'You will also learn that, although he has a brilliant mind, Benjamin has a lot to learn. He was naïve. He misplaced his trust in business tycoons who preyed on his youth and good nature. Ladies and gentlemen of the jury, let us correct that wrong. Let us bring justice to Benjamin and kids like him. Kids we want to encourage to be educated, to be special, and to strive for greatness. Let's inspire others, our sons and daughters, our nieces and nephews, to follow in his footsteps.'

I take my seat and listen to the drivel the opposition spins to the jury, all the while feeling my buzz grow. There aren't many better highs in the world than being counsel in a trial. Until a few weeks ago, I'd have said there were none.

My adrenalin builds as I call my first witness to the stand.

* * *

'I thought you said a few hours, Drew? I can't go through another day of this.'

Standing in the corridor outside the courtroom, I tell Ben, 'We had a good day. We've got this. Everything went according to plan; it's just taken longer than anticipated. We'll close this out tomorrow, and you can get on with doing what you're great at.'

He exhales slowly, his breath trembling. I swear the kid hasn't stopped shaking all day. 'Okay. Okay.'

'Now, go and get some food and try to sleep. I'll see you tomorrow.'

As Ben walks away along the marble floors of the corridor, his sparkly new trial shoes sliding against the smooth surface, Marty pats a hand against my shoulder from behind.

'You crack me up, Harrington. That shit about inspiring the youth of today or whatever. Brilliant.'

We walk out of the courthouse together, both fastening our jackets by one button when we step into the late afternoon gusts.

'You saw the jury. They were lapping it up.'

'I won't argue with that. The case is yours. I've got to tell you, Drew, another win looks good ahead of the vote on Thursday.'

'Certainly can't hurt, can it?'

'Not at all. Steak?'

'Read my mind.'

We walk to a grill house a few blocks from the court and are seated in a red leather booth.

A waitress makes her way over to us. 'Hi guys, I'm Cassie.' She hands us each a menu, and I start looking. 'I'll be taking care of you this evening. Can I get you started with some drinks?'

I don't know why I bother looking at the menu, knowing the rump steak here is particularly good. The waitress comes back with two glasses of ice water.

'I haven't seen you here before, Cassie,' Marty says. I don't need to raise my head to see he's flirting. That shift in his voice to somewhere between casual and low husk tells me all I need to know. 'I'm sure I'd remember.'

She's laughing, girly and high-pitched, and talking back as I look down the wine list for the reds by the glass. I won't have more than one since I have to be back in court in the morning.

Cassie takes our order and leaves.

'You've really got it bad, huh?' Marty asks.

I know what he's referring to, but I still ask, 'What do you mean?'

'I mean, that Cassie has the best rack I've seen in a while. She sticks her tits in your face, and you don't even notice she exists. I've got to tell you, Drew, at first, I thought Becky was just another notch. Then I thought you were taking my push for you to appear human to the extreme. Then I started to think you actually liked her, and I was worried, buddy. You made a few slip-ups that aren't like you. As a partner, I was concerned.'

I roll my jaw, slightly uncomfortable with where this could be going. His comments kind of feel like an insult.

He leans back in his chair and accepts a glass of wine from a different waiter. 'As a friend, though, I have to admit, I've never seen you happier. Your work is back on track, and whatever she's doing, she's keeping a smile on your face. You're not quite such an arrogant bastard. The other partners are noticing, and I think it's working out well for you.'

'Well, not that I was looking for your blessing, Marty, but I do like her.'

*I like her a lot. A real lot.*

My stomach tightens, and I sip my Pinotage to take the edge off.

'Does she feel the same?'

That twists the knot in my abdomen tighter.

*God, I hope so.*

I shrug. 'She seems happy when we're together. She wants to be with me.'

'Am I detecting a but?'

*Yes: but there are things she holds back from me. Some kind of barrier I can't penetrate.*

All I say is, 'No buts. We're keeping it casual.'

The conversation sticks with me through dinner. Instead of having my mind on Ben's case, I'm focused on keeping the sick feeling in my gut at bay. Does Becky like me as much as I like her? She still hasn't said she would consider a relationship. And, yeah, I want one. I mean, we're having one. Aren't we? Are we?

By the end of dinner, I accept that I'm afraid. I'm no longer afraid of wanting more from her. I'm afraid that I need more, I'm craving more, and she isn't in this with me.

I say goodbye to Marty outside the grill house and we flag separate cabs. I take out my phone and see nothing. No missed calls, no texts. I'm not supposed to be seeing Becky tonight, but the panic that's set into my chest is making me desperate to be with her. When we're together, I don't worry about how she feels. She soothes my worries with every look and every touch.

I consider sending her a text message asking her to come to my place. My thumb rolls over the letters on my cell. But I decide against it. I said we'd do what comes naturally, that's what I agreed to, only I don't know if what feels natural is the same for both of us anymore.

I make my way to my apartment and let myself inside. The place actually smells of Becky: her perfume, the general sweet scent that isn't anything other than her own skin. I consider texting her again, then head to the living room without doing so. I need to get a handle on these feelings before I ruin everything.

As I'm placing my briefcase and phone on the kitchen counter, I notice the electric hearth flickering. My heart starts to beat harder in my chest. I pad through the living room to my bedroom and see the door ajar. The anxiousness in the pit of my stomach turns to excitement.

I push open the door to find Becky lying on her side in my bed in only black lace underwear. One leg bent. Her head propped up on her hand. The lights are dimmed low and cast a soft glow across her skin.

My first thought is, *She's beautiful.* My second is what I would like to do with that body. The third, as I slip out of my jacket and shoes and step closer to the bed, is that she came to me. She wants to be with me too. That thought forms a lump in my throat that stops me from being able to speak. I can only look, completely captivated by her, as I take her hands and bring her to sit on the edge of my bed.

She eyes me as she unbuttons my vest, then pulls my shirt from my slacks and unbuttons that too, pushing both to the ground. I run my hand through her long, silk waves, and watch her slowly unfasten my pants.

I don't just like her a lot. I'm in love with her. I love everything about her. I hold her face in my hands and press my mouth to hers. I kiss her slowly, tenderly, because that's how I feel. I don't want to ravage her. I want her to understand how I feel. I want her to know the things I can't say. And I want her to make love back to me.

When we're done, I fall to her chest, my breathing more erratic than if I'd gone at her hell for leather. I lie against her heart, listening to it pound as hard as mine. She strokes my hair as I drop kisses to her chest. I will her to say something. I want her to tell me how she feels. More than that, I want her to tell me what I want to hear. I want her to tell me she's in love with me.

She says nothing.

With each second of silence, I feel weaker, more broken, shattered.

## 20

### BECKY

*10 months ago*

'Becky, what's going on tonight? Is everything okay?'

I glance up from the service station where I am putting the finishing touches on a dessert and see Edmond. With unsteady fingers, I place the sugar nest over the last of four plates.

'They're ready,' I tell the lingering waitress. I force a smile when I stand, facing Edmond. 'I'm fine.'

'You're not fine. You've messed up two plates tonight. That's two more plates than you've messed up the entire time you've worked in my restaurant.'

I tuck my towel into the belt of my white coat and rub a hand across my clammy temple. 'I know. I'm sorry.'

'Listen, I can finish up tonight. There are only a few tables left. Why don't you take yourself home? It's been a busy night.'

'No, really, Edmond, I'm fine. I can finish here.'

'You look tired, Becky. Stop being a martyr. Go home.'

I'm not being a martyr. Going home to Mike is the last place I want to be.

Sighing, I nod and unbutton my chef's jacket.

I strip out of my uniform and leave it in a bag for the restaurant porter to pick up for dry cleaning. Then I pull on a pair of leggings and a hooded jumper and leave the restaurant to catch the train home.

I take my time walking through central London. First, I catch the underground to King's Cross Station, where I'll take the train to Kent.

I am tired. I'm tired of my shitty life.

More than anything, I'm tired of worrying about the baby growing inside me.

Instinctively, I press a hand to my belly. It's only been a week since I found out I'm pregnant. I'll love it. I will. But the thought of bringing a baby into this world – the world I share with Mike – I can't bear it.

I'm trapped. My one sanctuary is work, and now he's threatening to take it away from me, owing to the long hours and long commute. He doesn't want me to risk our baby's life. At least that's what he says. In reality, he doesn't want me to have anything for myself. He doesn't want me to have independence.

God, what a mess.

Why couldn't I have been stronger? When he found out I was still taking my pills, why didn't I leave or find another way to keep this from happening?

I cowered away from another barrage of abuse, that's why. I've spent years under his leash, and I can't do that to a baby. Our baby. The thought brings bile to my throat.

I make my way down the escalator to the underground and wait on the platform.

The digital overhead sign tells me it is one minute before the train to King's Cross arrives.

As I hear the tube approach, a pain strikes low in my abdomen. I press my hand to it, and it fades.

I take a seat on the tube. There are only eight other people in the carriage. The pain comes again, then recedes to a dull ache.

It's been a long night. Fridays are one of our busiest nights at the restaurant. That's all it is.

I start to sweat with the continuous dull throb and count down the stations to King's Cross, relieved when I can finally exit the tube.

I make my way up toward street level, in the direction of the overground trains. The pain strikes again when I'm in the middle of a concrete staircase. This time it's bad, really bad, and makes me fold forward.

My foot slips, and I fall back, rolling down the staircase, cracking off each concrete step.

Everything goes black for a moment but I am conscious and face down on the ground. The pain in my stomach is still there.

'She's bleeding,' I hear a woman yell.

I groan as I roll over so I'm facing up, not sure which is hurting more, my spine, my ribs, or my stomach. I try to sit, but I feel dizzy and fall back.

My vision comes in and out. I can make out a man and woman talking quickly and hovering over me.

Two men in green uniforms move toward me and my vision starts to clear. 'I don't need an ambulance,' I tell them. 'I'm fine. I just slipped.'

'All right. All right. Don't try to sit just yet. Can you tell me your name?'

'Becky.'

'What day is it, Becky?'

'Friday.'

'Where are you headed?'

'Home. I need the overground.'

'Do you live in London?'

'No. I work in London. I've just finished work.'

'Okay. Can you tell me if you're in pain?'

'My stomach and my back.'

'Is your vision clear?'

'Yes.'

'Okay, Becky, let's try to sit up.' The man holds me under the arms and brings me to sit. It's then I notice blood on my jeans.

I reach up to my head and get blood on my fingers. 'I cut my head.'

'You did.' He moves around me and mumbles with his co-worker. 'We're going to pop you in a chair, Becky, and get you to the hospital, okay?'

'Please, I don't need to go to the hospital. I have to get home.'

They don't listen, and within minutes, I'm being strapped into an ambulance chair with a pink knit blanket over me.

In the ambulance, the man who spoke to me asks, 'Is there any chance you could be pregnant?'

I feel my brows furrow. 'Yes.'

'Okay.' The smile he gives me is so fake, it tells me exactly where the blood is coming from.

* * *

I'm lying on the hospital bed in a white gown, my eyes closed to shield them from the overhead fluorescent lights. Yet my tears keep falling.

They confirmed I lost the baby.

I've cried for the baby I didn't know. But that's not why the tears keep falling. My tears keep falling because I am a cold, heartless bitch. Because when they first told me, I felt choked. I'd lost the life that had been growing inside me. The life I was supposed to protect. Then, I felt relief.

How can I possibly feel relieved?

I don't want a baby to come into this world and live with Mike, with his constant verbal abuse. I don't want a baby to see how weak I am. To know that I can't protect it because I can't even protect myself from him.

I don't want to be trapped anymore.

I've wanted to leave for so long and never found the strength. The baby finally made me think I could do it. That I had to leave Mike's hold to protect my little boy or girl. Yet, I still hadn't done it because a part of me knew I would be taking my baby away from its dad.

Now, there is no baby, and I can go. I want to go. I will leave him.

'Rebecca.' I hear Mike and open my eyes. He's glaring at me. He moves toward me and hovers over me, close to my ear.

'You did this. You did this on purpose, you selfish cunt.'

My willpower is immediately zapped by this man. 'Mike, please. I swear I didn't.'

'I told you to leave that job,' he snarls.

I'm saved by a doctor who enters, wearing a white coat and carrying a clipboard.

'Hi, Becky. I'm going to sign you off now that you have someone to take you home.'

*Please. Please don't send me away.*

'Your head wound is superficial, and you can take painkillers for your muscle soreness.' He pauses, and his eyes fill with pity I don't deserve. 'I'm sorry for your loss.' He looks at Mike too and places a hand on his shoulder.

Maybe I am a bitch. Mike lost a baby too and all I can think about is myself and how to get away from him.

I dress and meet Mike at reception, feeling emotionally drained more than in physical pain. I climb into the passenger side of our rusty Volvo in silence. Mike doesn't speak the entire ride home, but his grip on the steering wheel tightens to the extent his knuckles are white under the broken flashes of streetlights.

My heart races in my chest. I've done things wrong in the past. I've seen his temper. But this... He knew I didn't want a baby. He almost hit me when he found my stash of pills. Now he believes I murdered our baby.

'Mike. Please talk to me.' *Talk to me now, here, in the car, where I know you can't hurt me.*

'What the fuck do you want me to say? Tell you what I'm thinking? Because right now I'm thinking you killed my baby.'

'Mike. I was in pain and bleeding. That's why I fell. I didn't—'

He reaches out and grabs my thigh, digging in his fingers so hard I yelp. 'I told you to leave that job. You did this.'

My tears roll down my cheeks again.

'Stop crying like a crying fucking bitch.'

'I'm sorry.'

'Sorry? You think sorry is fucking good enough?'

'No. I know it isn't.' I say the only thing I think might end this before it begins. 'We'll try again. I do want your baby. Of course I do.'

It pacifies him enough to finish the drive. He screeches to a halt outside our house, forcing my body forward against the dashboard.

He storms into the house and I take deep breaths, willing myself to be strong. I push through the front door of the house tentatively. He slams it behind me and pins me against it by my throat.

'You killed my fucking baby.'

'I didn't,' I sob.

It happens in slow motion. He pulls back his free hand, and though I raise my hands to protect myself, his knuckles connect with the corner of my eye. I scream, part in shock, part in pain, and he lets me go.

I fall to my knees and look up at him, seeing his own shock on his face. He's never hit me before. He's bashed me verbally, called me every name for a whore he can, but he's never hit me.

I stare at him, holding my hand to my stinging cheek, and I find my strength, my resolve.

No more. I'm going.

I stagger to my feet and get a good look at his ghost white face. 'Rebecca, I'm sorry.'

'It's okay. You're upset. Go to bed. I'm going to ice this.'

He reaches out his arms and it takes all the strength of my will not to flinch. 'Becky—'

'It's okay, Mike. I'm okay.'

Because in the morning, I'll be gone.

* * *

When Mike goes to work, I pack what I need. I'm already late for my shift at work. I told Mike I would quit. I won't. If there's one thing I know about all of this, I need money. I need a job. And my work is the one place I feel safe and worth something.

I take my suitcase to the train station and ride into London. People stare at my blackened eye on the train. Two women whisper among themselves. I rest my head back against the window, trying to block them out.

I take the underground and receive similar reactions. When I get to work, I walk through the hotel with my suitcase, keeping my head down.

In the kitchen, I say good morning to the staff already in and take my suitcase to Edmond's office, where I'll leave it until the end of my shift. Meanwhile, I need to figure out where on earth I'm going to go. Where in the hell I can go that Mike won't find me.

I punch the code into the keypad on Edmond's office door and let myself in.

'Oh, I'm sorry, Edmond, I didn't realize—'

'Becky, what happened to your eye?'

'I...' Haven't even thought of a lie. 'It's nothing. I fell in the train station last night.'

He stands from his desk and comes toward me, taking hold of my chin and looking closer at the bruising.

'And the pavement shot up and punched you in the face?' The anger in his words is clear.

I don't have a lie to tell him. He knows he saved me once by bringing me to this restaurant, and in a way, I've let him down every day I've continued to be with Mike. I'm fed up with letting people down. I'm fed up with being controlled. I'm fed up with my life.

An audible sob escapes me and opens the floodgates to what I think might be endless tears. Edmond seats me at his desk, then leaves the office, returning with two cups of tea. He sets them down with cookies, telling me I could use the sugar, and I tell him everything he needs to know, leaving out the pregnancy and the full extent of just how fucked up my relationship with Mike really is.

'I knew you weren't right last night.' He shakes his head. 'I never should have sent you home to him.'

I place my hand over his on the desk. 'Edmond, you're not to blame for any of this. It's been my weakness, my decision, to stay with him.'

'You're not going back to him, Becky. He hit you.'

I shake my head. 'No. I'm not going back.'

'What are your plans?'

I suck in a breath. 'I haven't got that far yet. I've packed some things and left, that's all. I need to get away, far enough from my usual life that he can't find me.'

Edmond leans back in his chair. 'Stay here. At the hotel. Just for now. I need to make a few phone calls, but I don't want you to leave. You don't have to work. I just mean you should stay in the hotel.'

I shake my head again. 'No, please, Edmond, I want to work. This is the only thing I have left.' My eyes fill again, but I fight back the tears.

'Okay. I will spread the word that you fell. If you start working and you don't feel up to it, you can go to your room.'

'Thank you.'

\* \* \*

I get to the end of my shift without any questions and without having time to think about anything but the Saturday night service. The decision to work was a godsend.

I'm cleaning down the pastry station when Edmond asks me to follow him to his office. I finish wiping the disinfectant from the steel benchtops and go to him.

He's sitting on the edge of his desk, his hands folded in his lap. 'You look better tonight. Do you feel better?'

'I still have no clue where to go from here, but working has helped.'

He nods. 'I have a proposition for you. Take a seat.' I do. 'How would you feel about taking a job in my New York kitchen? Same role. Same pay.'

'I...' I feel my jaw drop. 'I... New York? America?' My mind frantically tries to piece together the request.

I would go to New York. To Edmond's signature restaurant. I'd leave London. I would leave Mike, forever. I'd work out who the hell I really am. I could start again. Free of my family. Free of everyone who has put me down for as long as I can remember.

'When can I start?'

# 21

## DREW

Becky didn't come to me on Tuesday, and I didn't go to her. I told myself I was drinking scotch after scotch with Marty to celebrate winning the trial against Codaware. I know I was really drinking to forget. To be numb.

She didn't come yesterday. And I didn't go to her.

Since I made love to her, real love that rocked me to the core, we've sent a few friendly text messages to each other. For my part, forced.

I don't want to lose her. I can't. But I can't do that again. I can't give her every single part of me and get nothing back.

She felt it too. She had to. It's not possible that something could be so overwhelming for one person and not affect the other. But she didn't say a word.

I didn't tell her how I feel. But she had to have sensed it. And she said nothing. Nothing. Not a thing.

'Ladies. Gents. Thank you for being here. This is obviously a sad and momentous time for the firm.' Marty addresses the conference room. The partners sit around the large board table. The most junior stand around the periphery, leaning against windows and walls. 'For more than thirty years, this firm has thrived under the Turner name, no matter what changes have been encountered along the way. I know my own father couldn't speak highly enough of Richard. It is with a heavy heart that we say goodbye to him as a managing partner, but his legacy will live on in the ethos of our firm. Before we take the vote on the next named partner, Richard would like to say a few words.'

As Richard recounts tales of his time at the firm, sharing anecdotes of bloopers and awkward clients, I glance around the room. My nerves are jangling as I silently count which partners I think will vote in my favor and then count those whom I really couldn't take a guess at. I only hope that my efforts over the last few weeks have won over those who might have chosen Patrick initially. Others, those who vote on billables, I know I have them in the bag.

'Without further ado, then, let's vote on my replacement,' Richard says. 'Take a voting slip. Mark down Drew or Patrick and drop your response in this box. Drew and Patrick will not be entitled to vote on this matter. Gentlemen, you both deserve this. Good luck.'

Purely for show, I offer my hand to Patrick, leaning across both Marty and Richard. He takes it. I avoid looking at the other partners as they place their votes. I could try to see where they're placing their mark. I could look for a subtle nod or wink that might give me an indication of their choice. But it wouldn't change a thing at this stage.

Instead, I interlace my fingers and place my hands at my waist, trying to hide my anxiety. Patrick drums his fingers on the tabletop, and I swear, if the man doesn't stop, I'm going to tear off his goddamn fingers.

As partners begin depositing their slips in the sealed black box, Sarah comes into the room, her presence calming me slightly. She winks at me, then makes her way to the far end of the table. When the last slip is in the box, Marty asks Sarah to break the seal and count the votes.

She unfolds the first piece of paper and places it down on the table. 'Drew.' She does the same again, placing the next piece on the left side of the box. 'Patrick.' She continues through the slips.

We're neck and neck with three partners left. When Sarah meets my eye, her look is no longer calming my agony; she's worried.

'Drew.' I hold my breath. 'Patrick.' Even.

She takes the final voting slip and opens it. She closes her eyes.

Fuck. All these years. All these years of being an asshole and thinking performance alone could get me where I wanted to be. I've lost.

She opens her eyes and her lips begin to curve. 'Drew.'

I try to stay outwardly calm. I try to act as if it was always a sure thing. It never was.

My heart is racing. My mind is in some incomprehensible state.

I stand and shake the hand Patrick offers to me. It's only when Marty takes hold of my shoulders and rocks me once that I absorb what just happened.

'Welcome to Statham Harrington, buddy.'

'Fuck.'

Marty laughs, as does Richard. Richard thumps my back and says quietly to me. 'You always had my vote, son. I'm glad you took your head out of your ass long enough to win the other votes you needed.'

Sarah throws her arms around my neck. 'All these years were worth it, huh?'

All these years of denying myself things that might make me happier than spending my life in an office.

'We did it,' I whisper as I hug her back.

'No, Drew, you did it.'

'Actually, I think someone else deserves some of the credit for making me see the bigger picture.'

And she's the person I want to tell first. She's the person I want to drink champagne with. The person I'm madly in love with.

I pull back from Sarah's hold. 'I've got to go.'

The grin that pulls on her face lifts her cheeks. 'Go tell her.'

I shake more hands and thank people as I leave. When I'm finally free of the boardroom, my strides turn to a jog. I leave Lexington Tower and run to Edmond's place.

I'm panting when I pull open the door to the restaurant. The kitchen looks busy, and staff are already behind the bar and setting tables, but the first diners aren't yet in.

The restaurant manager, Beatrice, is looking at a computer screen at the hostess station.

'Drew. Are you okay?'

'Yeah. I think so.' I'm about to put myself out there and see whether the woman I don't think I can live without feels the same.

I rub my hand across my chin, suddenly wondering whether this is insane. I could lose her. I could scare her away and I don't think I can take it.

'You look pale, Drew. Do you want water?'

I shake my head. I also can't keep going with this sick feeling in the pit of my stomach. The hell of not knowing.

'Could you get Becky for me?'

'She isn't here. Some kind of emergency came up this afternoon.'

'Emergency? Is she okay?'

'I'm not sure what happened. I think maybe she was sick. Edmond sent her home.'

My thoughts are so erratic, it takes me a beat to process the conversation. 'So, she's at her apartment?'

'I believe so.'

I release my held breath. 'Okay.'

Well, if she's sick, that's not ideal, but in the history of mankind there must have been declarations of love less timely.

I thank Beatrice and outside the restaurant I flag a cab.

I thought waiting for the partnership vote was agonizing. That was before I sat in this cab, going over the words I want to say to Becky. Everything sounds ridiculous, or just not enough to make her understand how I feel.

'Can we make this any faster?' I ask the driver.

'Sorry, man, it's seven thirty. This is Manhattan.'

Tell me something I don't know. The night seems to get warmer as we sit in traffic. I loosen my tie, then take it off and undo the top buttons of my shirt. When we're a few blocks from Becky's place, I can't bear the waiting any longer. I pay the driver and walk the rest of the way.

I slip through the door to her building behind another tenant and go up to Becky's floor. I'm frantically trying to string words together, and I'm still trying when I knock on her apartment door.

'Drew.' She opens the door in yoga pants and a sweater. She's surprised but doesn't look sick.

'Hi.'

She steps into the hallway and pulls the door shut behind her. 'I thought you were at the partners' meeting.'

My brow furrows as I consider the closed door, but I concentrate on her, on getting out the words I need to say.

'I am. I was. I got voted in.'

Her face breaks into a smile and my entire body aches to hold her. 'I'm so happy for you, Drew.'

I force my arms to stay by my sides and take a calming breath.

'Listen, Becky, I... Damn it.' I rub my hands roughly over my face. 'When I got voted in, Sarah was there, Marty was there, but the one person I really wanted to tell was you.'

She glances across her shoulder to her apartment door. When she looks back at me, her eyes are glazed.

'Becky, I know what we said. I know we said we'd take it slow...'

'Drew—'

'Please. Let me finish. The thing is, I'm hoping that... Christ, I have no fucking idea how to do this.'

'Drew, please, there are things I need—'

'I love you, Becky. I'm in love with you.'

Her eyes widen and she presses her lips together as her eyes fill again. I feel helpless as I wait for her to say something. Anything.

The door to her apartment opens, stealing our attention. A man stands on the threshold, wearing nothing but a towel around his waist.

'Rebecca, what are you doing out here?'

I look from his dark, wet hair, to his bare feet, then I look at Becky.

'Rebecca?'

'I...'

The half-naked man moves toward us. 'Who's this?' he asks, his voice thick and deep. British.

Becky clears her throat, shifting her focus between the man and me.

'This is my friend Drew.'

He doesn't make a move toward me, he just lifts his chin in acknowledgment, eyeing me suspiciously.

Her friend? Right.

As he holds out his hand to me his expression is anything but amiable. 'I'm Mike, Rebecca's husband.'

It's as if someone just tackled me, crashing into my chest and taking the air from my lungs. I look at Becky, waiting for her to tell me it isn't true. Silently begging her. She only looks at me through wet eyes, her mouth opening and closing without making a sound.

I take a step back and feel everything inside me start to crumble. Pain sears my body and stings my eyes.

I push out of the fire door and into the stairwell. I head down two flights of stairs before my legs give out and I sit on a step. I drop my head into my hands and dig my knuckles into the corners of my eyes. Bile rises to my throat.

She's married. How can she be married? That makes no sense.

It hurts like hell.

## 22

### DREW

I walk for a while before I flag a cab, trying to make sense of what just happened.

I can't.

I replay every conversation we've ever had, searching for a clue. She said she had left a long-term relationship. I knew she had a past and that she was keeping something from me. But a husband?

My phone rings. My heart leaps until I see the caller is Sarah. I end the call and turn off my phone. I don't want to see her. I don't want to explain that I fell in love with a woman who made me commit adultery, who lied to me, who ripped out my fucking heart.

Drink. That's what I want. I want to go home and drink until this pain disappears.

That's where the driver is headed, until we drive by Edmond's place, and my hurt turns to anger. She said Edmond saved her. Did he know?

I throw bills at the driver, not bothering to count them, and storm like a raging bull into the restaurant. I walk right by Beatrice at the front desk and into the kitchen.

'Two steak. One rare, one blue.' Edmond catches my eye and

probably sees the murderous look on my face. 'One halibut. One lamb, pink.'

'Yes, Chef.'

'Chef.'

He moves from behind the counter. Rather than asking me anything, he says, 'Drew, you can't be in here.'

'You knew. You fucking knew.'

He holds up a finger. 'Keep your voice down. This is my work. And hers.'

I squeeze my eyes shut to stop the burning sensation. 'How could you know she's married and not tell me?' My anger wanes, and I'm looking at my friend through clouded eyes.

How can it hurt this much?

Edmond looks at me with sympathy. Something I've never seen when he's looked at me before. I realize I'm standing before him, not as a hot-shot attorney in the city, not as the friend he knows, but as a broken man.

'There are things you don't know, Drew.'

'So fucking tell me,' I snarl.

'It's not my story to tell.' He looks at the clock on the wall. 'Give me an hour, all right? Go to the Irish bar around the corner, and we'll talk.'

I don't know whether I want to throw myself on the floor like a child and beg for the pain to go away, or whether I want to put my fist in my friend's face. So I turn my back on him and leave.

I contemplate going home. The last thing I want is to be in a bar full of people. But I need to know what Edmond has to say. If nothing else, I'll have a drink in my hand sooner if I go to Paddy's than I will if I go home.

\* \* \*

She lied to me. She laughed and smiled and made love to me, and the whole thing was a goddamn lie. I wrestled with fear and doubt. I went against everything I've told myself is important.

She's made a fool of me. And I let her. I fell for the lie. I plant my empty shot glass on the bar. 'Another.'

'You might want to slow down, pal,' the Irish barman says as he refills my glass.

'You have no idea how fast or slow I want to drink.' I want to drink myself into oblivion. I want to drink myself into a stupor of ignorance. I think I want to drink so much, I don't remember anything. Not the bagel truck. Not her dimples. Not the way her skin feels against mine.

'I know you're starting to slur your words, and this is number ten.'

I slap a hundred-dollar bill down on the bar. 'I'm not paying you to count. I'm paying you to pour.'

Two hands come down on my shoulders.

'He's all right, I'm hanging around.' The voice is Edmond's. He orders a beer and takes a seat on a bar stool next to mine. 'Drinking yourself senseless isn't going to make this disappear, Drew.'

'Now you want to fucking tell me something.'

'Don't take this out on me, Drew. You're better than that.'

'Better than that? Am I? I've been sleeping with someone else's wife.' I mean the words to sound fierce, but they stick in my throat, catching on the emotion that's been balled there since I saw her standing next to her husband. Her fucking husband.

After downing my shot, I wiggle the empty glass in the air, catching the attention of the staff. Edmond says nothing. He doesn't defend himself. He doesn't defend her.

I stare at my glass, turning it between my fingers, contemplating smashing the thing into the mirror behind the bar, into the reflection of a man who barely looks like me. That man looks pale and red-eyed. He's skewed by the fog of liquor. And he let this happen to himself. One of his best friends let him get here.

Gripping the glass tightly in my fist, I grate the question through my teeth. 'Why didn't you tell me she's married?'

Edmond swigs his beer and puts the bottle down on the bar. 'I won't fight with you, Drew.'

I scoff. 'Maybe I'll be the judge of that when you tell me why the fuck you lied to me.'

He shakes his head, and I wonder whether he'll walk away. Maybe he should. Maybe I'm done with the whole damn farce anyway.

Or, maybe I need to hear what he has to say because our friendship might otherwise end right now.

My glass is topped up – the only thing stopping me from crushing it in my hand. I throw the liquor back and relish the burn in my throat and chest that momentarily masks what else I'm feeling inside. I will it to travel directly to my head and kill my thoughts.

'I don't know everything. I don't have the full story.' Edmond's words bring me back from darkness. 'What I can tell you is that marriage is the reason she left London. She hasn't seen him in months. Not since she's been here.'

'Then why is he here and dressed in a towel in her apartment?' My words are almost a bark.

'I can't answer that, and I can't answer everything for you. I'm here because I want you to appreciate it's not as straightforward as you think it is. She came to me on Tuesday and said she didn't know what to do about what's going on with you two. I told her to tell you about her husband. That's where it stopped. I'm not sure what she decided, and I don't know how it happened that he's here now.'

I snort and knock back my scotch. 'It seems fucking obvious to me. He came here for her.'

Edmond sighs, his cheeks puffing out. 'I hope not. And I hope she doesn't go back with him.'

I try to sit straighter but wobble on my stool and have to brace myself, palms on the bar. My scotch fog makes piecing everything together difficult. 'But she might.'

He nods silently.

'If she doesn't want to be back with him, then how did he find her?'

'I have no idea, Drew. He turned up at the restaurant this afternoon, and she left. I can't say what he's doing here, but I'll tell you this: Becky is not the person she was when she came to me in London. She's stronger and she's happier. You helped her with that.'

I know that's true. At least I thought I did. Then, I also thought she was falling in love with me. 'She lied to me.' My words have about as much strength as I feel.

'I know. And I can see you're hurting, my friend. You need to talk to her.'

'Maybe I do.' I push up to stand and find my legs unsteady beneath me. 'Maybe I don't. She could have talked to me for the last four weeks we've been together and she didn't bother. Why should I give a damn now?'

Even as I say the words, I know why. Because I love her. As messed up as it is. As fake as we've been. As fucked up as all this is. I love her.

Edmond puts a hand on my shoulder to balance me. Though I'm sour at him, I'm grateful to him for being the only thing keeping me upright. 'Before you make any decisions, you need to go home and sleep this off.'

'Or maybe I go there and tell him a few things. Let him be crushed by her too.'

He shakes his head. 'You need to let them talk, Drew.'

'So they can work things out?' I drag my fingers through my hair, pulling on the roots. 'Jesus.'

The word leaves me on an exhale. I was ready to give her everything. Give her all of me. And she's let me down more than anyone else in my entire life.

'Go home to bed and see how you feel tomorrow.'

I flop back down onto my stool and hold up my empty glass one more time. 'I think I'll still feel like someone punched me in the gut.'

I rest my head on my forearm on the bar and shut my eyes, willing myself to blankness. The last thing I hear is the sound of Sarah's voice.

'I'll take care of him, Edmond. He needs me.'

\* \* \*

I stir and try to open an eye but pin it closed again when the light feels like it's piercing my eyeball.

'Good morning, sleepy.'

I roll onto my back on my leather sofa, realizing I'm in my apartment, and try to piece together last night. Paddy's bar. Scotch. Home. More scotch. Sarah taking off my jacket and shoes on the sofa.

'I think I'm dying,' I groan, dropping my hands over my face.

'You look like shit.'

I can well imagine, if the throb in my head is anything to go by. 'What are you doing here?'

'Besides bringing you these?'

I open one eye again and see Advil and a coffee in her hands.

'You're an angel.'

'I know.' She takes a seat on the sofa opposite mine as I drag my sorry ass up to sit.

'What time is it?'

'Six.'

I groan again, dragging a hand over my face.

'Becky called me last night, I'm guessing as soon as you left her place. It didn't take long for me to work out where you were. I figured you'd think about taking this all out on Edmond. I also figured you'd turn to your nemesis: Johnnie Walker Blue Label.'

For all the good it did, because that same pain in my chest and in my gut is back. 'She's married.'

Sarah crosses her legs and purses her lips. 'She told me.'

I close my eyes because I don't want to see her sympathy, and I drop my head back on the sofa. 'How could she lie to me about that?' My eyes burn behind my lids and my throat tightens. 'How could she make me fall in love with her and not tell me?'

'I'm so sorry, Drew. I really am. I can only imagine how you're feeling. But... she called me and told me she's going to London.'

I swallow Advil as I bring my head forward to look at her. 'So, she's gone back to him.'

'That's not what she said. She just said she had to go to London.'

I can't remember the last time I cried. I was probably a kid. But now, I have to stand and walk to the window to distract myself from doing just that.

'Drew, I think she told me because she knew I would tell you. I don't know why she's going there, but I think she wanted you to know. I think it's a cry for help.'

'Or she's going back to him.'

'It's possible. But she's been here for months without him. She hasn't spoken to anyone about having a husband. In my experience, some things are too painful to talk about. She walked away from him.'

It comes back to me now, my conversation with Edmond last night. I turn to Sarah. 'Edmond said she was in a bad relationship. She told me she didn't want to be in a relationship because she was figuring out who she was. Maybe she figured out and wanted him back.'

Sarah nods. 'Perhaps. I can't answer that.'

I stare out to the horizon, searching for the answer. Looking for anything to tell me what in hell I'm supposed to do.

She's married. She loved a man enough to marry him. Maybe I should respect that. Let them work it out. God knows, if she was mine, there's no chance I'd let her go.

But she isn't.

With a sound that's somewhere between a wail and a growl, I thump the windowpane with the side of my fist. I see Sarah flinch from the corner of my eye, and I turn my back on her completely, resting my fists on the window and hanging my aching head between my arms.

'I don't want her to go back to him, Sarah. I can't give her up. At least not without a fight.'

She startles me when she speaks, her voice coming from right beside me. 'Drew, I get the feeling it isn't as simple as her having a husband she's been hiding from you.'

With a sense of renewed purpose, I nod. 'I need to talk to her.'

'I was hoping you would come to that conclusion sooner rather than later.' She moves to the sofa and reaches into her handbag. 'Go and get cleaned up. You've got an early flight to catch.'

I take the envelope she's holding out. 'You booked me a flight to London?'

'I know you better than you know yourself, Drew Harrington. She's staying at Chateau Belmont, where Edmond's restaurant is.'

## 23

DREW

The good news is, by the time I get to Chateau Belmont, I've slept off my hangover. The bad news is, now that I'm sober, I'm wondering what in the hell I'm doing here. I came for an explanation. I came to fight. But what if I'm too late? What if there's nothing to fight for?

I follow a bellhop through the pillared entrance of the hotel. The inside is even more grand than out. Black and white floor tiles gleam. Green marble pillars hold up the high ceilings. Everything is mahogany and trimmed in gold. The place smells of polish and vanilla all at once. I'd expect nothing less luxurious from the hotel that's home to Edmond's restaurant.

'Good evening, sir. May I help you?'

The porter stands behind me with my luggage as I check in with a suited woman who has immaculately combed hair and insanely red, painted lips.

'Our concierge will take your bags to your room, sir. If there is anything we can do to make your stay more comfortable, please do let me know.'

'Actually, there is one thing. Can you tell me which room Becky

Fletcher is staying in? She used to work here, in the restaurant. I'm... a friend from New York.'

'I'm sorry, sir. I'm not at liberty to share that information with you. I'm afraid it is hotel policy.'

Hotels and their damn adherence to rules. 'Fine. Could you at least get a message to her for me?'

She smiles, revealing perfect white teeth. 'Of course, sir. Would you like to write it down?'

She hands me a note pad and a pen. I hover the pen over the paper, not having a clue what I'm here to say. Except...

*I'm here.*
  *I want to know everything. I'll be waiting in the bar.*
  *Drew*

I nudge the note toward the receptionist, my heart hammering in my chest, my palms hot.

Will she come? If she comes, what will she tell me?

Jesus, I could lose her for good. Maybe I already have.

As I sit at the bar, nursing my first scotch, needing to kill my nerves but remembering too well how my body ached from the after effects of the same taste just hours ago, it occurs to me more than once that I might have lost my mind. I've chased a woman halfway across the world, and I have no idea what to say to her or what she might say to me. I keep thinking about the way she looked at me when I saw her husband. She gave nothing away. She looked sorry, sure, but she didn't necessarily look like she wanted to be with me instead of him. She didn't tell me in that look that she didn't want to be with him.

Was her telling Sarah that she was in London a message to me? Was it a cry for help, or was she telling me we are over? Were we ever more than friends in her mind?

It's nine on the dot when I lean my wrist toward the bar lamp and check my watch. I order a second scotch on the rocks and wait.

To everyone else, I must just look like a man sitting in slacks, his shirt tucked in beneath his jacket, having a drink. Normal. I feel anything but normal. I feel like a nervous wreck.

As if I'm tuned in to her presence, I sense her before I see her. I take a slow breath to calm the anxiety running through my blood and making me dizzy, and I turn on my stool. Her hair is pulled across one shoulder. Her gray dress is elegant and plain yet hugs every curve of her body. Her black heels make her already fine legs to die for.

Her lips are straight, once again telling me nothing, as she walks toward me. I get off the stool and look down at her slightly, despite her heels.

'Hi.'

'Hi.'

I want to fist my hands in her hair and kiss her pink lips, but there's so much passing between us. Such a mess. I have no idea whether she's single or married. I have no idea whether she still even wants to be friends. I pray she wants something more.

One thing I do know: I love her just as much now as I did yesterday.

Becky orders a martini, and I get another scotch. Then it's just us, with no distractions.

'So...' is all I can think to say. When I really want to scream, *Tell me, goddamn it! Tell me you're not with him. Tell me it wasn't all a lie! Tell me you love me.*

She sucks in a deep breath. 'I'm sorry, Drew. I should have told you about Mike.'

'You should have.' My words are abrupt.

She nods. 'I never meant to hurt you.'

I snort. *You fucking ripped me apart.*

'Please, don't be like that. I'm... I'm so pleased you came here. I didn't expect you to, but I hoped you would.'

I swirl the scotch in my glass. 'Why?'

'Because there are things you need to know, and there are things I had to come here to fix before I could be truly honest with you.'

I don't know whether she expects me to talk, but when I don't, she sucks in another breath and continues.

'I ran from London. I ran from Mike.'

My pulse judders. Perhaps my heart stops. She ran from him.

'Edmond got me straight out of London. He arranged the job in New York for me.' Her eyes cast down to her delicate fingers in her lap. 'Mike wasn't good to me, Drew.'

He hurt her? Someone dared to hurt her?

I feel rage building inside me. Her eyes fill with unfallen tears and I can't stay away from her any longer. I reach out and take her hand from her lap, locking her fingers between mine.

'Don't shut down on me, Becky. Talk to me.'

'I once told you we ended over babies. Well, that was kind of true.' She takes a large mouthful of martini and presses her eyes shut, opening them before she continues. 'We got together when I was a teenager. I had a horrible home life. Nothing like yours. My dad died when I was young. I don't even remember him. And the others, my mum and her multitude of boyfriends, they really couldn't have cared less about me. Mike was older than me. He was stronger. And I thought he was something I needed. Someone to look after me. We moved in to his place fairly quickly, and everything started to go wrong.'

A tear rolls down her cheek. She swiftly swipes it away as if I might not have seen it. I squeeze her hand tighter, not sure if I can bear to see her hurting.

'I didn't notice at first. It was just small things. He would tell me not to go places, not to see people or do things. Then he'd tell me how to dress. Tell me...' She clears her throat and stares into her half-empty glass. 'He'd tell me I was ugly. Or too fat.' She laughs but it's not an amused laugh at all. It's a somber sound. 'I was a UK size eight. I mean, Christ, what size did he want me to be?'

'You're beautiful, Becky. More than beautiful.'

At my words, another tear rolls down her cheek. I rub it away with the pad of my thumb.

'I just became this shell. He didn't save me like I thought. He caged me. And I was... intimidated by him. Scared, even. He had never actually hit me, only threatened it, but I was afraid of the possibility, I guess. And I was young. I had nowhere else to go. I lost the few friends I had. My family... Well, that wasn't a good option. I was alone. I was lost. I didn't know what to do and I had no one to talk to. Somewhere along the line, I agreed to marry him.' She shakes her head. 'You must think I sound pathetic.'

I gently place my knuckle under her chin and make her look at me.

'You have no idea what I'm thinking. It definitely isn't that.'

I'm thinking I would like to get my hands on this guy and beat him to a pulp.

She drops her gaze to our hands in her lap and rolls her finger-tips over my knuckles.

'The only place he let me go was work. The café I worked in became my sanctuary. Then, one day, like I told you, I ended up working in a branch in London, and I met Edmond. He was kind and honest. It was as if he saw right through me, like he could see that I was trapped.'

I think of Edmond last night in Paddy's, and I feel like a dick for challenging him.

'After I started working for Edmond, I was commuting in and out of London, and it meant I spent a lot of time out of the house. Over time, Mike got angry about it. He started talking about children and saying I should stay home. Rather than telling him I didn't want to have children with him, I told him I should keep my job, for money to help our family.' She wipes another tear and drains the drink in her glass. Then she looks me in the eye, as if she's building courage. 'I got pregnant.'

I try not to react outwardly, though everything in my body is screaming at me.

'I'm sorry to disturb you. Will you be dining with us this evening?' We look to the waitress, accept menus. For my part, I'm grateful for a short break to get my head straight. I don't know what I was expecting, but it definitely wasn't this.

I barely take in the menu, selecting dishes I probably won't even eat. My mind is awash with thoughts of Becky, babies, her being hurt.

The waitress takes our order and leads us to a table. Whether she took her cue from Becky's red eyes, or just has good intuition, she places us in a secluded table in a dimly lit corner.

Becky gives me a meek smile and thanks the waitress. Before she sits, I place a hand on the small of her back. I'm terrified of what comes next in the story, but she's hurting more than me, and I can't stand it.

I move my table chair from opposite her until we're adjacent. The waitress adjusts our place settings, and the sommelier brings a bottle of wine. We both take a drink, our silence unbroken.

'Becky, you don't have to tell me more if you don't want to.'

'I don't want to, Drew. That's why I didn't. But in not telling you, I risked everything. I might still. But you flew to London to hear what I'm keeping from you. The least I can do is be honest with you now. And...'

'And what?'

'And hope that... you'll still want me.'

I want to tell her I can't imagine a circumstance in which I wouldn't want her, but the words don't come because they're locked behind fear. Fear of what she might tell me.

She looks away and runs her fingers around the base of her wineglass. 'I had an accident one night. I left work. It was dark. I slipped down the steps at the underground station.' Her face contorts as she fights back sobs. I take her hand beneath the table, and she grips me tightly. 'I lost the baby.'

A slow, unsteady breath leaves me. 'I'm sorry.'

I'm not sorry that she doesn't have someone else's child, but I'm sorry that she lost her baby.

She pulls her hand from mine and sniffs, pressing the corner of her napkin to her eyes.

'Drew, I... When it happened... I felt relieved. What kind of person does that make me?'

My throat is dry, and I have no words. All I can do is watch her pain.

'I would have loved that baby. It would have been mine, and I would have given it everything I could. But, when I miscarried, it was like a second chance. It was as if something woke up inside me. I knew I couldn't bring a life into the world with someone like Mike. I knew I wanted to be stronger. To be a better person. Otherwise, I'd never be able to show my child how to be strong. The night I lost the baby was the one and only time he hit me. I left.'

I don't know what makes me lean in and kiss her, but I do. I hold her face and keep her lips pressed to mine, smoothing her hair as she cries against me. When she calms, she kisses me back.

I allow myself to hope.

She holds my hands when she separates from me. 'I was afraid to tell you. I thought you would think I'm a monster.'

'I don't think you're a monster, Becky. I think you're strong. I think you're amazing.'

'Drew, you... you know a different version of me. I started to become the person I wanted to be in New York. Then I met you, and for the first time ever, I felt wanted. You make me feel confident and attractive. I didn't want to lie to you, but I didn't want you to know the old me. The weak me. I just wanted to be Becky. The Becky you know. I wanted you to see my wings.'

'I see your wings, Becky. And I want to be your roots too. I'll never try to control you. I never want you to be anyone other than who you want to be. But I'd like to be by your side.'

Her tears come again but they merge with a happy laugh and she presses her smile to my mouth. 'I'd like that.'

When we break our connection, she digs her teeth into her lip.

'What is it?' I ask.

'I... I don't know if it's fair to ask. Not now. Actually, forget it. Maybe you should take some time, you know, to think about things. Not that I want you to change your mind, I just—'

'Becky, you're babbling. What is it?'

Her chest rises as her eyes connect with mine. I brace myself, wondering how much more she can tell me tonight.

'The reason Mike came to New York, or the way he managed to find me, is because I started divorce proceedings. I wanted to be strong enough to finally break from him, for good. I also wanted to be able to tell you, but I wanted to be able to say I was getting a divorce. Maybe that seems crazy now, given the mess I made of everything. I could just feel things changing between us, then on Monday, when you... we slept together. I don't know, it felt different to the other times, it felt...'

'Like we made love?'

Her mouth curves at one side. 'Yes. I knew then that I'd fallen for you, with all of me. I think I knew it before then, but the words were right there, and I felt like I couldn't say them, not until I had taken care of things here.' Her words wrap around my heart, warming me, taking hold of me. She hasn't said it, not exactly, but she feels the same.

'I'm here because I have a meeting with Mike and our lawyers tomorrow to sort out the divorce.'

'And you want me to go with you?'

'I'm not asking you to represent me or anything, I wouldn't do that. I just, what I would really love to do is walk into that room tomorrow, look Mike in the eye, and tell him to go fuck himself.'

Her level of hatred for this man is appropriate but hearing it from her surprises me.

'The thing is, he has this kind of hold over me, and as much as I want to break free of him, I know I'll sit in that room and not say anything. If you were there, it would just... I would just feel...'

I reach out and pull her in to kiss me. 'I'll be there with you.'

She kisses me with such urgency it leaves me desperate to hold her, to take care of her, protect her, and make love to her.

'I would really like to have our food brought up to my room.'

She presses her forehead to mine and lets out a short giggle. 'Me too.'

'God, I've missed that smile.'

## 24

### DREW

We step out of a black cab in front of an old English building: white with dark wood beams and windows. It's like something from a Charles Dickens novel. It harbors a small family law firm.

Rain is pounding against the sidewalk. I hold up a large umbrella, borrowed from the hotel, that both Becky and I can fit under. Becky straightens her black tailored dress and fusses, replacing her handbag over her shoulder and smoothing her already perfect hair.

'Are you okay?' I ask her.

She nods too quickly and tightly to be convincing.

'Let's just take a breath, okay? Look at me.' I run my fingertips down her cheek, and she leans in to my palm. I want to tell her I'm here with her, that we'll do this together, but that's not what she needs. Instead, I tell her, 'You've got this, Becky. You've come this far all on your own. Go in there with your head held high and finish this.'

'You're right. You're right. I'm ready.'

'That's my girl.' I kiss her temple, then take her hand as we walk inside. The building smells musty, like an old library. Becky takes the lead, speaking to the receptionist. I stand behind her.

'It's this way,' she tells me, even though I heard the directions from the receptionist.

'Lead the way.'

We walk down a wooden corridor that's decorated with gold-framed portraits of the founders or ex-attorneys of the firm. It screams old, stuffy British law school to me.

Outside the meeting room, a man introduces himself to Becky as the attorney she spoke with on the phone from New York. He has a rotund belly, and what is left of his hair is gray. He's a short man, and his suit pants ripple at the heels. I inwardly roll my eyes. I could do a better job of this, and I don't have the first clue about handling a divorce.

'Victor, this is Drew.'

We shake hands and he eyes me suspiciously, as if weighing up whether I'm going to cause trouble. Wearing an Omega, chinos, and a tailored shirt, I hardly think I look like the type, but in my mind, I would love to lay my hands on the bastard who hurt Becky.

'If you're ready, Becky, we'll go in. Mike is in there with his lawyer. Are you sure you don't want anything?'

'Not a thing. I just want rid of him.'

'All right then.'

She could take whatever she wants. Damn, she could press charges against the asshole. But this is her show, not mine. I run a hand down her back, letting her know I'm with her, before Victor opens the door. I feel her body tense when she sees her soon-to-be-ex sitting on the far side of a mahogany table. He stays seated, his eyes fixed on me. I notice more about him this time: his dark eyes, his harsh, angular features, his broad shoulders. It doesn't deter me or make my anger wane in the slightest. In fact, it gets my hackles up. I want to put this guy's nose across the other side of his face.

'Ms Fletcher. My name is Harold.'

After introductions, we take our seats opposite Mike and his attorney. The air is charged, tense, in the heat of the room.

'Well, this should be very simple,' Victor begins, shuffling papers in a cardboard file as if this is the nineteen fifties. 'My client wants only to have divorce papers signed today. She isn't interested in dividing assets. She wants only to walk away.'

'Rebecca, you don't want this.' I feel myself go rigid as Mike looks at Becky. His words sound like a plea, but his eyes say they're a threat. I'd like nothing more than to ram my fist into his throat.

She closes her eyes. 'Mike, you have nothing to offer me. Don't make this difficult. Just sign the papers.'

'What if I won't? What are you going to do about it, Rebecca?' His words are low, ominous even. I have to bite my tongue to keep from defending her. She needs to do this herself.

'Then we'll go to court if that's what it takes.'

He stands from his chair with such force, the wood clatters against the wall behind him. 'You're a manipulative bitch.'

I count to ten in my head. When I haven't calmed, I count to twenty, then thirty. At this rate, there will be someone ending up behind bars and it might not be him.

'Mr Fletcher, my client would like this to remain amicable,' Victor begins.

'Amicable? She fucking stole nine years of my life, and you want me to play nice? She killed my baby. Our baby.'

I watch Becky's eyes fill. Her voice is weak. 'That wasn't my fault.'

I place my hand on her thigh and lean into her ear. 'He knows that, Becky. Don't let him get to you.'

She looks at me with surprise, as if she's just remembered I'm here with her. I will her to be strong, to do this for herself. I want her to be the Becky from New York. The Becky she wants to be.

'I should be filing for fucking adultery,' Mike snarls. 'You expect me to believe you weren't shagging this American twat? Is that why you left?' He places his hands on the desk, leaning toward Becky, making himself taller than her, more intimidating.

'Mike, sit down; this isn't helping anyone,' his attorney says.

Mike shrugs him off. 'Do you enjoy fucking my wife?'

I stand from the table and give him a sadistic grin. 'She hasn't been your wife for a long time. She should be hauling your ass through assault proceedings, you son of a bitch. Consider yourself a very lucky man that she just wants to walk away. And by the way, if you and I have a problem, we can step outside. I'd love to give you a beating.'

'Gentlemen, gentlemen. Let's all calm down.'

'Victor, I just want to sign the papers, that's all,' Becky pleads. 'I want nothing from you, Mike, only a divorce. Behaving like this won't change that fact. If you don't want to spend thousands of pounds in legal fees, just sign the papers.'

'That's it? Nine years and that's all you have to say to me?'

Becky looks down at the table.

I take a seat beside her. 'Actually, Becky did have something she wanted to say to you. She told me so, right before we went to bed together last night.' I turn to her. 'Do you remember?'

She looks at me and I give her the slightest nod, trying to say, *You've got this*. She squeezes my hand, then slowly rises to her full height, facing Mike. The feeling of her strength growing is palpable. She signs her name on the divorce papers, then pushes them across the table.

'There was one thing I wanted to say. Go fuck yourself, you sick, hateful bastard.'

With that, she turns on her heel and struts out of the room. I can't help smirking, proud as hell of my girl. I rise from the table. 'Gents, it was a pleasure.'

Then I go find Becky. She's in the reception area, trembling, when I get to her. I fold her straight into my arms.

'You were so fucking amazing. Confident. Hot.'

I feel her shudder against me, and when I pull back to look at her, I realize she's laughing. 'I was a little dramatic.'

'Spend enough time with us Yanks and it'll happen.' I wink at her and press my mouth to hers. She kisses me back deeply, as if she's letting go of everything she has held inside for so long. As if she's telling me she'll be mine. I try to tell her in that kiss, she won't ever fight alone again.

In the distance, I see Mike head into the toilets. Perhaps there's just one thing left to do.

'I'm going to use the bathroom,' I say. 'Then let's get out of here.'

Becky lets go of my hand and I follow Mike into the restroom.

He watches me in the mirror above the urinal as he zips himself back into his jeans.

'You motherfucker,' he snarls, his lips trembling with hatred.

He turns quickly and throws a swinging hook at me, but I duck and he misses.

I lunge at him, ramming my forearm into his neck and pinning him to the tiled wall. Then I drive my fist into his gut so hard, he retches.

'You want to pick a fight, champ, pick it with me.'

I pull my fist back and drive it so hard into his jaw his head rocks back against the tiles. His eyes roll. I rear my arm again and enjoy the crunch when my knuckles connect with his nose. Blood starts pouring from his face. When I release him, he falls to the floor.

I leave him there, holding his stomach and spluttering blood. I look back once and feel no regret, not even an ounce. Just wonderment, that any man would dare to touch a woman like Becky. Never again, for so long as I live.

'All set?' I ask Becky, slipping my hand into hers, trying not to wince when she interlaces her fingers with mine.

'I'm ready to go home.'

I stroke her hair behind her ear. 'How would you like to meet my brother for lunch, then spend the night running up a tab courtesy of Edmond? Then we'll fly home tomorrow.'

'Sounds perfect.'

# 25

## BECKY

I stand in front of the dress bag that's hanging on my wardrobe door, my hair curled and loosely pinned up, my makeup complete. My nerves have stayed at bay so far, but now I've gotten to the point of actually putting on the dress, it seems more real. I'm going to be by Drew's side as his firm celebrates his accession to named partner.

I can honestly say, an evening like this – black tie, champagne – will be the fanciest event I've ever attended. I only hope I don't say anything out of place, and that I look like someone he can be proud to have on his arm.

Since the day I met him, I've wanted to blow him away, the way he does me. Sure, he's gorgeous. His body is, well, incredible. But it's more than that. He has a goodness in him. In his blue eyes. I see it when he looks at his family, when he laughs with his friends, and when he looks at me.

He wants to take care of me, but not like Mike. He wants me to be whoever I want to be. He doesn't want to trap me or control me.

I've never met a man quite like Drew Harrington.

For all his success, for all the cut-throat attitude I'm sure he displays at work, he still has the most tender of touches. The way he looks me in the eye and strokes my face, the way he never wants me to look down; he makes me feel extraordinary. I want to be strong for me, and for him.

I had nine months in New York before I met him. In that time, I started to find myself. I became more than someone's daughter to be ordered around and put down. I realized I could be free of a husband's hold and try things, go places, for myself.

I was afraid to lose the strength I'd found. But being with Drew, I don't lose anything. I gain everything. And I still have my independence. It's something so precious to me now, I'll never give it up. The best part is, he doesn't want me to. And he wants to keep his too.

I unzip the dress bag and lift out the gray silk gown, letting the train fall to the floor. We bickered over the dress, in the way we do, a kind of playful way where we always know which one of us will win – and that changes each time. Yesterday, we bickered because I wanted to buy my own dress for the dinner tonight. Drew said he was the reason we were going and he should pay.

I was always going to win this one. I had to buy the dress myself. I wanted him to know that he doesn't have to fend for me. I needed him to know that I'm so proud of him, I want to look special for him.

Now, nervous as I am, I'm pleased I am standing in front of the most extravagant purchase I have ever made.

I draw the zipper down the back and step into the dress, lifting the silk and crystal woven straps up to my shoulders. Once I've fumbled with the zipper, I take my new silver shoes – the second most extravagant purchase of my life – from their box and sit on the edge of my bed to strap them around my ankle.

When I'm done, I can't stop the smile that pulls on my lips. I move in front of the floor-length mirror. My reflection seems to waver as I bite my lip, my stomach in knots, my heart beating fast.

When my eyes clear, I see what I knew I would see. I am finally Cinderella.

'You're breathtaking.'

I spin quickly to see Drew in the doorway of my bedroom.

'I let myself in.' His dark-blond hair is intentionally messed with product, reminding me how much I love pulling my fingers through it. His dinner suit hugs that perfectly toned body just enough to tease me with the thought of what lies beneath. His shirt is buttoned up and a bow tie in place.

My mouth is suddenly dry. He's like something out of a movie.

'This can't be real.'

I don't realize I've said that aloud until he strolls, casual and so bloody sexy, toward me. He raises his hand to my cheek and looks at me as if I am the most special person in the world.

'Sometimes I don't think you're real either, baby. How did I ever find you?'

I run a hand over his shirt beneath his jacket, unable to resist. 'I believe it went something like, you were being an arrogant arse and couldn't wait for me to order my bagel.'

His lips part into his devastating smile. It shows his perfect white teeth – Manhattan teeth – and lights up his irises. 'You're beautiful, Becky.'

My cheeks heat. I'm a little overwhelmed and a whole lot giddy to spend the night with this man.

'I feel like I'm Cinderella and you're my prince.'

He moves slowly and presses his lips to mine. My body melts against his. His touch. His hold. His taste. The assault of his scent on my senses. I've been waiting for the perfect moment to say what I've thought since I watched him sleep in my kitchen at work, just days after I met him. It hasn't come yet. We both had things to sort out. I needed to close the door on my old life and start the life I used to lie in bed at night and cry for.

This life.

I pull back from his kiss and open my eyes to his.

'I love you, Drew.'

He presses his forehead to mine and pins my body to his. 'God, I love you too, Becky. So much.'

My eyes fill and I giggle. 'I don't think I've ever understood happy tears.'

'They're the only kind I'll ever make you cry, baby. I promise.'

I kiss him again, pouring into the touch every single thing I feel for him. It's so much, I could burst when I'm around him.

'Shall we go, Cinderella?'

I nod and slip my hand into his.

'Oh, before we do...' He reaches into his inside pocket and pulls out a black velvet box. 'I conceded on the dress.'

I take the box from him and open the lid, gasping when I see a fine chain with one large, gleaming stone.

'Is that a...?' My words get lost in my tight throat.

'Diamond. Yes.' He turns me to face the mirror and fastens the chain around my neck. The diamond falls perfectly into the sweetheart neckline of my dress.

I look at him through the mirror. 'No one has ever...' I shake my head quickly and force away my tears.

He kisses my neck. 'They're happy tears, right? I don't want to break my promise right after I've made it.'

I chuckle and sniff. 'Yes. They're happy tears.'

'Good. Come on. I want to show you off.'

He leads me out of the bedroom. As I reach back to flick off the light switch, he asks, 'You won't turn into a pumpkin at midnight, will you?'

'Have you even seen *Cinderella*?'

'I could answer that honestly, but then I'd have to kill you.'

'That's a yes.'

'Of course I haven't seen *Cinderella*. It's for girls. Little girls.'

'So was *NSYNC, Drew, and that didn't stop you.'

He tugs me against his side as we both laugh.

# ACKNOWLEDGEMENTS

I first wrote The Law of Attraction in 2016, when I lived in the British Virgin Islands. In the hours I spent walking on the beach with my dog, Rocky, I plotted the original version of this book. So, thank you to my furry bubba, forever in my thoughts.

In the original acknowledgments for this book, I thanked my husband, for his patience and willingness to be neglected, make dinner and do the grocery shopping, all to allow me to write. I also thanked him for making me laugh and understand love because without those things, I could not write romantic comedies. Fast-forwarding seven years to the re-write of this book, he no longer does the grocery shopping! But he does still make me laugh like no one else can. I will love you always.

My friend, Jennifer, got a mention in the first acknowledgements, for being one of the first people to read this book and for her endless bookish support. This stands. More importantly, thank you for your friendship and near daily voice notes, making me chuckle.

Now, I must thank my incredible agent, Tanera Simons, who encouraged me to revisit the Brits in Manhattan series. I'm so pleased we did this! Thank you for your support, your time and your wisdom. A huge thank you to my new and wonderful editor, Emily Yau. Thank you for seeing the potential in this series, for being a champion of these books and my writing, and for giving me the freedom to turn The Law of Attraction into a book I can be proud of. I can't wait for our journey to continue. Of course, this book and the rest of the series could not reach my fabulous readers without the help of an army of people at Boldwood. Thank you to each and every member of the editing, marketing, sales, accounts, production, art and publicity teams. How lucky I am to have such a fantastic team!

Last but by no means least, thank you, dear reader, for choosing my books and allowing me to take you on a trip to Manhattan with Drew and Becky. I hope you love their story.

Laura x

# ABOUT THE AUTHOR

**Laura Carter** is the bestselling author of several romantic comedies including the *Brits in Manhattan* series. She lives in Jersey.

Sign up to Laura Carter's mailing list for news, competitions and updates on future books.

Visit Laura's website: www.lauracarterauthor.com

Follow Laura on social media:

instagram.com/lauracarterauthor
x.com/LCarterAuthor
facebook.com/LauraCarterAuthor

# ALSO BY LAURA CARTER

# LOVE NOTES

### LOVE IN EVERY CHAPTER

WHERE ALL YOUR ROMANCE
DREAMS COME TRUE!

THE HOME OF BESTSELLING
ROMANCE AND WOMEN'S
FICTION

 WARNING:
MAY CONTAIN SPICE

SIGN UP TO OUR
NEWSLETTER

https://bit.ly/Lovenotesnews

# Boldwood

Boldwood Books is an award-winning fiction publishing company seeking out the best stories from around the world.

**Find out more at www.boldwoodbooks.com**

Join our reader community for brilliant books, competitions and offers!

Follow us
@BoldwoodBooks
@TheBoldBookClub

Sign up to our weekly deals newsletter

https://bit.ly/BoldwoodBNewsletter